Bound by revenge, a woman turned outlaw and a knight sworn to reclaim his birthright band together to vanquish an enemy of Scotland . . .

After her family is slain and her home seized, Elspet McReynolds flees into the forests surrounding Tiran Castle, where she resorts to thievery to survive and save her sole remaining kin. There she finds an unexpected protector and ally in Sir Cailin MacHugh, rightful heir to the earldom of Dalkirk—a noble rumored to have perished at sea . . .

Sir Cailin owes his life to the Brotherhood for saving him from a murderous plot. But what is the Knight Templar to do about the fearless, sword-wielding beauty who has enlisted his aid—and awakened his desire? In the face of devastating betrayals and traitorous enemies closing in, can Cailin and Elspet dare claim a love that makes no promises—for a future they may not live to see?

Visit us at www.kensingtonbooks.com

Books by Diana Cosby

The Forbidden Series
Forbidden Vow
Forbidden Knight
Forbidden Legacy
Forbidden Alliance

The Oath Trilogy
An Oath Sworn
An Oath Broken
An Oath Taken

MacGruder Brothers Series
His Enchantment
His Seduction
His Destiny
His Conquest
His Woman
His Captive

Published by Kensington Publishing Corporation

Forbidden Alliance

The Forbidden

Diana Cosby

LYRICAL PRESS
Kensington Publishing Corp.
www.kensingtonbooks.com

LYRICAL PRESS BOOKS are published by
Kensington Publishing Corp.
119 West 40th Street
New York, NY 10018

All Kensington titles, imprints, and distributed lines are available at special quantity discounts for bulk purchases for sales promotion, premiums, fundraising, educational, or institutional use.

Special book excerpts or customized printings can also be created to fit specific needs. For details, write or phone the office of the Kensington Sales Manager: Kensington Publishing Corp., 119 West 40th Street, New York, NY 10018. Attn. Sales Department. Phone: 1-800-221-2647.

Lyrical Press and Lyrical Press logo Reg. U.S. Pat. & TM Off.

First Electronic Edition: August 2019
ISBN-13: 978-1-5161-0887-9 (ebook)
ISBN-10: 1-5161-0887-6 (ebook)

First Print Edition: August 2019
ISBN-13: 978-1-5161-0889-3
ISBN-10: 1-5161-0889-2

Printed in the United States of America

This book is dedicated to Sally Pelkey, an incredible woman who has been a part of so many amazing memories in my life. I deeply appreciate the gift of her friendship. Sally, you're truly a blessing in my life. *Hugs*

Acknowledgments

My sincere thanks to Cameron John Morrison, Kathryn Warner, and Jody Allen for answering numerous questions about medieval Scotland and England. I would also like to thank The National Trust for Scotland, which acts as guardian of Scotland's magnificent heritage of architectural, scenic, and historic treasures. In addition, I am thankful for the immense support from my husband, parents, family, and friends. My deepest wish is that everyone is as blessed when they pursue their dreams.

My sincere thanks to my editor, Esi Sogah; my agent, Holly Root; production editor Rebecca Cremonese; copy editor Randy Ladenheim-Gil; and my critique partners, Michelle Hancock, Cindy Nord, and Ella Quinn for helping Cailin and Elspet's story come to life. A huge thanks to the Roving Lunatics (Mary Beth Shortt and Sandra Hughes), Nancy Bessler, and The Wild Writers for their friendship and support over the years!

*A very special thanks to Sulay Hernandez for believing in me from the start.

Chapter 1

Scotland, November 1308

Snow pelted Elspet McReynolds as she clutched her dagger, her gaze riveted on the two roughly dressed men paces away.

"Hand over the sack!" the stocky one with a jagged scar across his cheek demanded.

His partner, with a scraggly beard, narrowed his eyes.

Heart pounding, she tightened her grip. God in heaven, how had her simple plan gone so horribly wrong? She'd despised robbing these strangers. An action she'd never have done if not for the Earl of Dalkirk's treachery.

Horrific images of the day before stormed her mind. The grizzly death of her mother and stepfather, her stepbrother Blar's screams as he was dragged away by the murdering cur's men, and how the earl had hauled her to his chamber.

Nausea choked her at memories of her struggle for freedom. How dare the arrogant bastard believe she'd ever willingly share his bed? Had he not deflected her dagger, she would have driven the *sgian dubh* deep into his vile heart. She found grim satisfaction that her blade had left a long gash across his cheek.

With the noble howling in pain and demanding that she be captured and killed, she'd fled Tiran Castle. However much she yearned to leave Dalkirk land, she couldn't allow her stepbrother to die in the earl's dungeon.

Terrified for Blar's life, she'd begged her family's friends to help her discover whether he was alive. They'd agreed. Except once they'd believed her asleep, she'd overheard them planning to turn her in to gain favor with the noble.

Devastated by their betrayal, after they'd found their beds, she'd crept to the door and, with painful slowness, opened the hewn entry and fled.

Earlier today she'd found a castle guard out on his rounds, a man she'd met several times before, who'd sworn that her stepbrother still lived. For a pound he'd agreed to help Blar escape. That had been on her mind when she'd stumbled across the camp in the woods and had seen both strangers at the river, propelling her to foolishly try to rob them.

A brief search had revealed where the travelers kept their coin. Except, before she could slip away, they'd spotted her and given chase.

Body trembling, she glared at the angry faces of the furious men, damned that she hadn't stolen one of their horses and ridden away. With the earl calling for her death, she had naught to lose.

Another snow-drenched gust whipped past, blinding her from her ill-chosen victims. Too aware of the steep slope behind her, and the harsh landscape of the Highlands, she edged to her left. If she could only reach the trees a short sprint away, she might lose them in the dense woods.

The man with the scraggly beard stepped closer. "Hand it over!"

Elspet's blade trembled in her hand. Somehow, she must distract them. "Stay back."

"Nay one steals from me!" Teeth bared, the scarred man moved to the side and cornered her against the dangerous incline.

Fear a bitter slide in her throat, the icy ground crunched beneath her as she edged back. "I am sorry. I needed but a few coins, I—"

The scarred man lunged.

With a scream, she slashed out with her blade.

A thin line of blood streaked his chin. "You bloody bitch!" Snarling, he caught her arms. After twisting both wrists behind her back, he seized the bag of coins.

Panicking, she struggled to break free. "You have your money; release me!"

Scowling, the thickset man shoved the leather sack into a ragged, worn pocket. "Nay, lass, you have earned naught but punishment for your thievery." He wrenched open her cape. "Penance," he said, his eyes darkening with lust, "I shall enjoy delivering."

His friend gave a cruel laugh. "A comely wench indeed."

"Nay!" Fresh terror building in her chest, she drove her foot against her captor's thigh.

With a curse, the stocky man fisted his hand, swung.

Pain exploded in Elspet's head, and she collapsed onto the snow-covered ground.

* * * *

A woman's scream had Sir Cailin MacHugh reining his warhorse to a stop. Gaze narrowed, he scanned the forest.

Another shriek rang out.

God's blade! He whirled his destrier toward the sound, kicked him into a gallop.

Through the break in the trees ahead, a burly man stood over a slender woman garbed in a torn, pale-green gown. At his side leered a man with a scraggly beard, as shabbily dressed as the other.

Fury exploded in Cailin's mind as memories of a woman he'd cared for deeply, had sought his protection after she'd been badly beaten. As he'd held her bruised and bloody body in his arms, prayed for her to live, she'd drawn her last breath. From that moment he'd sworn that never again would he allow a man to harm a lass.

Jaw clenched, he leaned low and urged his horse faster.

The attacker hauled her up, drawing his fist back to land another blow.

Cailin jumped his steed over a fallen log and into the clearing, drew his broadsword. "Release her!" he roared.

Her attacker whirled. Outraged eyes shifted to fear as they locked on his weapon. "You bloody want her," he snarled, "here!" He shoved the lass down the steep incline, nodded to his partner. "Run!"

Brush snapped as both men bolted to their horses.

Instinct urged Cailin to give chase as they galloped away but lost against his need to protect. He kicked his mount to the edge.

Like a broken doll, her fingers splayed against the snow-covered ground, the woman lay at the bottom of the hill.

An icy burst of wind howled past as he dismounted, then hurried down the slope.

Half-frozen rocks loosened, clattered ahead of him.

With a curse, he shifted to the right to avoid any falling debris hitting the unconscious woman.

Once he reached the bottom, he knelt by her side. Chestnut-brown hair dusted with the fall of snow framed her angelic face. A gash creased her right brow, and a bruise darkened her cheek, both in stark contrast to her pale skin.

Praying she was alive, Cailin gently touched her shoulder. Once, twice. "Lass."

Eyes the color of water-drenched moss flickered open, focused on him. Their depth, intensity stole his breath.

She gasped, rolled and stumbled to her feet. Favoring her right ankle, she backed away.

Cailin slowly stood. "Dinna be afraid," he said, keeping his voice gentle. "I am here to help you."

A shiver racked her body, then another. Her mouth tightened in pain as she tugged her cape together, then glanced toward the knoll where one of the attackers had seized her moments before. Her gaze narrowed on him. "W—who are you?"

"Sir Cailin." Though years had passed since he'd ridden on Dalkirk land, he couldn't risk her recognizing his surname and warning his uncle, let alone the rest of the earl's reprobates, of his return. "And your name?"

The beautiful woman hesitated, her eyes dark with distrust. "Kenzie."

By her proper speech and the quality of her torn green gown, he suspected she was a woman of noble birth. The lass's reason for keeping her nobility a secret could be endless and as worthy as his own. Nor would he seek an answer.

"Are you from around here?" he asked.

Wary eyes held his. "Are you?"

Blast it. Did her family live within Dalkirk, or had they given the earl their fealty?

"You know the men who attacked me?" she asked, suspicion raw in her words.

He shook his head. The combination of her physical struggle and swelling jaw made his gut twist. By God, he'd catch the scoundrels. He gestured to her leg. "'Twas a nasty fall. You are injured."

Face taut, she shrugged. "Bruised is all."

He grunted. "That I doubt. I will carry you. From how you are favoring your ankle, you canna climb back up on your own."

Defiance blazed in her eyes. "I can make it without your help."

Regardless of the pain, if he let her, no doubt she'd try. "Aye, but 'tis rest and a warm fire you would be needing, not climbing up the brae," Cailin said with emphasis, "in pain."

In a calmer setting he would have pondered her bold manner. But with her injury, the snow falling at an increasing rate, and the howl of the bitter wind, they needed to find shelter.

Scraping her teeth over her lower lip, she scoured the surroundings, then stilled

He followed her gaze.

A step to his left, half-buried in snow, lay her *sgian dubh*, a smear of blood across the blade.

Before she could move, he retrieved the knife and wiped it clean. Handle facing her, he offered her the dagger.

Wary eyes held his as she accepted her weapon. "Why are you helping me?"

"You were in danger."

She sheathed her blade. "As simple as that?"

"Aye." He held out his hand. "We must go before the weather makes travel impossible."

After a brief hesitation, during which her gaze seemed to pierce his and evaluate his trustworthiness, she placed her hand upon his open palm.

At the silkiness of her skin against his, Cailin smothered the flare of awareness. Irritated by the desire she stirred, he lifted her in his arms.

Snow crunched as he carried her up the steep, icy incline. He tried to ignore how good her body felt against him, failed. At the top of the cliff, more than ready to put distance between them, he gently set her on her feet.

Cheeks flushed, she moved back, clearly trying to shield that her ankle caused her pain. "I thank you, Sir Cailin. I owe you much. I—" Her face paled as she twisted around with a gasp. "My horse!"

Blast it, the thieves had circled back and taken her steed. "Do you know their names?"

She paused, then shook her head. "I have never seen them before today."

No doubt the robbers had believed her a lady, and easy prey. "Why are you riding without a proper guard?"

* * * *

Dismayed by the turn of events, Elspet studied the handsome knight. Dark red hair framed blue eyes that no doubt had made many a woman desire. His muscle-hewn body and confident stance that of a man used to taking charge.

Was this warrior one of the Earl of Dalkirk's men out searching for her? She struggled for an explanation that would satisfy the formidable knight so she could leave before he recognized her.

"I was en route to my aunt's home in the Western Highlands when thieves attacked my guard. He was…" She drew in a ragged breath, allowing the terror, the fear that at any moment she'd be caught haunting her since she'd fled Tiran Castle to fill her words. "H—he died. I escaped, or believed I had. But the men caught up to me and…" Her breath hitched. "Thank God you arrived."

"They willna touch you again," he said, his voice somber. "That I swear."

A sense of rightness flowed from this man, a strength, an integrity that left her feeling vulnerable and exposed. Shaken, Elspet dragged in a steadying breath. "How I wish you could promise such."

Intense blue eyes held hers. "I mean what I say."

However foolish, more so after her neighbor's betrayal hours before and with him possibly one of the earl's men, she believed him. "Never have I seen you before."

The daunting knight's eyes grew unreadable. "I am but traveling through."

Tension in her body eased. Thank God, he was not in service to the noble. "You are a stranger to Dalkirk lands. What you witnessed today was but a pittance of the lawlessness the earl allows his men."

Surprise flickered in Cailin's eyes. "Your attackers are men within his guard?"

She hesitated. Regardless if he was an outsider and ignorant that the earl had ordered his knights to catch and kill her, 'twas wisest to take care with what she revealed. Another shiver swept her. "Ignore my ramblings, 'tis exhaustion feeding my words."

A frown creased his brow. After a moment, he nodded. "'tis time to leave."

"Where are you going?"

"*We*," he said with emphasis, "are going to an inn where I have a room for tonight. You will have a meal, and a place to rest while your injury mends."

One she'd passed earlier this day. Though far enough away from where anyone would recognize her, without coin or time, she'd avoided the tavern. Neither did she wish to go with him.

She shook her head. "I canna—"

"While we sup," he continued, "we will discuss arrangements for you to reach your destination."

"You would accompany me to my aunt?"

"Nay. As you are without sufficient funds, I will arrange for an escort."

"I..." Elspet smothered another surge of guilt. "Your generosity is appreciated, but I refuse to disrupt your travels further. If you would kindly spare a pound, which will cover fare, meals, and lodgings for the remainder of my trip, I willna delay you further." Lowering her lashes a degree, she gave him a demure look. "Money I assure you, once I know where you are headed, that I will repay."

He shook his head. "I dinna carry such a large amount when I travel."

She smothered a burst of panic. Merciful saints, what was she going to do?

"I understand and appreciate your kindness," she forced out, "but I nay longer need your assistance."

A red brow lifted in stunned disbelief. "You want me to leave you here, injured and without a horse or protection?"

Straightening her shoulders, she limped back a step. "Aye. If I find the need to rest, as you said, there is an inn nearby."

He frowned. "With the way the storm is worsening, *we* will be fortunate to reach the tavern by horse, much less on foot. Or, in your case, hobbling. Nor, by your admission, can you pay for a room."

Blast it. She scowled at the thick flakes tumbling past, damned the throb in her ankle. All she needed was the coin, not more time spent with a man who made her notice the hard cut of his jaw, nor his eyes as blue as the ocean, not to mention the delay that may cost her stepbrother his life.

An errant ray of light broke through the clouds and shimmered off the knight's broadsword.

Elspet stilled. Atop a leather grip, a carved gold crest lay etched within the pommel, with intricate carvings on the guard. She'd believed him but a knight, though a warrior could far from afford such a superior weapon, garb of such quality, or a destrier of such caliber.

Unease rippled through her. God in heaven, who was he? If of nobility, why had he not proclaimed his title? Regardless, a sword of this quality would bring more than enough to pay the guard to free Blar.

She lifted her gaze to his, distaste swirling on her tongue. The last thing she wished to do was to steal this courageous man's weapon, nor did she wish to risk trying to rob an unsuspecting traveler. She brushed her fingers against the bruise on her cheek. Too well she understood the danger in such a foolish choice. Though she despised her decision, time to reach the guard was running out. "I agree."

A dry smile touched his mouth. "I thank you, my lady, for allowing me to offer you escort."

She didn't correct him. Let him think she was of noble birth, not the daughter of a farmer. 'Twould make it more difficult when he tried to find her.

The warrior swung into his saddle. With ease, he lifted her before him.

Elspet tried to ignore the hard ripple of his muscles against her body, his warmth, the strength of his arms as they circled around her to lift the reins, or how, for this moment, she felt safe. Given her predicament, she had no business noticing anything about this handsome knight.

Cailin draped his cloak around her. "I will protect you," he said, as if sensing her need for reassurance, then he kicked his steed into a gallop.

Protect her? If he knew what she had planned this night, he would have abandoned her to her fate.

* * * *

A short while later, settled in their room at the inn, the savory scent of food filled the air and firelight from the hearth illuminated the chamber with a soft, golden glow and warmth. Elspet scowled at how the swelling in her ankle had grown steadily worse.

"I fear my aunt will be worried when I do not arrive," she said.

Cailin tore off a piece of bread, dipped it in the hearty stew, popped it in his mouth, then swallowed. "Given the ferocity of the storm, she will understand the delay."

As she ate her portion of the fare, she scanned their tiny room. Aside from the hearth, a bed with extra blankets folded atop stood in the corner, and nearby sat a small table holding a pitcher of water.

However sparse the furnishings, Cailin's presence seemed to fill the chamber, a potent reminder of her predicament. "'Tis unseemly for us to share this chamber."

"If another room were available, I would agree." He took a sip of ale, grimaced. "God's blade, they must have scraped the dredges of the barrel for this rot. Still, we were fortunate that I had already paid for a room. Given the steady flow of travelers seeking shelter since our arrival, by now even the stable is filled."

Indeed. With the throng of people below, they were lucky to have acquired a meal and drink.

He refilled his goblet. "Sleep in the bed. I will make a pallet beside the hearth."

And once he was asleep, she would leave, though…Another wave of guilt swept Elspet as she glanced toward the finely crafted broadsword hanging near the door and damned the action she must take. If only he'd had the coin to loan her, she wouldn't need to resort to thievery.

While he continued to eat, she fingered the sack of powdered valerian root hidden deep in her gown pocket. A healthy dose would make him sleep, and the bitter taste of the brew would mask the herb.

Though she regretted taking his weapon, except for any personal attachment to the broadsword, for a powerful man of wealth, procuring another would be naught but an inconvenience. More important, on the morrow she'd meet with Wautier Brecnagh, a merchant known for purchasing stolen goods.

Her heart stumbled whenever she thought of Blar locked away in that gruesome dungeon, and prayed the merchant would give her enough to pay the guard to save Blar's life. Beneath half-lowered lashes, she studied Cailin. At least once she departed, she'd never see this handsome warrior again. Given the stakes, neither could she afford to care what he would think of her.

Elspet rubbed her arms. "'Tis cold."

Eyes dark with concern swept over her. "Exhausted and injured, you might be coming down with a chill." He crossed to the hearth.

With his back to her, on a trembling breath, she withdrew the valerian root. After a quick glance to ensure he hadn't turned, she sifted a liberal amount into his ale, stirred.

Logs clunked in the hearth, and her fingers jerked. A swath of powder spilled on the table. Nay! She swept away the residue, secured the sack, and then stowed the herb.

Sparks swirled within the churn of smoke as he laid several smaller pieces of wood into the flames. Brushing the dirt from his hands, he stood. "That should keep us warm for the night." He walked over, settled in the chair, and lifted his mug. Cailin's brow furrowed.

Her heart pounded. God in heaven, had she missed some of the powder? "Do you have a large family?" she blurted out, desperate to distract him.

Weary blue eyes shifted to her. "If I reply, will you be answering my questions about yourself as well?"

Tension eased within her. He suspected naught. "Nay."

With a grunt, he lifted his cup in a mock toast, downed the brew, then hissed, shoved aside the mug. "'tis dreadful, but it wets the throat."

She forced a smile. "As you said, we were fortunate that any food or drink remained."

"Nay doubt until the storm arrived, they had planned on dumping this foul brew." He shoved aside the goblet, then stood. "Go to sleep."

"I thank you." Mindful of her throbbing ankle, Elspet limped to the bed, then slipped beneath the covers. Feigning sleep, she watched for signs of the herb taking effect.

At the hearth, he made a pallet. Instead of lying down, he knelt and then made the sign of the cross.

Soft whispers of the Lord's Prayer reached her, each word thick with grief, each verse as if dredged from his soul. Once Cailin finished, he began again.

Mesmerized by the intensity, riveted by the passion, she couldn't look away. What had happened to cause him such torment? A part of her tried to ignore the anguish in his voice, but another longed to offer him succor.

Elspet's heart ached. His faith was a potent reminder of how, days before, her belief in Him had been just as strong. But after what she'd witnessed yesterday, she could no longer fathom believing in a God who would allow people to endure such horror.

After whispering several more Paternosters, he again made the sign of the cross and then sat back.

On a yawn, the warrior glanced toward her.

Through her lashes, she watched him.

For a long moment, he studied her.

And why wouldn't he be curious? She'd revealed naught about her past, and during their brief discussion of her travels, she'd remained vague. Neither had she pressed him for information.

However ill-timed and destined to be short-lived, she found herself drawn to this handsome warrior. Foolish indeed when soon she would be leaving.

He started to turn away and almost tipped over. Muttering a curse, he righted himself.

"Cailin?"

His lids raised, and she caught his slightly dazed look. She gave a relieved sigh. The valerian root was beginning to take effect.

"Aye?" he replied.

"I want to thank you for rescuing me this day."

"'Tis naught."

"I disagree. Many would have ridden past without a care."

"That, I f-find," he slurred, "hard to believe."

"I would have agreed," Elspet said, "but since Gaufrid MacHugh, Earl of Dalkirk, took control of Tiran Castle years ago, he rules with a brutal hand."

He sat, braced himself against the wall, giving his head a quick shake, as if to clear the confusion. "Explain?"

What could it hurt? He was unlikely to remember this conversation. "He is a cruel man. All within Dalkirk fear him."

"As do you?"

Horrific memories of the day before rolled through her. "Nay. I despise him."

"Why?"

Far from pleased by the shift in the conversation, she looked away.

"Kenzie?"

Tears burned her eyes, and Elspet damned that he'd ask or care. The crackle of flames echoed within the chamber, melded with a faint yell and laughter from below, as if the night was like any other.

A soft thud had her turning.

Eyes closed, Cailin lay on the floor, his red hair flopped against his cheek. On his next breath, he gave a soft snore.

Anxious as she'd been for this moment to arrive, now regret weighed heavy in her mind. Though she'd known the knight for mere hours, he seemed good, decent, and kind.

Refusing to let her conscience outweigh what she must do, Elspet pushed from the bed and hobbled over to him as quietly as she could. She allowed herself the luxury of skimming her finger along the hard line of his jaw, then slid the pad of her thumb along his firm mouth.

In sleep, his expression had softened, as if he were a gentle man, though she saw the faint scar on his cheek, and another across the side of his neck that disappeared beneath his garb.

He was a man of war, one who would not tolerate being crossed. When he awoke, he'd be furious.

Something that couldn't be helped.

Pulse racing, Elspet pulled a blanket up to his chest, then moved across the chamber and withdrew his broadsword from the scabbard. The weight of the weapon surprised her, but her gaze shifted to the gold crest etched within the pommel, then to the intricate carvings on the guard. However wrong, this valuable weapon would save Blar's life.

After securing the sword beneath her cape, she opened the door. Throat tight, she glanced back. "I am sorry, Cailin." Favoring her ankle, Elspet stepped into the hallway and quietly closed the door in her wake.

* * * *

Through the fog of sleep, Cailin forced his lids open, peered out. He cursed the pounding in his skull, the dizziness blurring his thoughts, and the awful taste coating his tongue. Blast it, where was he, and why did he feel as if he'd drunk too much? Foggy memories of the men assaulting Kenzie rushed through his mind, of saving her, and then their travel through the blizzard to the inn. He sat. Pain spiked his head. With a slow sweep, he scanned the unfamiliar chamber. Coals glowed in the hearth, the sheets on the bed turned back; a slight impression of where she'd slept remained, but the lass was gone. He rubbed his brow. Mayhap she'd headed downstairs for food. Foolish, when the inn was filled with men and without his protection.

Cailin shoved to his feet, damned another blast of pain. He started to turn, stilled.

His scabbard was empty.

Unease prickled up his spine. Had she taken his weapon to fend off any threats? He grunted. As if with her ankle injured she could swing the sword with any force. Blast it, why hadn't she woken him?

Muttering a curse, he turned, paused at the smear of powder on the floor beside where he'd sat for supper. His mind churned with several reasons for the residue.

None good.

Wanting to be wrong, Cailin stalked over, swiped his finger through the powder, sniffed.

Valerian root!

He glared at the closed door. Nay, he hadn't slept, nor were his ailments the result of too much ale. Kenzie had drugged him and then stolen his broadsword. His anger surged. God's blade, the lass was in league with the men he'd found her with yesterday. They weren't robbing her; 'twas naught but a bloody ploy to fleece him!

Fury seething through his veins, against the splintering pain in his skull, Cailin jerked on his cape, gathered the few belongings he'd brought, then stormed from the chamber.

Aye, he'd find her.

God help her then.

Chapter 2

Her fingers numb from the cold, Elspet tugged open the thick entry of the merchant's cottage. A hand's width above her, metal bits hanging against the door to warn those within of someone entering clanked.

"Shut the bloody door!" a surly voice boomed.

The cold bite of wind blasted against her as she hurried inside, shoved the heavy wood shut.

Warmth permeated the chamber from a fire roaring in the weathered stone hearth, and the rich scents of leather, oil, and age, along with a faint wisp of cooked meat filled the air. Staggered upon the side wall hung several baskets, helmets, swords, a wide array of tools, and, centered against the back, a large woven blanket curtained off a room.

On a table to her right, half buried beneath various pieces of leather, lay an anvil with a hammer atop. Seated behind the disorganized heap on another table to her left, a reed thin, balding man, his mustache infused with gray that curled into a thick beard, scowled at her, a strip of leather in one hand and an awl in the other.

Elspet's shoulders sagged. Thank God Wautier Brecnagh was here.

The merchant set down the leather tool. "'Tis a poor day to be out."

An understatement. Falling snow was now knee high, and the wind blew with merciless disregard. Though binding her ankle had allowed her to walk with bearable pain, she'd had to travel throughout the night and a good part of the morning to reach his hut. If desperation hadn't forced her hand, she would have found shelter and hid until the storm passed.

She shrugged as if she wasn't freezing. "A bit of snow."

"And did the snow give you the gash above your eye or the bruise upon your cheek?"

"I–I slipped and fell in the woods. Hit my face against a rock."

With a disbelieving grunt, he set down the piece of leather, then crossed his arms over his chest. He nodded to the bundle wrapped in her arms. "To sell or trade?"

Thankful he hadn't pressed further, her fingers tightened on the covered hilt, and she damned the guilt weighing upon her. "To sell."

Unfurling his arms, he shoved aside the pile of leather, clearing a large swath of the table. "Place it here."

Her hands trembled as she lay down the heavy bundle and unwrapped the blanket.

Firelight glinted off the blade as Wautier lifted the weapon, turned it. Shrewd eyes cut to her. "'Tis a common enough weapon."

"There is little common about this broadsword," she scoffed. "Look at the detail of the engraving on the pommel and hilt."

The lean man shrugged. "I have seen such weaponry before, forged with craftsmanship of higher quality."

A lie. Over the years, when she'd accompanied her stepfather and mother to festivals, she'd seen many knights' swords. Never had she witnessed anything this exquisite. She ached to rewrap the weapon and storm out, except she didn't know of another merchant who dealt in stolen goods, and neither did she have the time to find one.

Nor could she blame him. He did naught but barter to his advantage. Elspet met his gaze square on. "How much?"

"Eight shillings."

Her breath caught in her throat. Moireach had demanded a pound! "'Tis worth at least two pounds."

"Two," he blustered as he lay the weapon down. "'Tis the cost of a palfrey."

"'Tis," she agreed. "But the broadsword is well worth the price."

He rubbed his chin, paused for a long moment. "I will give you nine shillings."

So close to what she needed. Taking a chance, she scowled as if insulted by his pathetic offer. "Never mind." She clasped the sword's hilt.

Wautier's boney hand moved atop hers, his eyes narrowed. "A pound."

Relief filling her, Elspet gave him a cool stare. "The gold on the pommel alone is worth more."

"The reason I raised my offer. Take it—" A gust of wind slammed against the side of the cottage as he withdrew his hand. "Or leave."

"'Tis thievery!" she sputtered with indignation.

"A fair price when I have not questioned how you came by such a fine weapon when you arrive in a tattered gown and cloak, looking little better than a thief." He shot her a sly glance. "Had you purchased the blade through a legitimate venue, never would you have traveled here in the middle of a snowstorm."

Fear building, her stomach clenched.

Aged brows slammed together. "Was the man who owned the blade old?"

"Nay."

"Did you know him?"

"Never had I seen him before." Merciful saints, she must have the coin before he changed his mind. On a shaky breath, she withdrew her hand from his. "I accept your offer."

A cold smile curved his mouth. "You are fortunate I am in such a generous mood."

Generous? With ease he would sell the broadsword for more than two times what he offered her, if not more. Thankful he hadn't pressed for further details of who she'd acquired the weapon from, she focused on the fact that within moments she would have the money and could leave.

The merchant lifted the sword and started to turn.

She caught his arm. "Until I receive the coin, the broadsword remains with me."

Anger flared in his eyes. "So be it." Wautier set the weapon down, crossed to the hanging linen, and shoved the blanket separating the rooms aside, exposing the back of a younger man working, a saddle, tools, blankets, and various items stacked inside the room.

The merchant entered the chamber, and the cover settled into place, cutting off her view.

Again, Elspet glanced around the work area, pausing at the array of swords mounted on the wall. Blackened leather grips from heavy use stained the handle of each one, fractures marred some of the blades, while others displayed chips in the cutting edges. None could begin to compare to Cailin's impressive broadsword.

She worried the finely braided strip of leather around her neck holding a forged Celtic cross of silver with a ruby embedded at the center shielded by her garb. Where was he now? A foolish question. Nay doubt searching for her. But he sought a noblewoman named Kenzie, one he would never find. Once he grew frustrated, the knight would continue on his journey.

Another gust battered the exterior, and she tugged her cape tighter. She far from looked forward to the travel to pay the guard who'd promised to aid her, but her discomfort was a small price. But what if Moireach took her coin and refused to help free Blar?

No, she refused to cling to doubts. She'd met the guard several times. Moireach had always smiled at her as she passed, and once at the castle had helped her load oats she'd purchased into her stepfather's wagon. By this time tomorrow, her stepbrother would be free, and they would be headed toward...

A sinking feeling settled in her chest.

Where?

During yesterday's mayhem, the Earl of Dalkirk had seized their home.

Grief built in her chest. As if where they went at this moment mattered. Blar was her only remaining family. They would be together and free. With the earl furious at their escape, they would go wherever necessary, do whatever they must, to keep safe.

"You want me to travel to Tiran Castle in this weather?" the young man grumbled from behind the curtain.

"Keep your voice down," Wautier hissed.

Elspet stiffened. Why would the merchant want to send his assistant to Tiran Castle and hide the fact from her? She crept closer.

"Tell the Earl of Dalkirk," Wautier whispered, "that I have purchased his brother's broadsword from a thief. I am unsure how 'twas acquired, but warn him that I suspect his nephew, Cailin MacHugh, has returned intending to claim his rightful title."

Confused, she frowned. Sir Cailin was the earl's nephew? How could that be?

"But he died as a lad," the man replied in a low voice.

Something she'd been told in her youth as well.

"Dinna question me!" Wautier hissed.

"A-aye." The youth stumbled out.

"Tell him that the coat of arms on its hilt is proof to those within Dalkirk that Cailin MacHugh is the rightful claimant. A fact," the merchant grumbled, "that will infuriate the earl."

A chair scraped.

With a gasp, Elspet stumbled back. Merciful saints, the warrior who'd saved her, the knight she'd robbed, was the rightful heir of Dalkirk!

With a frown, she stared at the curtain. Why would news that Cailin lived displease his uncle unless... Heart pounding, she took another step back. The Earl of Dalkirk was behind Cailin's supposed death, which must explain why Cailin hadn't ridden straight to Tiran Castle, or disclosed his full name when they'd met.

"And dinna discuss this with anyone but the earl," the merchant said with soft warning.

"A–aye," the lad replied, fear thick in his voice.

She must inform Cailin! Elspet grasped the hilt, hesitated. As if after she'd lied and stolen his weapon Cailin would believe anything she had to say. What if after she explained, he refused to help her? Breath unsteady, Elspet stared at the broadsword. Should she stay for the coin to pay Moireach to free her brother?

How could she? After Cailin had saved her, he deserved to know that his uncle was being informed of his presence on Dalkirk lands. As well, if his uncle was involved in attempting to kill him, Cailin must despise the earl as much as she and would indeed help her free her stepbrother.

Calmer, she accepted the logic of her decision. He had a horse and could make the trip to the guard in but a few hours, when on foot and with her injured ankle, 'twould take her a day. As for how she'd convince Moireach that he could trust Cailin, she would worry about that when the time came.

Steps thudded on the other side of the curtain. The hanging blanket shifted as the outline of the merchant bumped against it. Wautier whispered something too soft for her to hear.

Quickly enfolding the sword in the blanket, Elspet hobbled to the door, scowling at the bits of metal hanging above. With a glance toward the blanket, thankful the makeshift curtain remained in place, she propped the sword against the wall. Withdrawing her *sgian dubh*, she stood on her tiptoes and caught the tied bits of metal in her fist. With a slash, she severed the string, then secured her dagger.

After another glance back, thankful the cover hadn't moved, she picked up the covered weapon, eased the door open, and crept out. Once she'd secured the entry, Elspet tossed the bits of metal, then fled.

Ignoring the shooting pain with each step, the lash of bitter cold wind, she pushed on. At an outcrop of rocks a distance from the merchant's home, she collapsed beneath the stone overhang.

Her breath rolling out in a cloud of white, pain screaming up her leg, she glanced at the covered broadsword, fought the rush of nerves. What if another knight named Cailin had come into possession of the previous Earl of Dalkirk's sword and, as Cailin had claimed, he was doing naught but passing through? Or what if the merchant had misidentified the crest upon the sword?

Or, in her panic, she had erred and sealed her stepbrother's fate? No. After losing her mother and stepfather, she couldn't lose Blar.

Frustrated, she jerked open the blanket. Flakes of snow hurled past as she stared at the gold crest etched within the pommel.

Faded memories of Cailin's sailing to Rome to study came to mind, then news of his death. Much loved as he was, all within Dalkirk had mourned his passing. She slid her finger across the tip of the hilt as she recalled how Cailin's father's sword had disappeared. Rumors of a witch's curse upon the blade, of fairies taking the weapon to the Otherworld, or a ghost hiding the sword to preserve it for Cailin's return were among many reasons for its disappearance. Regardless, the broadsword had never been seen since. Until now.

Memories of how Cailin had faced the two braggarts without hesitation, of his chivalrous actions to ensure she had food and rest flickered in her mind. Nor could she overlook how his confident actions, quick decisions, and intelligence bespoke a man of noble birth.

Elspet's finger stilled on the crafted hilt. The sword belonged to Cailin and, God willing, she would return it to him.

With a grimace, she shoved to her feet and shifted the weapon to her other arm. Ignoring the stabbing pain in her ankle, she pushed on.

* * * *

Cailin shielded his face as he rode, damned the sharp sting of snow that had buried Kenzie's tracks hours before. Blast it, where was she? Injured and slowed by his heavy sword, he found satisfaction in knowing that wherever the lass was, she couldn't have traveled far.

If, indeed, she was alone.

When he'd first begun his search, he'd expected to find naught but hoof tracks leading away from the inn. Then he'd picked up her awkward steps with ease.

As he'd trailed Kenzie, he kept waiting for her steps to merge with the hooves of her accomplice's steed. Proof she was in league with the two miscreants he'd found her with yesterday, men who'd awaited her departure from the inn and were long gone. But her tracks had remained solitary as they headed north.

Over time, snow had begun to fill her trail; then any signs of her passing had become undiscernible against the bulky blanket of white. That her path never wavered from its direction kept Cailin pushing on, searching for a fragment of her torn gown or broken twigs to expose signs of her passing, anything that would alert him that he was closing in on her.

What tragedy had she endured to convince her to join such a disreputable lot? Her quick wit, bearing, bravado, and, though ruined, her quality gown, assured him that she was a woman of means. More perplexing, he was a good judge of character. That he hadn't an inkling of her deceit until too late left him unsettled.

Cailin tried to dismiss his draw to her beauty, the ease with which he'd been able to speak with her. Regardless of her duplicity, there was something genuine about her, an innate sense of hurt she tried to shield.

With a frustrated sigh, he shook his head. 'Twas a sad day when after her deception he'd seek a motive for her thievery.

He kicked his steed into a canter and hardened his heart. When he found Kenzie, regardless of her nobility, she'd be answering his questions. However beautiful, and though she stirred his blood, she'd proven she was a lass he couldn't trust.

He scowled at the steep incline ahead. How much longer until he found her? Blast it. The broadsword was proof of his claim as the rightful earl.

The soft thud of hooves upon snow accompanied Cailin as he rode through the weave of leafless birch. Slashes of black smeared the white bark, thin strips he'd used many times over to start a fire or, in times of urgency, to pen a missive. But today, the majestic trees laden with snow upon their barren branches were naught but a reminder of the oncoming winter.

Cailin nudged his steed around a large copse of rocks, then guided him higher up the incline. A short distance ahead, pine, alder, and ash stood like sentinels to the windswept valley below, one as a child he'd ridden through many times over with his father.

Tragic memories of how he'd lost his parents twisted inside. When his uncle, Gaufrid MacHugh, had stepped in to become his guardian and to run Tiran Castle until Cailin was of age, he'd been an innocent child struggling with the loss of the parents he loved, and had been thankful.

A month later, Gaufrid's decision to send him to Rome for a proper education to prepare him for the day he claimed the title of earl was one that made sense.

But 'twas a lie.

Once away from port, the ship's captain had revealed that his uncle had paid him a handsome sum to kill Cailin. Instead, swayed by greed, the miscreant had sold Cailin to pirates, believing the lad would die at sea and his uncle none the wiser. A cruel plan that would have succeeded if the pirates hadn't attacked a cog of the Knights Templar.

Rescued by the Brotherhood, without coin, connections, experience, or a fighting force to reclaim Tiran Castle, Cailin had remained with the Templars while he'd struggled against the grief at his parents' death and his uncle's betrayal. But, in the back of his mind, thoughts of one day avenging Gaufrid's betrayal remained.

Once of age, without means, he'd set aside his thoughts of vengeance and joined the Brotherhood. There, he'd found a life he'd cherished until King Philip's treachery two years before.

Fury slammed through Cailin at thoughts of the French monarch's duplicity against the Templar Knights, elite warriors who'd protected him over the years. Men of honor who, in the sovereign's desperation to replenish his coffers, he'd sacrificed without hesitation.

Though absolution was the teaching of the Church, for the wrongful accusations and slaughter of warriors who'd vowed to protect the innocent, men who'd given their lives to serve the Brotherhood's cause, Cailin could never forgive King Philip.

With the Templars secretly disbanded, he, as many within the Brotherhood, had fled to Scotland to serve King Robert, whom few knew was a Templar. Knowledge Cailin still found incredible.

Cailin was thankful he'd gained the Bruce's support in reclaiming his birthright, his lands and the title of Earl of Dalkirk, from his treacherous uncle, who'd supported King Robert's adversary, Lord Comyn. More so the Bruce's promise to send troops as soon as possible to support Cailin's cause. With the lull in fighting the king's bid to claim Scotland, knights that would soon arrive.

Nor had he expected his sovereign's gift of Cailin's father's broadsword. A weapon he'd never again thought to see. The Bruce had explained how Father Lamond, a priest faithful to Cailin's father, had seized the weapon, then secretly delivered the blade to the king.

A snow-littered gust of wind swept past. His horse slowed, snorted as he half-walked, half-slid down the steep incline. "Easy, boy." He scanned the valley below.

Sparkles of sunlight glinted off the pristine white like diamonds scattered. A smile touched his mouth as he thought of the way his mother used to tell him the shimmers were magic dust sprinkled over the land by the fey.

His fingers tightened on the reins. Nay, the glitters upon the frozen ground were naught but tricks of light, a tragic reminder that the woman he'd loved was lost.

A grimace settled upon his mouth. He had more important forces to face than fairies.

Several paces from the copse of pine at the bottom, branches shifted and snow tumbled from the limbs.

He halted his destrier and withdrew his dagger.

Tangles of chestnut-brown hair tossed within the snow-whipped wind as Kenzie limped into view, a bruise dark on her cheek, minimal swelling on her jaw, the gash on her right brow showing signs of healing, and his father's sword partially wrapped in a blanket in her arms.

Rage pulsing through his veins, Cailin scoured the area. Naught but another gust of snow whirled past.

She lifted her head and her eyes seared him, an action at odds with someone who'd wronged him. Her shoulders seemed to stiffen beneath her bulky woolen cape as she clutched his stolen sword, yet her gaze remained unwavering.

"I am alone," she called with impressive confidence for one who had committed a treasonous act, yet managing somehow to look as if she was the victim.

That he doubted. "Where is your horse?"

"As I explained yesterday, I have none."

Cailin grunted. "You said the men had taken your mount."

"I lied." She limped toward him. "Never had I planned to see you again."

"And the men who supposedly robbed you?" he demanded. "Am I to accept that injured, you somehow hobbled this far, or after you have given me naught but mistruths, am I to believe anything you say?"

"Suspicion I would deserve." Favoring her right ankle, the one bound with sturdy cloth, she limped forward, struggling up the incline. "I came to return your broadsword." Kenzie paused a pace away and unwrapped the weapon. Cloth fluttered in the wind as she raised the forged steel, hilt first, toward him. "'Twas wrong of me to take it."

"Wrong?" Ignoring a twinge of pity at her struggle, he leaned forward, retrieved his blade. "'Twas thievery."

Her face pale, she nodded. "'Twas. I was desperate and needed coin to save my stepbrother."

Far from persuaded by her demure demeanor or that anything she shared was the truth, he sheathed his sword. "And your companions?"

"Travelers whom I had robbed earlier in the day." She captured several strands of hair fluttering against her face, secured them in her braid. "When you rode in, they had caught up with me and seized their coin, which I had taken earlier. Only"—a blush swept her cheeks—"I had not planned on their..."

Wanting her for their pleasure, he silently finished to himself. Could he believe her, or was this yet another deceptive tale? Though Cailin hesitated to accept any of her claims as the truth, her having stolen from the travelers explained their anger. "And your stepbrother?"

Hope ignited in her eyes. "The reason I am here. I seek your help to save him."

Cailin crossed his arms. "A request you could have made without drugging me *or* stealing my weapon."

Her breath rolled out in a broken cloud of white. "I–I am explaining this poorly."

God's teeth, why the devil was he allowing her to ramble on? With his weapon recovered, he should leave her to her fate. "Save your lies for another." Cailin shot her a cool glare as he picked up his reins. "Away with you before—"

"I know you are Cailin MacHugh," she burst out, "the rightful heir of Dalkirk!"

He wanted to dismiss her claim, but there could only be one way she'd discovered his identity; she'd heard it from another. "Explain."

In detail, she described how she'd brought his sword to Wautier Brecnagh, a merchant known to purchase stolen goods. While awaiting payment, how she'd overheard him send his assistant to warn the Earl of Dalkirk that Wautier had purchased a broadsword bearing the earl's family's coat of arms from a thief. And how the merchant suspected the earl's nephew had returned to claim his rightful title.

So bloody much for anonymity, or time to refamiliarize himself with his home and plan how best to confront his uncle and seize Tiran Castle.

On trembling legs, Kenzie knelt, bowed her head. "I swear my fealty to you, my lord."

"I am not the Earl of Dalkirk," he snapped.

Emerald eyes lifted to him. "You are the rightful heir." At his silence, she continued, her gaze unwavering. "Years ago, your uncle informed the people of Dalkirk that you had tragically died at sea. Obviously 'tis a lie. On my word of honor, I swear I will do all within my power to ensure you receive your title."

"I am unsure if you are brave or stupid," he charged, anger seeping through his words. "After your deceit and theft, do you honestly believe I will ever give your word any weight?"

Frustration flashed in her eyes. "I risked my life to warn you!"

A muscle worked in his jaw as he scanned their surroundings. Naught but tree branches rattled in the wind. Far from convinced, he glared at her. "Nay, you risked your life to help save your stepbrother." He reined his horse back. "I canna help you."

"I returned your sword!"

He refused to be swayed by the desperation in her emerald eyes. However beautiful, she'd proven herself a woman he couldn't trust. "Fear guided your hand in returning my weapon," he said with cold warning, "one you were foolish to have dared taken. Rest assured, had you not come before me, I would have found you."

"You dinna understand; without your help, my stepbrother will die!"

A sliver of doubt wedged inside him. Damning he'd waste time to ask, he nodded. "Tell me, why should I believe you?"

* * * *

Elspet didn't know why but thanked God he was giving her another chance. "A fair question. One I would ask in your stead. More so as I have given you little reason to do more than see me hang." Her voice wavered despite her willing it to be strong. "But I swear what I tell you from this moment forward is the truth."

He arched a skeptical brow, then again scanned the area before his wary gaze cut back to her.

Merciful saints, she had to convince him to help her! The last thing she wished was to again steal his weapon for coin or, with him suspicious of her now, was that even possible?

"Where is your stepbrother?"

She ignored the condemnation and focused on the fact that he hadn't ridden away yet. "I believe Blar is locked in the dungeon at Tiran Castle."

"Believe?" he drawled.

"After the earl killed my mother and stepfather," she rushed out, "they hauled my stepbrother to the stronghold."

"And you know this how?"

"Because after his butchery—" she fought past the bile in her throat— "the earl hauled me to his chamber, intent on making me his mistress."

Anger darkened the knight's eyes, and a chill swept her at the cold fury within them. "Yet you escaped."

"Aye," she said, struggling against the horrific memories that would haunt her for the rest of her life. "When he tried to take me, I jammed my knee into his groin. While he lay screaming in agony, I fled. As I ran from the castle, I heard his shouts for his men to kill me."

Blue eyes narrowed as Cailin studied her a long moment, as if weighing her words. "Why did you remain on Dalkirk lands? You must know that the earl isna a man to offer false threats."

Emotion burned her throat. "I–I couldna leave Blar to die."

"How was robbing the men, or me, providing you with a hope to save him?"

Elspet exhaled an unsteady breath. "I found a guard, Moireach, who, for a pound, agreed to free my stepbrother."

Cailin arched a doubtful brow. "And with the earl calling for your death, you believed one of his guards would help you?"

"I have seen Moireach several times over the years. Though not a friend, neither is he a stranger. I thought..." A shudder ripped through her as she clung to her desperate hope. "Aye, I believed him."

"Then you are a fool," Cailin stated, his words as frigid as the snow-covered ground. "Once you paid the guard, he would have hauled you before the earl. That is, once he'd slaked his lust and *if* he'd allowed you to live."

"You are wrong!" She staggered back, damning him, damning the sense of hopelessness engulfing her. "Go to the devil. I dinna need you. I will save Blar myself!"

Elspet whirled and half-hobbled, half-stumbled down the incline, refusing to focus on the panic rising in her chest. Cailin was wrong. Moireach would aid her; she only needed to acquire the coin he'd demanded.

The thud of hooves was her only warning a second before Cailin's strong arm swept her up and plopped her before him on his destrier. She tried to dive off.

His hold tightened.

Elspet whirled, but he caught her arms as she tried to attack. Breath coming fast, she narrowed her gaze. "Let me go."

"If you somehow procure the necessary coin and reach the guard, you will be dead."

"Dinna you realize that if I do not, my stepbrother will die!"

Cailin's eyes bore into hers. "Had the earl wanted to kill your stepbrother, he would have slain him, not hauled him to the castle."

Through the fragments of lucid thought, she focused to his words. "Then you will help me?"

A muscle tightened in his jaw. "Nay."

Chapter 3

Grief tore through Elspet as Cailin held on to her as he rode. All her risks, her foolish belief he would aid her, for naught. She should have hidden Cailin's sword and secured his agreement to help save Blar before giving it back. Foolishly, she'd convinced herself that with the earl destroying both their lives, and with her returning the sword, Cailin would help her.

"Lass," Cailin said, his voice laden with ire as she continued to struggle against him.

"You bastard, I was a fool to ever think you would help me!"

"Blast it, I—"

Elspet twisted free, raked her nails down his face.

With a roar of pain, he jerked back.

Pulse racing, she dove from the horse, hit the snow, then shoved up. Clenching her teeth against the pain in her ankle, she ran.

The thud of hooves sounded behind her.

She scrambled beneath a line of thick, snow-laden brush. Thankful the steep bank forced him to circle around, she climbed to her feet and took off again.

"Kenzie!"

She ran faster.

The crusted ledge beneath her suddenly shifted. Tremors rippled in the frozen shelf.

No! She grabbed for a limb.

The outcrop crumbled with a loud whoosh, gave.

A scream ripped from her as she plunged within the hurl of snow, the blur of white broken by glimpses of blue that she managed to glimpse above. After a final tumble down the incline, Elspet rolled to a halt.

The soft clop of hooves halted nearby.

Gasping for breath, the sky clear, as if mocking the way her entire body hurt, she glanced over.

Cailin jumped down, his expression fierce.

Another burst of pain shot through her as she tried to struggle to her feet. Her legs wobbled and she collapsed.

He stepped toward her.

Blast it, she'd almost escaped. "Dinna touch me!"

"That answers whether you are alive," he grumbled.

"As if you care? Leave! If I never see you again, 'twould be none too soon."

His scowl darkened as he studied her. "And where will you go? Or are you willing to stake your life that a guard, one who demands coin to champion your cause, is a man you can trust?"

Heat burned her cheeks. "As I explained before, Moireach and I have spoken a few times."

"A few times?" Cailin muttered a curse. "Knowing his name doesna make him less of a stranger."

She angled her jaw. "Was trusting a man I had met but a few times a decision easily made? Nay. After my escape from Tiran Castle, terrified, betrayed by people I believed were friends, and frantic to save Blar's life, I made the choice I believed best."

Though now, she realized the recklessness of her decision. However much she damned Cailin's intervention, he was right. If she'd achieved her goal and given Moireach the coin, with the guard's loyalty to the earl, odds were she would find herself locked in the dungeon.

Or raped.

Or dead.

The futility of the situation threatened to overwhelm her, but she smothered her despair. She refused to do nothing.

She eyed Cailin, and an idea came to mind of how she might convince him to assist her. Though she far from trusted him, he'd proven himself an honorable man when he'd rescued her from harm and offered her shelter. Neither was he a brutal man, proven when he hadn't beaten her after she'd stolen his blade and he'd caught up to her, but sought the reason for her less-than-honorable actions.

Nor, in the brief time they'd spend together, would she have to do more than keep a close watch on him. Once they helped Blar escape, she and her stepbrother would flee Dalkirk land and never see Cailin again.

* * * *

Snow smeared Kenzie's face, hair, and her tattered gown as she stared up at Cailin. Arching a fierce brow, he folded his arms across his chest. "I should *leave* you. 'Twould be a lesson for your stubbornness."

She eyed him as if on a dare. "But you willna."

God's blade, the lass had bravado, that he would give her. Far from wanting another confrontation, he rubbed the back of his neck at the tension gathered there. He should abandon the willful lass to her fate. Yet, for some unexplainable reason, he couldn't. "And why is that?"

"Because you need me to aid you in your quest."

"Indeed?" he asked, his voice dry. How in Hades did she think she could help him?

"You have been away for many years. Though you know names from your childhood, could perhaps recognize a few people, you dinna know who to trust, or the places we can hide until you seize Tiran Castle."

The matter-of-factness in her tone had a smile tugging at his lips. A Knight Templar, he didn't need a lass, more so one of the nobility, hindering him.

Nor was discovering those within Dalkirk who would be loyal to him a significant challenge. King Robert had bid him to find a trusted contact, Sir Angus McReynolds, a stalwart man Cailin had met on several occasions. One who had brought the Bruce secret missives from Father Lamond, and a person who would take Cailin to the priest without question.

"I will find my way about without your aid," Cailin said, "along with discovering those who remain loyal to me."

"Mayhap, but with your presence revealed to the earl, an exposure I sincerely regret, your travel within Dalkirk, as with every contact made, will be at great risk."

He rubbed his jaw. A valid point. Once Gaufrid discovered the arrangements for Cailin's death years before had failed, the blackguard, would do whatever was necessary to keep the earldom, including ensuring Cailin's death this time.

No doubt his uncle would not only send his guard in search of him but keep a close watch on friends from Cailin's past to see if he tried to approach them, or if their actions grew suspicious. Regardless, he refused to allow this complication to alter his intent.

Frowning, Cailin reached down to her.

She pushed his hand away. "Wait, where are we going?"

Blast it, did she not realize the danger they were in? "You are staying with me *only* until I decide what to do with you." He leaned a hand's width from her face. "Try to fight me again and I will leave you to the wolves."

"I—"

"You lied to me, stole from me. If I were you, I would count my blessings I am taking you along."

Fire flared in her eyes, but Kenzie remained silent.

Though tempted to leave her, if she was indeed alone, which, considering her condition, he was beginning to believe, cold and injured, she would die.

After swinging up on his horse, he hauled her up before him and headed west.

* * * *

Later that day, deep in the cave, Cailin added several dry limbs of ash to the growing fire, thankful the curve of the chamber shielded any glow of light from outside. He rubbed his hands before the growing flames, glanced over at Kenzie curled up beneath the blanket, her eyes closed.

During their ride, she'd fallen asleep. Given the distance she'd traveled on foot before meeting up with her, he wasn't surprised.

He grimaced, unsure if she was more foolish or brave. She'd risked great injury in travelling through such miserable conditions to at first escape and then to find him. A fact that supported her claim of her family's fate. Regardless, neither his regret for her loss nor her plight swayed him.

While he reclaimed his birthright, the dangers would be many. Unseasoned in war, there were risks she wouldn't understand. 'Twas best to leave her where she'd be safe.

Where was the question.

Flames snapped as they slowly consumed the dry wood, and the waver of light from the growing flames shimmered over her.

In sleep, with wisps of her deep chestnut hair framing her face, she looked like an innocent maiden. A far cry from the brazen lass earlier this day, her emerald-green eyes dark with fury searing into his own.

If all she'd shared was true, she was a woman who would hold her own against the odds, fight for those she loved, go to any lengths to right a wrong.

A rare lass indeed.

Cailin grunted. He'd known few women of such caliber. All whom were now married to his friends. Not that he cared about her. He couldn't afford to. When it came time to leave, he would walk away without looking back.

Her lashes flickered, opened. Confusion shadowed her eyes as she looked around, then her gaze landed on him and grew wary.

A sliver of regret shimmered in his mind. Cailin sat back.

With a wince, she sat up and looked around. "Where are we?"

"In a cave."

"There are several nearby."

He tried to ignore the soft roughness of her voice, thick with sleep. "Aye." Annoyance sparked in her eyes, bolstering his irritation with himself for noticing anything about her.

Kenzie tugged her cape closer and she glanced toward the flames. "I know you dinna believe you can trust me, misgivings I have more than earned, but I swear to you, from this moment on, I will speak naught but the truth."

"There is little you could disclose that I would find useful."

"As I stated earlier this day, I know places where we can hide until you seize Tiran Castle. More importantly, I know people who will help you."

Cailin lifted a stick from the fire, watched the curl of smoke. "Such as?"

"I risk much by telling you," she said, nerves making her voice waver.

Doubtful, he remained silent. If she indeed proved herself reliable, once he claimed his birthright, 'twould be beneficial to have another person on Dalkirk land he could trust. Cailin gave a curt nod.

She wet her lips. "I am a friend of Father Lamond, who I know was a confidant of your father. A man I believe will help you."

He stilled. Father Lamond, a trusted adviser of King Robert and the priest who'd risked his life to recover his father's broadsword and deliver the blade to the Bruce. The weapon the king had presented to him but days ago, and the man Sir Angus McReynolds was to lead him to.

Refusing to allow Kenzie to know the significance of the cleric to him, Cailin shrugged, cast a flaming twig into the blaze. "I heard he was banished."

"He was."

"Yet he remains nearby?"

Kenzie reached up, touched the edge of a finely braided strip of leather around her neck. "Father Lamond is important to you, is he not?"

Pleased by her uncertainty, he added several more sticks to the flames. Sparks popped, curled up within the thin wisps of smoke. "He is a man I wish to speak with."

Hope brightened in her eyes. "If I tell you where he is, will you help me save my stepbrother?"

Cailin slanted her a cool look. The lass was like a dog with a bone. "Nay, for the reason I have already explained."

Her fingers tightened on the braided leather. "I must know if Blar is alive. Can you not at least agree to discovering that?"

The last thing he wanted was to concede to any condition, but Father Lamond was a crucial contact who would help him claim his legacy. Bloody hell. By now he'd intended to have found Sir Angus McReynolds, who would have led him to the priest. The events of the past few days had waylaid his plans. Also an issue she'd shrewdly pointed out, with his uncle warned he was in Dalkirk, Cailin didn't have the luxury to travel unheeded.

With the detour this night, travel back to Sir Angus McReynolds's home would take a day; given the possibility they might need to hide from guards in search of them, more. Time and risk he could avoid if she indeed knew Father Lamond's location.

"If the situation presents itself where we can learn of your stepbrother's fate," Cailin said, "I will find out."

"And if Blar still lives?"

"A decision I will make if the circumstance arises."

In the shimmer of flames, green eyes darkened with frustration. "'Tis little to offer me after I dare expose the location of the priest, whom I know the earl has banished, a man of the cloth who risks his life by remaining nearby." She started to shove to her feet.

Cailin caught her wrist; awareness surged through him. Irritated, he shoved the unwanted draw aside. "Sit. We have much to discuss."

Her eyes narrowed with defiance.

The stubborn lass. "If we learn your stepbrother is alive and his life is at risk, I will try to save him. But if I discover you have lied to me, regardless in how trivial a way, I will abandon you to your fate."

The tension in her body eased. "I thank you and swear you willna regret trusting me."

Though she seemed sincere, he was far from convinced. After her mistruths since they met, he'd be a fool to believe her without proof.

Cailin released her hand. "Where is Father Lamond?"

She tugged the blanket tighter around her, edged closer to the fire. "He lives in a small crofter's hut on the edge of Dalkirk land."

Cailin was stunned his uncle would allow the priest's presence after he'd stolen Cailin's father's sword, an act he knew from his discussion with the king that had led to the earl banishing the cleric. Only fear of the church's power had forced the earl to spare the priest's life.

"The earl consents to his presence?"

She shook her head. "Lord Dalkirk doesna know he is here. Father Lamond changed his appearance, and the earl believes he is Finnean Howe, an ailing man with a malady that is highly contagious."

"Which explains why he is left alone."

"Indeed. He keeps to himself, except for those who covertly visit. When outside, he wears a hooded cloak to shield his face."

Brilliant, and the reason why the priest had seemed to disappear. Even King Robert was unsure of his whereabouts, hence the instructions for Cailin to find Sir Angus McReynolds.

Though this far from explained one critical matter. "Why do you know where the priest lives?"

"'Twas by accident I learned," she admitted. "One night last summer, when I couldna sleep. As 'twas a full moon, I went outside for a walk. When returning, I heard a soft whinny from outside the stable. Worried that intruders may be about, I crept close. In the moonlight, I saw my stepfather saddling one of our horses. After he rode off, I followed him on one of our mares."

"He never saw you?"

A blush swept her cheeks and she shook her head. "Not until after I had arrived at the priest's home. Though upset, my stepfather grudgingly introduced us. It is incredible, but when I met Father Lamond, 'twas as if I had known him my whole life. 'Tis why, after, my stepfather allowed me to join him on his visits to the cleric. But that first night, after my stepfather and I departed, he made me swear never to disclose that we'd met."

"Yet you told me?"

"Because you are the true heir to Dalkirk." She paused. "I have sworn my fealty to you, and though you dinna know me, once my word is given, 'tis not done lightly."

He stared at Kenzie, confused and impressed by the complex passions that defined her. "I regret that I will never meet your stepfather."

"As am I. We were so close, and," she said, her voice growing rough with emotion, "he would have liked you."

Cailin found himself believing that however odd the circumstance came about, he would have liked her stepfather as well. "Mayhap we met during my youth. What is his full title?"

She hesitated. "If you had been introduced, I doubt you would have remembered him, as neither he, nor I, are of nobility."

A muscle worked in his jaw as he stared at her, unsure if he was irritated by her deceptions or impressed by her nerve. He threw another stick into the fire. "Yet you allowed me to believe such."

"I did, but that was when we first met. Then, you were never to find out who I was. When you tried to locate me, which given your determination I discovered during the short time we were together, I knew you would do. Your thinking that I was of nobility, would help ensure that you failed."

"It would, but I know your name." He paused with a shake of his head at her cleverness and understood, impressed further. "Kenzie isna your name."

A smile touched her lips, faded. "Nay, 'tis Elspet."

"Your surname?"

"McReynolds."

A chill trickled down his neck. No, it couldn't be. Though 'twould explain why Father Lamond had trusted her stepfather.

Cailin fought for calm. Look at him, getting ahead of himself. He wasn't sure if there was a connection. Her surname being the same as that of the man King Robert had sent him to find could be naught but a coincidence.

"Who is your stepfather?" he asked with indifference, as if the information wasn't of critical importance.

"Sir Angus McReynolds."

"God's blade," Cailin rasped.

She gasped. "You knew my stepfather?"

"We have met." Regardless of her tie, before he would have kept his word. But her stepfather being Sir Angus McReynolds, a trusted confidant of King Robert, changed everything. He must send word to the Bruce of Sir Angus's death. Bile curdled in Cailin's gut as a darker thought creased his mind. "You said your stepfather was killed by the earl. Why?"

Grief filled her eyes. "He was accused of stealing hart on the earl's land, but I swear, 'tis a lie. My stepfather was an honorable man and would never do such!"

"He wouldna," he agreed. Aware now of her stepfather's secret life, Cailin suspected the earl's motive had little to do with any game Sir Angus may have illegally caught, and prayed he was wrong. "Do you remember there being anything odd or out of the ordinary in your stepfather's days over the past few weeks?"

She frowned. "Odd?"

At the pallor of her face, he gentled his voice, understanding the grief of loss, more so when she'd battled the death of her family days before.

"I know this is difficult, but 'tis important. Did you notice that your stepfather traveled more, had visitors who were strangers, or was doing something around your home you had never seen him do before? Or acting in a secretive manner?"

Her knuckles squeezed the blanket. "Why?"

"Tell me. I swear 'tis important or I wouldna have asked."

"I... A man came to the house about a sennight ago. I thought little of it as we often had strangers stay with us who were passing through. My stepfather was kind that way; he never turned away a traveler."

Because the men who were given shelter weren't strangers, but contacts in league with King Robert, no doubt at times carrying missives to and from Father Lamond. "Do you know the man's name?"

"Nay. Though he bore nay signs of his being a nobleman, his bearing commanded respect. After their meeting, my stepfather seemed on edge, or..."

"Or?"

She frowned and rubbed her forehead. "This will sound strange, but I caught my stepfather looking at the man with a mixture of apprehension and pride." She shrugged. "I know 'tis little."

"Did the man leave anything, say anything you remember as noteworthy?"

"Nay, he...wait. A day after the man left, I noticed that my stepfather was troubled. When I asked him, he wouldna explain. Never had I seen him this anxious. He rode out soon after, when my mother and stepbrother were working in the fields. Worried, I searched through his things in hopes of discovering the reason. I found—" She closed her eyes.

"Steady, lass."

Red-rimmed eyes met his. "I found a map of Tiran Castle, with entries of improvements recently made. At the bottom, along with a brief note, 'twas signed, *Yours in faith, Father Lamond.*" She sniffed. "'Twas the day after that my stepfather was charged with poaching and killed."

Cailin stilled. God's blade. Sir Angus's death was far from serving justice from theft.

"What is it?" Elspet asked, her voice trembling.

Cailin met her gaze, damned what he would reveal. "Your stepfather wasna killed because of false charges of stealing hart but because my uncle discovered his loyalty to King Robert."

Chapter 4

"My stepfather was loyal to King Robert?" Firelight wavered against the cave walls as Elspet fought the grief, the anger surging through her at Cailin's assertion. "You are wrong. His fealty was to Lord Comyn, and he was often called upon and involved with planning significant battles for our liege lord."

Cailin slowly shook his head. "His supposed loyalty was a cover, proven by Father Lamond's name on the document in Sir Angus's possession, a man my uncle knows is loyal to King Robert. Your stepfather gathered information valuable to King Robert, aiding him in his rightful claim of Scotland."

A slow throbbing built in her head as she stared at Cailin, struggled to accept his words. Elspet stilled, finally understanding. "A fact you know because your allegiance is to King Robert as well."

He nodded. "I swore my fealty over a year ago."

"And my stepfather?"

"I first met Sir Angus during a meeting with the Bruce this past summer."

Merciful saints. The time when her stepfather had traveled to take care of important business. She could barely breathe at the enormity of the disclosure. The news shattered the beliefs of the life she'd known. "I never thought, never imagined that…"

"Sir Angus McReynolds was a man trusted by Scotland's king," Cailin continued, his voice filled with respect. "A knight who worked alongside others faithful to the Bruce to quell any who fought to deny him his rightful crown."

She rubbed her brow. "'Tis much to accept. But my stepfather secretly working for King Robert would explain why the Earl of Dalkirk, a loyal Comyn supporter, would want him dead."

"Elspet..."

Questions flooded her mind. "Did my mother know? Was she a supporter of King Robert as well?" Had she died because of the politics of men? Livid, Elspet held up her hand. "Even if you knew, it matters little. Both are dead, murdered by the Earl of Dalkirk."

"Nor," Cailin said through clenched teeth, "will he escape his crimes. That I swear."

The raw violence in Cailin's voice matched that raging through her blood. And why wouldn't he loath his uncle? The Earl of Dalkirk had also killed Cailin's parents during his youth. "How did the earl discover my stepfather's ties to King Robert?"

"As your family lived unharmed until recently, I suspect something raised my uncle's suspicions and so ordered your home watched. His knights must have captured a recent visitor of consequence to Sir Angus, mayhap the knight you spoke of or another, and the information was pried from him."

Bile again crawled up her throat. "You think whoever it was, they were tortured?"

"If he is loyal to King Robert, aye."

The thought of such brutal actions made her want to retch. "Nor should I be surprised," she whispered. "Lord Dalkirk is known for his cruelty, for making people suffer."

She swallowed hard. The crackle of the flames and the scent of smoke within the cave carried on as if everything was normal when 'twas anything but.

"Elspet, 'tis imperative that you help me," he said, his tone soft but firm. "Nor, for your safety, except for Father Lamond, can you tell anyone what I shared with you."

"I willna, I swear it." She hesitated. "You believe my mother knew?"

"I would think she was aware of Sir Angus's involvement. It may be the reason why she was hanged. And," Cailin said, "I seek your allegiance to King Robert."

"If my family's loyalty was given to the Bruce, the decision is simple. I only wished they had told me. Only wished that..." She shoved aside the rush of sorrow. Now wasn't the time for regrets but action. "I give my fealty to King Robert Bruce."

Cailin nodded.

She gasped. "You think my stepbrother is ignorant of his father's true loyalty?"

"Mayhap, 'twould explain why his life was spared, but"—his red brows drew together—"something still feels out of kilter."

"Regardless," she said on a relieved breath, "'tis a reason for which I am thankful. More, it makes sense that my stepfather wouldna want me or his son involved."

"It does. Nor will we have our answers until we speak with him." Cailin sounded distracted. As if he was thinking things out as he spoke.

"Then you will save Blar?"

He gave a curt nod. "I will try."

"I thank you." She wanted to throw her arms around him. He would never know how much this meant to her.

"What of the map to Tiran Castle? Do you know if 'tis still there?"

"Nay. When the guards stormed inside, two grabbed my stepfather. Under the direction of Lord Dalkirk, three others tore apart our belongings until one found the map and handed it to the earl."

"Which makes sense if it was one of the men who visited recently who exposed Sir Angus's loyalty to the Bruce." He grimaced. "And after the search?"

"I saw nay more. The earl ordered his men to haul me to Tiran Castle. When I was dragged into the noble's chamber in the stronghold, he didna have the map, and I..." A tremor shook her and she closed her eyes against the violent memories, her terror, the fear for her life.

"Elspet."

Fisting her hands against the rush of emotion, she turned away, feeling too fragile to combat another memory, afraid if he touched her now, she'd fall apart. "I am tired," she said, damning the tremor in her voice.

The shuffle of clothes was her only warning, then Cailin's strong arms drew her against him. "'Tis all right, let the tears come."

"Release me," she breathed, the swell of tears building in her throat.

Instead, he lay her head against his chest.

A sob tore free, then another. Any semblance of control shattered as great, heart-wrenching sobs poured out, each shaking her body until she was exhausted. In a combination of pain and grief, she collapsed against him. Cailin held her close, the steady rise and fall of his chest like an anchor of goodness against the horrific memories of her family destroyed.

How long she leaned against him, she wasn't sure, but when no more tears would come, she remained still. Shame had her wanting to pull away without looking at him, but pride had her raising her head and meeting his gaze.

* * * *

In the soft waver of firelight, her eyes, red with tears and dark with grief, lifted to Cailin's, and at that moment he couldn't look away. Though she hurt and suffered greatly, she had an innate strength he'd rarely seen. The intensity reminded him of three other special women he'd met: his friend Stephan's wife, Katherine; Thomas's wife, Alesone; Aiden's wife, Gwendolyn.

Yet, however exceptional, Elspet would never have a place in his life. He was a man of war. Though he sought to reclaim Tiran Castle, once it was secure, he would rejoin King Robert. Many years lay ahead before he would return to his home or consider an heir. When time came to seek a wife, no doubt King Robert would dictate who he would wed.

Nor would he allow himself to ponder the point further. Well he knew how war severed a man's dreams. No doubt a woman of such beauty would have many men interested in her, if not one who had spoken for her.

A trickle of possessiveness slid through him that another man would touch her. Cailin dismissed the unsettling thought. They had known each other but a few days, their first meeting far from inspiring trust.

His empathy came from anguish for her loss, a despair he well understood. After having witnessed her family murdered and a stepbrother seized but days before, she was heartbroken.

Understandably so.

A shudder rippled through her, then another. After a slow exhale, she nodded. "You may release me."

With care, Cailin set her away from him. To give her time to gather her thoughts, he tended to the fire, adding several sticks until the flames grew and warmth spilled around him in a slow wash.

"I thank you," she said. "I didna mean to fall apart."

"That you were able to hold in your grief this long is a testament to your strength. Few women would have been so strong-willed."

A fragile smile touched her lips, then faded. "I tend to be a bit more stubborn than most."

He grunted, pleased that her voice had steadied. "A trait I have noticed."

"How did you deal with losing your parents so young?"

Memories of his youth rolled through him, the old, familiar ache. "Years have passed, allowing the heartache to ease."

"Mayhap," she said, "but you remember, and however unwanted, are there not times your grief haunts you?"

"Aye, more than I wish." He picked up a stick and drew a line in the dirt. "When I learned my parents had died in a hunting accident, outwardly I handled the loss, but inside I was inconsolable. Each day was a blur, my grief so strong that I didna live but existed. Every day, everywhere I looked—" he struggled for calm, "there was something I would see that was a reminder of my parents. A reminder of what I had lost."

When he looked up, tormented eyes met his, the eyes of a woman who'd suffered, eyes that understood strife, and he found himself wanting to reveal more.

"Gaufrid assumed the duties of earl until I was of age to claim the title. Months later, when he advised me that he'd made arrangements for my education in Rome, I jumped at the opportunity to escape Tiran Castle, where around every corner 'twould be another memory, another reminder of the loss."

She touched the braided leather hanging around her neck. "I would give anything to have a place to return to, to have at least memories of our time together, but there is naught." Elspet lowered her hand. "As one of Lord Dalkirk's men hauled me onto his horse, they torched our home."

The bastard. Another sinful act to lay at his uncle's feet. "A wrong I will right once I have reclaimed my title."

"There is nay need. Once Blar is free, I will leave."

Cailin frowned. "Where will you go?"

"I am pondering that question, but before I depart, I will see my parents buried."

He touched her shoulder, and she stiffened. "Whatever happens, I swear I will ensure they are given a proper burial."

"I thank you," she whispered and sagged, as if a weight had been lifted from her shoulders.

"As for your departing Dalkirk lands, now isna the time to be making such a decision. Know this: you will always have a place within my home."

Her mouth parted. "'Tis a generous act after the mistruths I told you."

"After your family's fealty to mine, and now King Robert, 'tis an offer you deserve." And one that brought Cailin a sense of peace. Once he returned to fight with the Bruce, Elspet would have protection.

A gust of wind howled outside, and she tugged her cape closer. "'Tis a cold night. I am thankful we have shelter and a fire."

"As I. Once we reach Father Lamond, I will speak with him about finding a place you can remain until I have seized Tiran Castle."

"I willna be left anywhere." Her eyes narrowed. "My stepbrother is in Tiran Castle, and if he is still alive, I will be there to discover such."

He forced himself to be calm, given her recent suffering. "Though I admire your courage, I refuse to allow a woman to willingly place herself in danger. After I have spoken with the priest, whatever I decide, you will heed my decision."

Such arrogance. "Though Father Lamond will be of great help, remember, he lives beneath the name of Finnean Howe and canna risk exposing his identity." She angled her jaw. "However much you dislike the thought of my intervention, with your unfamiliarity of the people, you still need my help."

Irritated she spoke the truth, Cailin dropped the stick and wiped his hands. Given the criticalness of the situation, the last thing he needed was a lass who believed she could make demands, one with a stubborn streak that prompted decisions far from sound.

"*I* will decide what needs to be done *after* I speak with the priest," he stated. "For now, you are exhausted and need to sleep."

Loose strands of chestnut hair lay in frayed twists against her face, pale with exhaustion, but she didn't look away or show any sign of backing down. "As do you."

A grim smile tugged at his mouth. "You would argue with a saint."

"I state naught but fact."

Unsure if her defiance amused or annoyed him, Cailin decided 'twas prudent to shift the topic to safer ground. "How does your ankle feel?"

Far from appeased but giving in to exhaustion, she followed his lead to change the subject and unwrapped the bandage, then rubbed the swollen joint. "It throbs, but less so than yesterday."

"You are fortunate you didna break anything."

"I am." Another wave of weariness swept her, and Elspet glanced about the cave before meeting his gaze. "Do you always care for women you rescue with such thoroughness?"

A tight smile touched his mouth. "Nay. Normally I learn little more than their names."

"Names?" she said, irritated by his admission. Nor did his interest in women matter to her. She had her own life...or had. She quelled the rush of heartache. It had been a strife-filled day. She didn't need to add to it with ridiculous notions. Still, she gave into curiosity. "Have there been many?"

He shrugged. "The duties of a knight are numerous."

"Far from an answer." Neither did she miss how he evaded most questions when it came to details of his life. Though a mystery, nor could she forget how he'd held her when she'd broken down.

Another blast of wind howled outside, a sad, lonely sound.

She inhaled, the tang of smoke entwined with the chill. Though her throat felt sore from crying earlier, she was far from ready to end the conversation. "Why are you only now returning to reclaim your birthright?" His face grew taut, but she caught the shadow of grief in his eyes.

"'Tis a long story," he said, his voice terse.

Sparks burst from the fire, tumbled to the ground, then grew black. She arched a brow. "'Twould seem we have time."

He pushed to his feet. "You need to rest; dawn will soon be upon us. Travel will be difficult tomorrow, more so with Gaufrid's men searching for me."

Despite her invitation, she was almost glad he'd postponed the conversation. Postponed, she reaffirmed to herself, because she wanted answers. Her lids half-closed, she struggled to keep awake.

"Go to sleep."

"What of you?"

"I will keep watch."

Unease rippled through her as she glanced toward the cave entry. "You believe the earl's men are near?"

"I canna be sure, but I willna take any chances."

Warmth from the flames flickered over her, and guilt swept her that he'd sacrifice his comfort to protect her. "There is only one blanket."

"With the fire and your cape, you should be warm enough."

She gave a frustrated sigh. "I wasna concerned for myself but you. 'Twill be cold leaning against the stone."

He shrugged. "I have endured far worse."

"Mayhap, but for now there is nay need."

"I will be fine." Cailin strode to the wall near the entry, paces from the fire, positioning himself where he had a clear view outside.

She scoffed. And he thought she was stubborn? Lifting the blanket, Elspet forced aside exhaustion and pain and, with effort, stood.

As she limped over, Cailin scowled.

"Lean forward," she said.

"Why?"

The sharpness of his tone far from intimidated her. However terse, she was coming to understand this formidable knight. She held out a portion of the blanket. "'Tis said that shared body warmth is essential when in the cold."

His brows furrowed.

"You might as well accept it." She had to smile, which surprised herself, given the tumultuous times. "I willna quit bothering you until you do."

With a grumble, he leaned forward, secured part of the blanket around him. "Sit."

Pleased to have won this battle, she settled beside him and rested her head against his muscled shoulder. Feeling safe for the first time since the attack on her home, she closed her eyes and savored the heat from his body.

Her mind hazed, and slowly her thoughts tumbled onto one another, blurred until blackness enveloped her. An image of herself at home, wandering in the gardens, grew clear, then of knights encircling her and marching her into the castle before the Earl of Dalkirk. Eyes dark with malice, the noble reached out for her. "Nay!"

"Elspet!"

Caught in the nightmare of the earl's attack, she fought the guard's grasp.

"Elspet, 'tis Cailin."

Heart pounding, she stilled. The faint smell of smoke and man filled her every breath, and memories of Dalkirk's attack faded. She opened her eyes.

Illuminated within the flames, sitting by her side, Cailin's worried gaze held hers. "You were having a dream."

"I..." Try as she might, she couldn't push out the words.

He tucked the blanket around her. "More nightmares will come, but over time, they will fade."

His quiet assurance was said with such confidence, such belief. After all he'd endured, he would know. "What did you do to overcome them?"

He gave a bitter laugh. "When I knew that I would live, I poured myself into learning how to use my weapons to become a warrior."

"To reclaim your home?"

"In part, but more, to help those who needed my aid."

How many men would give so unselfishly of themselves? "'Tis noble."

"Nay, 'twas necessary to survive."

"You are making little sense."

"Try to rest."

From the flatness of his voice, it was clear he wouldn't entertain more questions. She yawned and closed her eyes, and in moments lost herself in sleep.

* * * *

Snow whipped against Cailin and Elspet, seated before him, as he guided his destrier through the growing drifts. "How much farther to Father Lamond's home?" he called as another gust hurled past.

Elspet shoved aside the whip of chestnut hair slapping her cheek and tucked it into her braid. "We should arrive before dark."

Blast it, the weather was growing steadily worse. If they hadn't traveled most of the morning, he would head back to the cave. Nor did it help that several times they'd caught sight of his uncle's knights and been forced to hide. Now, with the snow starting to deepen, 'twas slowing their travel further.

Cailin guided his warhorse into a dense stand of fir, then drew him to a halt. "We will rest here a bit." He swung down, lifted her to the ground. "How does your ankle feel?"

She gingerly walked around. "'Tisna worse."

He gestured to the flat expanse of a nearby rock. "Sit there until we depart."

With a nod, she complied.

A horse whinnied nearby.

Cailin placed his finger over his lips, then crept to the dense boughs. He slightly pushed them aside and peered out. Stilled. Several of the earl's knights were riding toward where they hid. Bloody hell!

Chapter 5

Wind hurled snow past as Cailin peered between dense branches of fir, thankful when the small contingent of Dalkirk's knights swerved from where he and Elspet hid then halted about twenty paces away.

A large bearded man, his face hardened into a frown, scanned the area before turning to the others. "We have seen naught all morning."

"I dinna think they have traveled this far west," a fierce-looking warrior to his right said. "We should keep our search closer to Tiran Castle." Snow flew from his mount's hooves as he kicked the horse into a canter, and the others followed.

"They believe we are near the castle." Elspet's breath feathered his ear.

He released the thick branch and met her worried gaze. "For which I am thankful."

She nodded. "We are nearing Father Lamond's home and need to move deeper into the forest."

Once they'd mounted, Cailin guided his steed deep into the weave of trees, thankful for the cover and the break from the wind. Though she hadn't complained, no doubt the hard travel irritated her injury.

After they'd ridden down a steep incline, she pointed toward a break in the shrubs ahead. "Once you reach the opening near the large oak, bear to the right, then we continue for another league."

At the break, he guided his horse through the gap. For as far as he could see stood ancient oaks, their limbs arching toward the sky like battle-seasoned warriors. Sunlight streamed through the branches, illuminating the endless tangle of limbs enshrouded in moss, and the greenish hue that filled the air as if cast by the fey.

Memories rolled through him, and his throat tightened with emotion as he took in his surroundings. "I had forgotten this area. 'Twas one of my favorite places to visit during my youth. I assure you, with the hues of murky green filling the air and illuminated in the sunshine, 'twas rich fodder for a lad's imagination."

Laugher sparkled in her eyes as she nodded. "I enjoyed riding here with my stepfather over the years. When I was young, he'd lower his voice, and with the skill of a bard, tell me tales about wayward lads who dared to challenge those from the Otherworld upon this sacred ground. And," she whispered with mock warning as she'd heard her stepfather do many times over, "those who disappeared for their defiance."

He shot her a wry smile as he guided his horse up the steep incline. "I heard several tales in my youth as well. The stories nay doubt meant to sway unruly children from misbehaving."

"Whatever the reason—" she glanced around with appreciation, "this unusual corridor inspires many an enchanted thought."

He inhaled a deep breath, appreciated the scent of aged wood, earth, and time unique to this locale. "Aye, 'tis a place of magic."

She arched a brow. "I am surprised a man of war believes in magic."

"There are many things I believe." He held her gaze, the weight of their situation far from allowing him to linger on whimsy. "Fewer that I trust."

The warmth in her eyes faded, and he damned the reminder that their perilous situation had stolen her moment of joy. Cailin scanned the dense woods, the enchanted aura of moments ago fading beneath the reality of dangerous shadows where those in pursuit could hide.

As they rode, clusters of stones came into view. "See the large boulders edged with a dense, impassable thicket?"

Cailin followed her arm as she pointed. "Aye."

"Where it ends, we circle to the other side, then continue until we reach a narrow path."

He guided his destrier along the thick tangle of branches, impressed when a short while later they came across a worn pathway on the ground barely visible. To anyone passing, the impressions could easily be mistaken for a game trail.

As they traveled, the mighty oaks gave way to a mix of alder, birch, and fir. Glimpses of blue sky came into view, then the dense swath fell way, exposing a snow-laden field.

Amazed, Cailin drew his steed to a halt. On the far side of the meadow, framed within a stand of birch, stood a stone hut, a crude window near the thick-hewn door, and smoke puffing from the aged, thatched roof.

"I traveled through this area several times during my youth, but never did I know this place existed. Then again, with the complex track we took to reach Father Lamond's home, one would have to know where to look."

"Exactly, which is why this cottage was selected."

"I recall your explanation that the earl, as others within Dalkirk, believe Finnean Howe is an ailing man with a malady that is highly contagious, a story concocted to sway those with thoughts of going near."

"Aye."

"Incredible. 'Twas as if..."

She frowned. "What?"

Given the complexity of the story, of the hideaway, and the false name, 'twas as if designed by the Knights Templar. A foolish notion. Except for deep faith and the priest's loyalty to King Robert, no ties existed between him and the Brotherhood. With the Bruce a member of the Knights Templar, if a link between Father Lamond and the Templars existed, King Robert would have informed Cailin, wouldn't he?

He wanted to dismiss the possibility of any connection. Though he recalled how his friends and fellow Templar warriors, Stephan, Thomas, and Aiden, had learned after the fact that a mission their sovereign had assigned them held Templar ties.

Did the priest support more than King Robert but the Brotherhood as well? 'Twould explain not only why he lived in seclusion and his life was wrapped in mystery, but why he held the king's ear, and why but a few knew of his true identity.

From this location, regardless of the secrecy of the mission, 'twould be easy to pass word unnoticed through the Highlands.

He studied the cottage. Many things could explain the priest's reclusiveness, the foremost being fear for his life after having covertly acquired Cailin's father's sword from Tiran Castle and delivering it to King Robert. He reined his horse into the clearing, keeping within the shadows cast from the trees. Regardless of his uncertainties, he knew one thing: Father Lamond had been loyal to his father, and a man he could trust.

At the hut, Cailin drew his warhorse to a halt, dismounted, then lifted Elspet to the ground. She grimaced, but given his stubborn intention to care for her, she'd long since quit insisting on dismounting herself.

"I will knock. If he doesna recognize your voice, he willna answer." She hobbled to the entry and pounded on the thick door. "Father Lamond, 'tis Elspet."

A gust hurled a cloud of snow past. The breeze gentled, and silvery glitters of white spiraled in a slow cascade to the ground.

Metal clunked and the door scraped open. A large hooded man, his face shrouded beneath a cowl stood at the entry. "Elspet?"

Though coarse with age, the deep, healthy boom of the priest's voice caught Cailin off guard. Given the passage of years since his father's death, he'd envisioned him as a frail, elderly man.

"I come with a friend," she said.

The tall man glanced toward Cailin, paused, then shoved his hood back and opened the door wider.

Except for strands of gray sprinkled within his hair, the tall, lean man exuded strength. Fire blazed in the cleric's eyes, a potent reminder of the young man, years ago, who had first arrived at Tiran Castle and sermonized so passionately.

"Father," Elspet said, "we come on an urgent matter. Let us go inside and I will introduce you and explain."

With a nod, the priest stepped back. Once they'd entered, he shut and barred the door.

The scent of peat, onions, venison, and a mixture of herbs filled the air as Cailin's eyes adjusted to the flame and candlelit interior.

Dried herbs were suspended from the ceiling bound in thick swaths, a large metal pot hung from a hook over the hearth, several aged chests were shoved against the stone wall, a plain rug lay upon the wooden floor, and several folded blankets rested atop a small bed on the opposite side of the room. On a nearby shelf, a handful of jugs sat haphazardly, along with baskets and numerous smaller containers hung from hooks on the far wall.

"Father Lamond, may I introduce Sir Cailin MacHugh, the rightful Earl of Dalkirk?"

The tall man studied Cailin for a long moment, then gave a somber nod. "I bid you a humble welcome, Sir Cailin. I have been expecting you."

He nodded. "Father." With the priest's close ties to the Bruce, no doubt King Robert had sent a writ that Cailin was en route to reclaim his legacy. A disclosure he should have anticipated.

Elspet glanced at the priest. "Expecting him?"

"A fortnight ago, your stepfather delivered a missive from..." The priest hesitated.

"King Robert," she said, understanding shimmering in her eyes, "informing you that Sir Cailin was alive and would be returning to claim his rightful inheritance."

The priest's face paled. "You know of your stepfather's loyalty to Scotland's king?"

She nodded. "I do."

"Given the circumstances," Cailin said, "I explained."

Elspet touched the woven leather hanging around her neck. "After my stepfather's visit, he was worried. Why?"

On a sigh, the elder walked to a bottle of wine. He poured three glasses, handed Cailin one, then another to her. "With the Earl of Dalkirk determined to keep what he stole many years ago, Sir Angus was concerned for you, for your family's safety in the confrontation once Sir Cailin arrived."

The glass in her hand began to shake, and she began to sway.

Cailin caught her, then set her goblet aside.

The priest's eyes narrowed on the strips of cloth binding her leg. "You are hurt?"

"I am fine."

"Far from it." The priest gestured to a nearby chair. "Sit."

"Father Lamond, my stepfather is dead."

The priest caught the back of a chair. "God in heaven." Grief filled his eyes. "I am so sorry, lass. Angus was a fine man."

"He was," she rasped. "Nor did he die alone."

"What happened?" the cleric asked.

"Lord Dalkirk charged my stepfather with stealing livestock. A lie," she hissed. "As they were hanging him, my mother ran... She t-tried to go to him, but they cut her down."

As her body began to shake at the memory, Father Lamond stepped forward, but finding a need to offer comfort, Cailin drew her against him. Too well he remembered learning of his family's death, of the grief, the pain so intense, 'twas as if it had stolen his soul. "I am here, lass," he soothed as he stroked her hair.

She brushed at the tears pooling in her eyes. "I canna believe they are gone."

"I know." Her every fractured breath resonated through him. "Your family will be avenged, that I swear."

Slowly, her body's trembling ceased and her breaths grew steady. Face red with emotion, she stepped back. "I am sorry, Father, I hadna meant to cry."

"Never apologize for your feelings." Controlled rage shook the priest's voice even as he sought to comfort her. "You honor your parents with your love." He hesitated. "And your stepbrother?"

Face ashen, she took the seat the priest had indicated. "The earl's guard took Blar to the castle."

"Is he alive?" the priest asked as he bent to inspect Elspet's injured ankle.

"I dinna know, but Sir Cailin has promised to find out. If he is, he will save him."

"Thank God." Father Lamond frowned. "This doesna make sense. As a trusted follower of the Bruce, never would Sir Angus do anything to attract the earl's attention."

"We believe that, somehow, the earl discovered Sir Angus's true loyalty," Cailin said.

Worry dredged the elder's brow. "Why?"

"After they killed my stepfather and mother, the earl ordered his guard to search our home. They discovered the detailed map of Tiran Castle signed by you hidden in my stepfather's belongings. After," she said with a shudder, "Dalkirk's men hauled me into his castle, but before the earl could bed me, I escaped. 'Tis how I injured my ankle."

The priest crossed himself. "Thank God you were able to slip away." His worried gaze shifted to Cailin. "Lord Dalkirk willna stop until he finds you."

"Mayhap, but he will rue the day we again meet." The anger in his voice whipped through the small confines. Cailin smothered his outrage, focused on what must be done. "Though I spent my early years in Tiran Castle, I will need another map to familiarize myself with any changes that have been made since."

"Of course." Pride filled the priest's eyes. "I will help however I can to reclaim your birthright and—" He glanced toward her, "to avenge both of your families' losses."

Cailin lay his hand on Elspet's shoulder in a show of support. "I thank you."

"I thank you as well," she said, and accepted the vicar's ministrations to assure himself that her ankle bore no serious damage.

The priest's mouth pursed as he probed the swelling, then he gently placed her foot on the floor. "After you eat, I will put some herbs on your ankle and wrap it tight."

She nodded. "Whatever is cooking smells wonderful."

The vicar waved Cailin to a nearby chair. "I made venison stew this morning. We can carry on our discussion while we eat."

He fed several small sticks into the fire beneath the cauldron. Flames shot up and the soup began to bubble. Cailin's stomach growled at the tempting aroma.

"I find it incredible that you met," Father Lamond said as he ladled healthy portions into the bowls. After placing a spoon in each, he set the steaming fare before them.

Cailin almost groaned at his first bite and resisted the urge to devour the rest. "I came across her in danger in the woods and offered assistance." He refused to embarrass her by revealing the truth about her theft. She'd done what she had to in order to survive.

"Sir Cailin saved my life, for which I will be forever thankful."

"You have my eternal gratitude. I have known Elspet since she was a child." The priest gave a tight smile. "She was always very special." Tenderness softened her expression. "Father, you are being kind. I was always getting into trouble."

The cleric poured them each a goblet of wine, then dug into his own meal. "There is that, but your intentions were always good."

Cailin swallowed another spoonful of his stew. "Seems little has changed about getting in trouble. If there is one thing I have learned in our short acquaintance, it is that Elspet is very strong-willed."

Her eyes cut to his with a flare of defiance.

"You are one to talk." The priest chuckled. "Your father said that, as a child, you were a handful and then some."

"I remember your sermons in the chapel," Cailin said with a quick smile. "They were powerful. Once I reclaim Tiran, I will ask that you return."

"With pleasure." His face grew solemn, and he sat back. "'twill be a challenge to seize the stronghold. 'Tis well-fortified. Your uncle is a harsh man who controls his people with a brutal hand, and some claim with a cruelty for his own perverse pleasure."

"That anyone could find enjoyment in the torment of others is reprehensible," Cailin snapped.

"'Tis," Father Lamond agreed. "I assure you, when the Bruce sent a missive asking me to support you, I agreed without hesitation. More so given the Earl of Dalkirk supports Comyn."

"How long have you known King Robert?" Cailin asked.

"We first met during the spring of our lord's year of 1304, when I was traveling with Bishop Lamberton. I was but one of a few select men of the cloth chosen as witnesses when the Bruce and Lamberton vowed a united front. Each swore that neither would enter into any major cause for Scotland without informing the other."

Cailin nodded slowly. "'Twas a sage move that allowed King Edward to believe that Bishop Lamberton had abandoned his support for Scotland. In addition, however vague, it was also an acknowledgment to the Bruce from Lamberton that naught but war would reclaim Scotland's freedom."

The priest gave a solemn nod. "Aye. After that, I met with the Bruce many times over the past years, and a strong bond of friendship grew between us. When he confided that he was claiming Scotland, as 'twas rightfully his, I pledged my support. And I was honored to be at Scone when he was crowned king."

"King Robert is blessed to have such a loyal man."

"A compliment I return to you." The cleric paused before taking his next bite. "When I received our king's missive that you were returning, I was stunned to discover that you were alive."

Elspet took a sip of wine. "As was I."

The priest swallowed his spoonful of stew, then set the utensil down. "What happened to you during these missing years?"

In brief, Cailin explained how his uncle had paid a captain to kill him at sea and how, once away from port, the captain had sold him to pirates, believing Cailin would die. "But the pirates made an error and tried to seize a Templar cog," he stated with satisfaction.

Elspet's eyes widened, but the laugh lines around the priest's eyes deepened. "Taught the fools to attack an elite fighting force."

"Indeed." Cailin remembered his relief when he'd been hauled aboard the Templar vessel. "'Tis a portion of my life I will never forget." A time when he'd joined the Brotherhood, a life he had loved, one destroyed by King Philip's greed.

"But you arena here to reminisce over the past but reclaim your birthright," Father Lamond said.

Cailin's jaw tightened, looking forward to the time when he confronted his uncle, a day that was coming soon. He nodded. "I was en route to see Sir Angus. King Robert assured me that he would have information I would need, which included the map you drew of Tiran Castle. In addition to leading me to you, he was to assist in building a force to confront my uncle and seize my home."

"Aye, he would have done both and more." Father Lamond gave his head a sad shake. "'Tis a tragic loss."

"Father—"

Elspet's voice broke into their conversation, drawing their attention to her. She had finished her meal and looked beyond exhausted but determined to participate. "I didna mention it to Cailin before," she continued, "as I thought 'twould be of little help. There was another man who visited days before the earl made false charges against my stepfather. By chance, did you send him?"

A deep frown furrowed the priest's brow. "Nay. It could have been another of the king's runners carrying a missive. What did he look like?"

"He was a large man, about as tall as Cailin. Brown hair, grayish-green eyes, and…" She looked at Cailin, her brows drawn in thought. "His dagger was like yours."

Cailin stilled. "Like mine? Explain."

"It had a leather-wrapped handle, along with the engraving on the cross guard." She paused. "And a cross was inlaid on the pommel."

A Knight Templar? With Sir Angus a secret envoy for the king, it made sense that on occasion he would meet with those of the Brotherhood. With the knight in Scotland, no doubt 'twas a man he would know.

"You said his eyes were a grayish green?" Cailin asked, knowing only a handful of Templars with that trait. "Was there anything else about him that you remember? Something out of the ordinary?"

She scraped her teeth across her lower lip. "My stepfather and the man spoke in low tones, so I heard little of what they said, but I..." A smile touched her mouth. "This will sound insignificant, but his voice had a lyrical quality about it."

"Lyrical?"

"When I was younger, a band of Irish mercenaries met with my stepfather. This warrior's voice had the same flowing tone."

"Irish," Cailin said, aware of only one Templar who was Irish, had grayish-green eyes, and had sailed with their crew when they'd fled from France to Scotland. "Did you hear his name?"

"Only his first. Rónán." Elspet met his gaze. "Do you think you know him?"

Know him? Cailin's throat tightened at thoughts of this unexpected twist. A Knight Templar and a man who was like a brother to him. "Aye, 'tis Rónán O'Connor."

Chapter 6

Why had Rónán O'Connor met with Sir Angus? A foolish question. In service to King Robert, there would be many reasons to have Rónán traveling through the Highlands.

"Is he someone you trust?" Elspet asked.

At the strain in her voice, he nodded. "With my life. We have fought together in many a battle. He is like a brother to me."

Hope ignited in her eyes. "Then he will help us?"

"If he is still here, aye. Though by now he could be leagues away." Cailin paused. "Had you seen Rónán visit your stepfather before?"

She shook her head. "'Twas the first time."

He turned to the priest. "Have you ever met a man named Sir Rónán O'Connor?"

"Nay, but for my protection, few were allowed to know where I was, less who were brought to my home."

The last sliver of hope that his friend was still nearby faded. Cailin glanced toward Elspet and noted her pallor, the sadness in her eyes, and how her body trembled with exhaustion. He finished the last of his stew, then the remaining wine in his goblet. "I thank you, Father, for the fine meal. There is much left to discuss, but for now, I seek a bed for Elspet."

"After the hard travel, you will both be exhausted. I regret that I have but my bed to offer. I will make up a pallet near the hearth."

Elspet gasped. "I canna take your bed."

"You will—" Father Lamond smiled. "The heat will be welcome to my old bones."

Lips pressed tight, she nodded.

A smile tugged at Cailin's mouth. She didn't like it, but her respect for the priest stopped her from arguing further. He stood. "After I bed my horse for the night, I will make certain nay one is about. Then I will make a pallet by the entry in case anyone tries to gain access during the night."

* * * *

After the door closed, the crackle of the fire filled the silence and the vague scent of cooked venison and herbs filled the air. Weariness swamped Elspet, tangled with her heartache at the memories of the past few days, and the horror.

Father Lamond sat next to her. "I am so sorry to hear about your stepfather and mother; they were fine people."

She'd thought she couldn't cry more, but now tears burned her throat. "'Tis difficult to believe they are gone."

"'Tis." He paused. "You are welcome to stay here for as long as you wish."

"I thank you, but once Blar is free, I believe we will restart our life elsewhere. Or, if we wish, Sir Cailin has generously offered us a place to live at Tiran Castle."

"He is a good man. 'Tis indeed a miracle you met."

"Our meeting was nay accident." Guilt weighed upon her, more so at learning the priest held Cailin in high regard, which had erased any lingering distrust toward him. She needed to confess her sins. "In truth, a guard I had met on several occasions agreed to help Blar escape, but for a price. So, several days ago, I robbed two men. After I fled, they caught up with me and…" She closed her eyes, shoved the harrowing memory aside, then met the priest's somber gaze. "Cailin heard my screams and rescued me."

He made the sign of the cross. "I owe him a debt of gratitude for saving your life."

"As do I, but instead I—" She dragged a steadying breath and rubbed her injured ankle. "Instead of giving Cailin thanks after he saved my life, I placed powdered valerian root in his ale at the inn he brought me to, to recover. Once he fell asleep, I stole his broadsword and brought the weapon to Wautier Brecnagh to sell for coin to free Blar."

Sparks snapped in the hearth and flames illuminated the displeasure rippling across the priest's face. "Your decisions were nay ones that would cull praise, but—" His voice softened, "—they were guided by desperation." He glanced toward where Cailin's empty sheath hung, frowned. "You said that you took Sir Cailin's sword, but he has it with him."

"I did. While waiting for Wautier Brecnagh to pay me, I overheard him whispering to his assistant that he had recognized the coat of arms on the sword. You can imagine my shock when I heard the broadsword belonged to Sir Cailin's father. Before the merchant returned, I slipped away and returned the weapon. But," she admitted, humbled by the knight's kindness, "Cailin was too much a gentleman to expose my duplicity to you."

He stared at her for a long moment, then sighed. "Though your actions were spurred by fear for Blar, you are fortunate that Cailin is an honorable man, more so than many."

"I am," she rasped.

"Nor will you risk such dangerous actions again." He scowled. "If you need help, come to me, or send a message. I have many connections."

"I will, Father. I ask for penance to atone for my transgressions."

Wizened eyes held hers with somber regard as he made the sign of the cross. "Say three Hail Marys before you go to sleep."

"I will. I thank you, Father."

The scrape of the door had her glancing toward the entry. Heat stung her cheeks as Cailin stepped inside.

"Did you see any sign of anyone out there?" Father Lamond asked.

"Nay." Cailin dusted the snow off his boots, then secured his broadsword in the sheath. "To make sure, I made an extra round along the perimeter, then sat and listened for a while."

The tautness in her body eased. They were safe, but for how long? Nor could she erase the worry. "Father, there are only three of us. What if the earl's men come during the night?"

Cailin stepped forward. "Elspet, I—"

The priest stood. "A credible concern, given the circumstances, and one in which I can offer a bit of ease. As you notice, this floor is made of wood." He walked to where the large rug lay atop worn slats, rolled it back, then slid his finger into what looked like a crack in the plank, lifted it.

Inside the opening, the top of a ladder disappeared into blackness.

Elspet gasped. "A secret hideaway?"

"Aye," the priest replied. "If 'tis necessary to remain there for a few days, a candle and flint are in the chest below, along with supplies and several blankets. If a threat requires that you escape, the chamber narrows to a tunnel that exits a distance into the forest."

Her shoulders sagged with relief. Though danger still existed, to know they couldn't be trapped inside... "You have thought of everything."

"I canna accept the praise of the design. "The cottage was prepared for my use," he said. "I but live here, and I assure you, I am immensely grateful for the details considered in the planning."

"As I and pray we dinna need to use the hidden chamber or tunnel." Elspet glanced at Cailin, perplexed at the lack of surprise on his face, as if he'd expected some such twist, then gave an internal shrug as exhaustion set in. He was as tired as she, and his concerns were no doubt focused on his uncle's men in search of them.

She picked up her mug and plate and cleaned them off before heading to her bed. As she climbed in, she glanced over, noted that Cailin and the priest were deep in conversation.

Wind howled outside, reminding her of their night in the cave, of how he'd held her and the comfort she'd felt in his arms. For that brief time, in contrast to the terror of the past few days, she'd felt a sense of rightness.

After making the sign of the cross, Elspet pressed her hands together in prayer. "'Hail Mary, full of grace,'" she whispered, pouring her soul into each word, each verse drenched with regret. After she finished, she repeated the prayer two more times, then again made the sign of the cross. Though she'd completed her penance, guilt twisted in her gut.

What of Blar? Please God let him be alive, and let them find a way to save him.

Her lids heavy with sleep, Elspet turned toward the wall. She ached for her parents as well, wished back the time, wished that she could tell them how much she loved them.

The quiet voices of Father Lamond and Cailin reached her, a reminder that she wasn't alone.

More than ready to erase her thoughts, she closed her eyes and succumbed to sleep.

* * * *

Hours later, at the slide of parchment, Cailin withdrew his *sgian dubh* and sat up, forcing the remnants of sleep from his mind. A fire blazed in the hearth, and Elspet lay unmoving on the small bed facing the wall. He glanced toward the hearth. A sliver of morning light slipped from beneath the cloth covering the window and fell upon the priest as he sat before the hearth.

The cleric glanced over. "I didna mean to wake you," he whispered, nodding at Elspet, who still slept nearby, her face relaxed and looking impossibly innocent.

Cailin sat up and rubbed his face, the grittiness of his eyes assuring him that he could sleep several more hours, a luxury he couldn't take given the situation. "'Tis time I was awake. I need to make another search of the surroundings to ensure nay one is about."

The priest raised a brow. "Again? But you went out several times during the night."

"Aye, and will continue to do so as long as Elspet and I remain here. Though I havena seen anything suspicious, with my uncle's men in search of us, we are far from safe." He paused. "How long have you been awake?"

"But a short while. I was gathering a few documents you will need."

The gravity in his voice had Cailin shoving up from the pallet and crossing the room to join the priest. In front of the aged wood chest, a complex Celtic design was carved around a cross. Inside lay several rolled parchments, one of them stamped with King Robert's blood-red royal seal.

Father Lamond lifted the one bearing the sovereign's stamp. "'Tis for you."

Cailin frowned. "King Robert mentioned no other documents than the detailed map of Tiran Castle."

"Our sovereign decided that due to the dangerous travel, 'twas best to say naught until you arrived. Open it; 'tis proof to reclaim your inheritance."

"I have proof," he said, more confused. "The sword you recovered years ago and gave to the Bruce bears my family's coat of arms."

"Indeed, but this will end any questions of those who dare challenge you once you seize Tiran Castle."

Cailin broke the seal. Wax snapped and red shards scattered upon the wooden floor. He unrolled the document and scanned the contents. His fingers tightened on the parchment as he lifted his gaze to the priest. "'Tis a writ bestowing on me the title of earl and the holdings of Dalkirk, signed by my father."

"Aye. Before your father and mother were killed, there was deep unrest upon Dalkirk lands. Your father confided in me that something was greatly amiss. Livestock was being slaughtered, homes burned, and families killed. Several times, your father found tracks leading away from the crimes. Even with the help of his brother, Gaufrid, he couldna discover who was behind the violent acts."

"Of course not," he scoffed, furious anew at his uncle's black heart, "as 'twas my uncle who was behind the evil. Then, once I, too, was dead, Gaufrid could claim my inheritance without challenge."

"Wisely, in case something untoward were to happen to your father, he drew up this document." The priest's gaze narrowed. "You need to know that your uncle was riding with your parents and me and several others during the hunt when the accidents occurred. Your father was horribly injured, but before he was taken to the castle with your mother, he confided in me 'twas your uncle who had attacked them. A short time after we reached the stronghold, Gaufrid came to me, visibly upset. He shared that both your mother and father had died, and due to your father's horrible wounds, he had already made arrangements for them to be buried and asked that I say a prayer where they now rested."

Images of standing beside his parents' gravestones flickered in Cailin's mind, and a fresh wave of fury surged through him. Aye, despising his brother and sister-in-law so, Gaufrid had even deprived his parents of a proper burial. Cailin ached to wrap his hands around his uncle's neck, to watch as the life ebbed from the bastard's eyes. "He will pay for his betrayal by my hand," he hissed, "that I swear."

The priest laid a hand on Cailin's shoulder. "I shall pray for you, but naught will be easy about reclaiming your birthright."

"It willna, but whatever risk it takes, I will prevail." Jaw tense, he returned the parchment to the trunk, then closed the cover. "Keep this, along with any other important documents that I will need until I have defeated my uncle."

"Aye." Father Lamond walked to the hearth, ladled out a bowl of porridge for Cailin, another for himself, and brought them over to sit on a nearby bench. "Here, 'tis a bit of ground cinnamon." The cleric stirred a pinch of spice into his food, then a touch into his own.

Though not hungry, Cailin swallowed a bite of the warm honey-and-oat mixture, enjoying the taste of the flavorful spice.

Father Lamond ate several scoops, then lifted his gaze to Cailin. "You have grown into a fine man. Your parents would have been proud of you."

His fingers tightened on the spoon as he stirred the dark brown spice. "You lived with the Templars after you were rescued?"

"I found a life there, but then," he said, realizing the priest's source, "King Robert probably told you my story."

He shrugged. "While talking about our Templar ties, he may have mentioned the fact."

Incredulous, Cailin's hand on his spoon stilled. "Our Templar ties?"

"Aye." Father Lamond's gaze grew faraway. "Many years ago, I was of the Brotherhood and fought in the Holy Land. But during battle, I was injured. I was blessed to find a home, along with the title of priest and a post at Tiran Castle. A position offered through the Bruce's influence."

And apparently another reason Rónán had visited. What else had King Robert not revealed to him? "Did my father know?"

"Know what?" Elspet's sleepy voice asked.

Cailin shot the priest a warning glare. "Of my uncle's treachery."

The pad of footsteps grew closer as she walked over, favoring her right ankle. She knelt beside the hearth, her chestnut hair neatly braided as she held up her hands to the flames.

Cailin's body tightened with awareness.

She glanced at the bubbling stew. "The porridge smells wonderful."

The cleric filled the bowl, sifted the spice atop. "Here, my child."

"I thank you." Pleasure shimmered in her eyes as she inhaled the rising steam. "Cinnamon!"

"'Twas always a favorite of yours when you visited," he said with a smile.

She sat in a chair opposite the bench, and her eyes warmed with appreciation as she took a taste. "'Tis wonderful."

Cailin ate another bite, wanting more time alone to speak with Father Lamond. Though injured, that the priest had knowledge and experience in the Brotherhood was a boon. A fact King Robert would understand and no doubt the reason he'd sent him to meet with the cleric.

Elspet dipped her spoon into the fare, then lifted her gaze to Cailin's with concern. "You slept well?"

He shrugged. "In between rounds."

She sighed and swallowed several more spoonfuls of porridge. "Have you decided what to do next?"

"'Tis imperative that I gain entrance into Tiran Castle, take stock of what I am up against: men, arms, defenses."

"I agree," the priest said. "I have a way for you to enter the stronghold without suspicion."

Cailin finished the last of his meal, then set the bowl aside. "How?"

"You will"—mischief glinted in the priest's eyes as he buttered a chunk of bread—"dress as a monk."

"And easily move about the castle without suspicion," Cailin said.

"Indeed. I will make you a list of trustworthy contacts within the stronghold and, hopefully," he said, his eyes shifting to Elspet, "you can find out about Blar."

"'Tis perfect," Elspet said. "No one will question us if we are but traveling through."

Cailin shook his head. "'Tis too dangerous. You will stay here."

Green eyes narrowed. "Nay more dangerous than for you. More importantly, too many years have passed since you saw anyone within the castle. As I said before, I doubt you will recognize, if you are lucky, but a few people. Nor do you have the luxury of time to covertly discover the answers you seek or the people you need to find."

Father Lamond raised his hand as Cailin opened his mouth to argue. "However dangerous, the lass is right. She has a good head about her, nor is she weak-willed."

Not weak-willed; stubborn. The lass would give a mule a run.

"And," the priest continued, "she is skilled with weapons."

"Skilled with weapons?" Cailin asked, his voice dry. "Why am I not surprised?"

"I am proficient with a blade and a bow," Elspet said, pride in her voice. "Plus, Father Lamond taught me how to use herbs to treat wounds."

And make a man succumb to sleep. God's blade, the last thing Cailin wanted was to keep Elspet with him as he traveled in harm's way.

"I wouldna recommend her accompanying you," the priest said, as if sensing his hesitation, "if I didna think she would be an immense help. As important, she is someone you can trust."

Cailin bit back a host of protests, recognizing the need to focus on the greater good of their mission. However much he wanted her to remain here, taking her along made sense. "She will go with me, but we willna travel until her injury has recovered. Time I will use to go through the documents in the chest and discuss the details of the plan."

The priest nodded.

* * * *

Elspet noted the slide of clouds in the purple-orange sky as the sun set. Two days had passed, and between the priest's herbs and rest, thankfully, her ankle was almost healed.

She tightened her cape as she walked to the stable, the whip of wind harsh across her face. Though she struggled with grief, the time with Father Lamond had allowed her to begin to improve.

With one last look at the fading sunset, she walked inside. The scent of horse and hay greeted her as she tugged the door shut.

With the stealth of a predator, Cailin stepped from the side, his red hair secured behind his back in a leather tie, his face taut.

Heart pounding, she jumped. "I didna see you."

His brows slanted. "I told you to remain in the hut. 'Tis dangerous."

"If I stay inside another moment without seeing the sun, breathing fresh air, I will go mad."

"You should have waited until I returned."

She scowled and walked past him to his horse. "I am far from a helpless lass."

Steps crunched on hay behind her as she stroked the horse's soft muzzle. With any issues of trust between them erased, too often these past two days her eyes had strayed to his mouth.

"How is your ankle?"

"The pain is all but gone."

He gave a rough exhale. "Still, I dinna like your placing yourself in danger."

She scoffed. "With your uncle's men trying to find me, I am already in danger."

For a long moment he watched her, the displeasure on his face easy to read. "Once we leave here, you will follow all my commands without hesitation."

"I am not a fool."

The hard look on his face eased and he rubbed the back of his neck. "Nay, you are not. I want you safe."

"I know." Moved by his concern, she stepped toward him. He was a knight sworn to protect. It was understandable that he struggled with her taking risks. Still, she couldna help but wonder if there was something more personal in his concern. "But you need me, and I will be there."

He blew out a rough breath. "My uncle is an evil man. He must be stopped."

"He will be."

Silence fell between them, the slap of wind on the wooden building echoing with a mournful sound.

She looked around the stable, and an ache built in her chest. "The last time I was here, 'twas with my stepfather. 'Tis hard to believe that."

A strong hand gently touched her hand.

She didn't move, didn't dare. Emotions storming her, if she spoke, turned, she'd break down. She wanted him to leave her alone, allow her to regain her dignity.

"Elspet?"

The empathy in his voice cracked the fragile hold on her emotions. "Go...please."

Cailin drew her against his chest and wrapped her within his arms. "I am here for you."

Wrapped within his protective embrace, the steady beat of his heart, his gentle words a potent reminder that someone cared, that she wasn't alone. Fighting to control the swell of grief, she held in the tears.

"'Tis the third time you have offered me much-needed comfort," she said, her voice unsteady.

"You are naught but trouble," he whispered, his words far from holding censure.

"I am." She lifted her head and met his blue eyes, and the tenderness in his gaze stole her breath. Without warning, desire slid through her. Shaken by the need he inspired, she stepped back. "We should be returning. As you said, 'tis dangerous."

"Elspet, there is naught wrong in grieving for those you love."

She swallowed the lump in her throat and wished she was still in his arms. A reckless thought. He made her care too much. "I know, but I despise the weakness my grief brings me." Refusing to linger on her sadness, or what he made her feel, she started toward the door. "I should finish altering the monk's robe I will wear. With my ankle well enough, 'tis best if we leave at first light."

"I will let Father Lamond know." Cailin strode ahead of her, opened the door, muttered a curse. Wood scraped as he shoved it closed. "Riders are coming across the field."

"Are they the earl's men?"

"I didna see anyone I recognized, but there is only one reason a small contingent would dare to approach a man who is rumored to have a contagious illness."

"Because," she whispered, "they suspect we are here."

"Aye."

Heart pounding, Elspet ran toward the exit.

He caught her arm. "What are you doing?"

"We must warn Father Lamond and prepare in case we need to escape!"

Cailin's hard gaze met hers. "'Tis too late."

Chapter 7

Cailin hauled Elspet with him across the straw-strewn floor toward a mound of hay as the steady thrum of hooves grew outside the stable.

Fear shimmered in her eyes. "We must hide!"

"Aye. Help me, quickly." Working in unison, they shoved armloads of hay aside to create a hole in the stack. "Get in, hurry. Once I have covered the gear, I will join you."

Moments later, he climbed beside her, tugged hay up to shield them.

"What if they see us?"

He ignored the sharp ends of the pungent blades poking his face and withdrew his dagger. "They may not enter the stable." And prayed he was right.

A snort from outside announced the riders had halted. "Do you think Finnean Howe is inside?" a man's deep voice asked. "He could be out hunting."

"I didna know as 'tis late in the day to be out, but if he doesna answer," another man said, "we will return in the morning."

"'Tis said that anyone who gets within an arm's length of him will catch his malady," the first man said, nervousness edging his voice.

"Which is why we will wait outside until he answers our call."

Elspet unsheathed her *sgian dubh*. "At least they dinna know that 'tis Father Lamond's home," she said, keeping her voice low.

"Aye," Cailin whispered back. "That my uncle's knights are brazen enough to risk confronting a man they believe is contagious exposes their desperation."

"Finnean," a man yelled.

A gust of wind battered the stable.

"Bloody cold," a man muttered.

"Finnean," another man called, "we know you are in there."

A faint scuff of the door, then a series of rough coughs sounded.

"What do ye want?" Father Lamond asked, his voice weak and disguised with a coarse rasp.

"Dinna come closer," the first knight warned. "We are looking for a man and a woman."

"I—" Another round of coughs broke the silence. "I have seen nay one."

"Open your door wider and move away from the entry," the second man called, "so we can see inside."

"My old bones are weak with cold," the priest called out. "I dinna want to lose the heat in my home."

"Do it, or we will burn down the hut," another man warned.

A grumble sounded.

The thud of hooves upon snow grew louder.

"What do you think they are doing?"

At the worry in her voice, Cailin glanced over. "They must be looking inside the hut."

"I see naught," a guard said.

"Nor I," another said.

"Search the stable," the deep voice ordered.

Hand tightening around his dagger, Cailin held his finger up to his lips. The door scraped open. The crunch of boots upon straw grew closer.

"Do you see anything?" a man called from outside.

"Naught but horses," the knight paces away replied.

"Fine pieces of horseflesh," the priest said, then began coughing. "S-should bring a fair price this spring."

The guard grunted.

Through the breaks in the hay, Cailin made out the man's boots heading toward the exit. Thank God.

The door banged shut.

"Who are you looking for?" Father Lamond called out.

"None of your concern, old man," the guard replied. "Let us go." The thud of hooves on snow faded.

"That was too close. If they had found us..." Elspet's hand trembled as she secured her dagger.

He sheathed his weapon. "We are all safe, which is what matters. But with the guards nay doubt returning to check whether we have taken shelter here, 'tis unsafe to remain. With you well enough to travel, we leave at first light." He shoved aside the shield of dried grass.

Elspet's hand touched his arm, and he turned. Pieces of hay stuck out from her hair, and chestnut tangles framed her face.

His body tightened with an awareness that he'd been struggling against throughout her recuperation, and he damned his senses for being so attuned to her faint scent of heather woven within the sweet fragrance of hay. Her lips softly parted, and he found his gaze lingering on their fullness.

"I thank you," she said.

"There is nay reason to thank me." Cailin ordered himself to stand, to leave her alone, reviewed every reason why. Needing to touch her, he brushed his mouth against hers.

"Sir Cailin, Elspet?" Father Lamond called from outside.

Straw flew as Cailin jerked back. God's blade, what was he thinking? "We are safe," he called out. Blood still pounding hot, he shoved to his feet, extended his hand to help her up, then took a much-needed step back. The desire and confusion in her eyes helped little in his struggle to keep from hauling her against him. Blast it! "I..." What should he say, *I did nae mean to kiss you? This was wrong?*

An understatement.

He hadn't meant to touch her, except with her taste lingering on his tongue, his body ached for her. Frustrated and aggravated with himself and his seemingly unstoppable reaction to her, he floundered for what to say. In the end, deciding 'twas prudent to remain silent, Cailin strode across the stable and tugged the door open.

Relief swept the priest's face as he shoved his cowled hood back. "Thank God. Years have passed since any of the earl's men have dared to ride to my home." He shook his head. "Given your uncle's desperation since your return to Dalkirk, I should have expected his guards."

As should have Cailin. But 'twas too late to worry about that now. "They found naught, which is what is important. Nor will it matter if they come back for another search. Elspet and I leave at dawn."

Her soft steps came up behind him, and she paused at his side, brushing the dried grass from her hair.

The priest tsked as he took her in. "You look pale, lass. I think a couple more days' rest would be wise."

"There is little pain in my ankle, and I need to see my stepbrother, or at least discover his fate."

With a sigh, Father Lamond nodded. "One of the men I recommended you speak with should know where he is, or at least how he is."

She nodded, but Cailin saw the tension in her eyes. Nor did he miss that she kept her gaze averted from his. Regardless if he was drawn to her, it wasn't a train of thought he could allow. Once he'd claimed his legacy, he would rejoin the Bruce until his sovereign had smothered the last of the resistance.

"Come," the priest said, breaking into his thoughts, "we dinna want to linger where anyone could see us." He hurried toward the cottage, Elspet on his heels.

Cailin grimaced. What he should have thought of. Irritated at his unsuitable thoughts, he scanned the area one last time. Thankful for no sign of the knights, he followed them into the cottage.

* * * *

A day later, the musty tang of damp, stale air filled the secret tunnel leading to Tiran Castle. The wash of candlelight exposed the dank, cobweb-littered walls as Cailin made his way, ever on alert. 'Twould seem a long while since anyone had used the passageway. Yet, after their near confrontation with his uncle's men yesterday, nor would he relax his guard.

The steady plop of water echoed overhead.

Behind him, Elspet's soft footfalls sounded.

He lifted the taper higher. Droplets clung to the ceiling, wobbled, then fell with a plop upon the ground. With a grimace, he glanced behind him.

The monk's robe, a match to the one he wore, shielded Elspet's face and any sign of her hair from view. As an extra precaution, he'd smeared a dusting of soot on her chin to keep any who caught sight of her from identifying her as a woman.

A while later, as the ground began to angle upward, the faint nicker of a horse echoed down the tunnel.

"We are nearing the stable," he said.

"Aye. I pray we willna have to wait long to see one of the men Father Lamond suggested we speak with."

At the worry in her voice, Cailin looked over. "Dinna worry, we will learn what happened to Blar." And prayed they would discover her stepbrother was alive. She'd lost so much, and he understood how losing the last tie of family, especially through treachery, could leave one devastated.

The scent of horse and hay filled the air as they grew closer. The clatter of hooves sounded, a moment later a whinny.

"Steady, lad," a deep voice soothed.

"'Tis the stablemaster," Elspet whispered.

"Aye, and not one of the men we are to trust." Cailin moved to the tunnel's hidden exit, the entry secured with a false door hidden in a complex weave of stone. He peered through the slits crafted long ago, allowing whoever looked to survey the entire stable along with the castle grounds.

Memories rolled through Cailin as he took in the familiar setting, from the lists where the knights practiced, the wall walk where guards patrolled, to the bailey where people moved about at their daily tasks.

An ache built in his chest. So long ago he'd taken his family and clan for granted. He'd had a home and had felt loved and secure until, through deceit, Gaufrid had stolen it from him

Though he despised his uncle, he was pleased to discover that he'd kept the castle in good repair.

A sharp clanging sounded from his right.

He glanced over, watched the smithy forge a red-hot wedge of steel, and recalled, as a lad, being taught how to wield a hammer to craft a blade.

Cailin scanned the stable. Down the generous corridor, two stalls away, a thin man was brushing a bay. The horse snorted, then backed up.

"You will be getting your oats once I am done with you," the man grumbled, then continued his task.

"What do you see?" she whispered.

"Besides the stable master," he replied, keeping his voice low, "there are a few lads mucking out the stalls, but nay one else." He gestured toward two nearby large flat rocks against one wall of the tunnel. "Rest while I keep watch."

"Is there a place where I can look as well?"

Cailin shifted aside a degree. "We can both see through this slit."

She moved beside him and peered out.

He could smell her scent, impossibly fresh despite their travel. Her closeness was one he had been avoiding since the stable. Ruthlessly, he now squashed any awareness of her. His preoccupation with her was dangerous when his thoughts must be on his surroundings.

"I never knew these tunnels existed," she said.

"They were created when the castle was built."

"Cailin."

"Aye?"

"Why did you kiss me?"

He could have groaned. He was doing his best to ignore his body's tightening at her nearness. "Now is not the time to discuss what occurred."

"When will be the time?"

"Never. 'Twas a mistake."

"I see," she said after a significant pause.

Guilt wrenched him at her subdued tone. Now she was far from the stubborn, relentless fighter he'd come to know. In his need for self-preservation, he'd hurt her. Unsure how to respond, but needing to say something, he turned.

Elspet gasped. "'Tis the master-at-arms heading this way," she whispered, "one of the men Father Lamond told us to seek out!"

Thankful for the diversion, Cailin studied the large man entering the stable, his shoulder-length hair threaded with gray, and his arms defined by muscles honed from long hours of training. A younger man walked at his side.

Though years had passed, Cailin recognized Sir Petrus Beaton. Sentiment stormed him at seeing his mentor from his youth, a man who'd taught him how to ride, hunt, and wield a sword.

Elspet touched his arm. "How are we going to speak with him alone?"

Cailin watched as the knights moved closer, then glanced toward the others in the stable. "I am unsure." If he created a diversion, Sir Petrus would run out. Yet there must be a way.

Brooms clattered as the lads working in the stable departed, leaving only Sir Petrus and the younger knight inside. The men paused before a destrier five stalls away. They began to talk. Cailin's mentor folded his arms across his chest as the younger man became animated over whatever they debated.

The master-at-arms scowled, then shook his head.

"Whatever they are discussing," Cailin said, "the younger knight isna pleased."

"'Tis Sir Donald Burke," she said. "He tends to be hot headed and often earns Sir Petrus's censure."

"Is he loyal to my uncle?"

"Aye," Elspet replied, "and not to be trusted."

Sir Petrus motioned for the younger man to depart.

Eyes narrowed with disgust, the knight stormed from the stable.

Cailin stepped back. "Stay here."

Her hand caught his. "What are you doing?"

"Hopefully catching the master-at-arms's attention before he departs." Cailin hurried to the secret exit. With extreme care, he unlatched the door, slipped into the stable, and crept behind a towering pile of hay. He peeked through a break in the dried grass.

His mentor halted at the next stall and rubbed the steed's muzzle.

Cailin whistled in two soft bursts, a signal they had used countless times in his youth.

Sir Petrus's hand flew to his blade as he whirled. A dark yet confused scowl marred his face as he scoured the stable. "Show yourself!"

Pushing back the hood of his cowl, Cailin stood.

The giant knight's eyes riveted on him, widened with shock. "Cailin," he rasped. "It canna be."

After ensuring no one approached the stable, he waved over his old friend. "Hurry."

Sir Petrus secured his dagger, then rushed over, his face pale with disbelief. "Why... How..."

"I will explain. Follow me." He entered the secret tunnel, securing the entry after his friend stepped inside. Elspet, he noted, had wisely retreated deeper into the tunnel, away from view.

Tears had filled the master-at-arms's eyes. Before Cailin could speak, he was enveloped in a giant hug that he returned, then the large man stepped back. "God's teeth, I thought you were dead!"

He struggled against the onslaught of emotion welling in his throat. "Aye, a fact Gaufrid tried to ensure." Quickly, Cailin explained how his uncle had paid to have him killed, and his escape.

The master-at-arms's hand had clasped his sword by the time he finished relating the tale, his knuckles turning white. "I will cut down the bloody cur!"

"Nay," Cailin said with soft fierceness that silently cautioned his old friend to lower his voice. There was too much at stake to allow feelings to guide their decisions. "When that day comes, 'twill be my blade that serves justice. However much I want to confront the bastard now, he holds the fealty of those within the castle."

If possible, the knight's face further darkened with fury. "Loyalty based on a lie and fear of his brutal ways."

"Aye, 'tis what I have been told." Cailin paused. "I have spoken with Father Lamond. In addition to your name to speak with, as well as others I can trust, he drew a map of the castle, of changes, and secret passages that have been added since I left."

Sir Petrus's brows raised as he glanced down the dark tunnel. "Father Lamond is with you?"

"Nay," Cailin replied. "After I arrived on Dalkirk lands, we stayed with him for several days."

"We?"

Aware she was watching, Cailin turned and waved Elspet forward.

Sir Petrus's gaze narrowed as her hooded form moved into the candlelight. "Who are you?"

"A woman who has risked her life to aid me," Cailin stated, "and one whom I will protect with my life."

She shoved her hood back and angled her chin with pride. "Elspet McReynolds."

"Sir Angus's stepdaughter," Sir Petrus breathed. His eyes shifted to Cailin's, shimmering with understanding. "Now Lord Dalkirk's order makes sense."

She frowned. "What do you mean?"

"My men and I were ordered to find you and whoever you traveled with." Cailin glanced her way before meeting his mentor's gaze. "You never knew it was me?"

"Nay. We were given a rough description, told that you had abducted Elspet and were dangerous. Once captured, you were to be killed and your body disposed of."

Cailin grunted. "With no one the wiser that I was alive or had returned."

"So it would seem," Sir Petrus replied with disgust. "You are here to reclaim what is rightfully yours, I take it?"

Cailin nodded. "I am, but I need your help."

Face solemn, the master-at-arms nodded. "Whatever you need, I am at your service."

"Though I trust you, before I say more, you will swear your fealty to me."

Without hesitation, Sir Petrus knelt, pledged his fealty, then stood.

"What I am about to tell you," Cailin said, "you willna repeat until I tell you."

"I swear it."

"The charges my uncle pressed against Sir Angus McReynolds were lies," Cailin said,

A muscle worked in the knight's jaw. "That I can believe. I have known Sir Angus my entire life. He was a fine and honest man." Sadness filled his gaze as he looked at Elspet. "After the deed was done, I learned of the earl's order, and that your stepfather and mother were dead." He shook his head. "A terrible loss." He exhaled a rough breath. "I am sorry, lass."

She gave a shaky nod. "I thank you."

Sir Petrus frowned. "What I do not understand is why Lord Dalkirk would falsely accuse such an honorable man of a crime."

"Because," Cailin said, "Gaufrid discovered that Sir Angus's true loyalty was to King Robert Bruce."

The master-at-arms's face paled. "Scotland's king?"

Hand clasping his dagger, Cailin drew himself to his full height. "Aye, a fealty I share. I would know if you feel the same."

His mentor's face relaxed, as if a burden lifted. "I always believed the Bruce to be Scotland's rightful ruler. As with you, I swear my fealty to him." Cailin nodded. "Father Lamond gave me a list of men who are trustworthy within the stronghold and will swear their fealty to me." Parchment scraped as he handed the roll to the knight. "I need you to speak to each one, swear them to secrecy, then explain the situation."

"I will." Sir Petrus unrolled, then scanned the document. He frowned. "There are several men not on the list who I trust and am confident will pledge their oath to you as well."

"Excellent. I will meet you here tomorrow. Once we learn how many men will shift their loyalty to me, we will begin plans to seize Tiran Castle."

"Aye," he replied.

"One last thing." Cailin's gaze moved to Elspet before returning to his mentor. "I need to know if her stepbrother, Blar, is alive."

Disgust clouded the master-at-arms's eyes. "He is, but—" He frowned at Elspet. Taking a deep breath, he said, "'Tis with great regret that I must inform you that your stepbrother isna a good man, nor one I would trust."

Chapter 8

Cold rage surged through Elspet at Sir Petrus's disparaging remark. "Y-you are wrong. Blar is a good man. Though he and I have not always agreed, I would trust him with my life!"

"Keep your voice down!" Cailin warned as he peered through the slit into the stable. Body tense, he turned to the master-at-arms. "Explain."

"I admit that I have never seen eye to eye with her stepbrother," the knight stated. "A fact not helped by the way, during his visits to the castle, he behaved as if he were above us and went out of his way to garner favor with the earl."

"Garner favor with the earl?" she sputtered, taking a step closer within the confines of the tunnel. "He offered Lord Dalkirk the respect his station demanded, a man I assure you, he despises."

The master-at-arms's mouth tightened, goading her to further defend her stepbrother.

"At times Blar may appear to be arrogant," Elspet admitted, her voice but a whisper beneath Cailin's hard gaze, "but 'tis confidence in his abilities that guides his actions."

"I find it odd that since Blar's supposed arrest," Sir Petrus said, "he now serves with the earl's guard. An interesting position for a man who *despises* Lord Dalkirk."

Body trembling with fury, Elspet took another step closer. "'Tis rubbish. Blar, and I, were brought to Tiran Castle as prisoners."

"Aye, but you escaped." Pride flickered in Sir Petrus's eyes. "An outrage that festers in the earl like a burr beneath a saddle. As for your stepbrother—" His expression darkened. "I canna tell you what convinced Lord Dalkirk to add him to his men's ranks. Whatever the reason, Blar now rides on patrol with the guard and practices daily with the others as if his due."

Nausea swirled in her gut. "It canna be true."

He gestured toward the opening. "Look for yourself. He is in the lists now."

Pulse racing, she moved forward. The master-at-arms admitted he didn't like her stepbrother, but if Blar indeed trained with the earl's men, she assured herself 'twas due to his being threatened with imprisonment or death. That he'd voluntarily join the earl's guard was unthinkable.

Elspet peered out. Sunlight struggled to break through the dense overcast, leaving the hard, snow-encrusted ground suffocated within a murky gray.

A gust whipped past, then another, hurling snow through the air as if another layer of gloom as she gazed past the bailey toward where the knights trained.

The clang of blades rang out as two men sparred to the far right.

She studied both, the distance making it difficult to see their faces. Frustrated, she slowly scanned the other fighters, searching for anyone resembling her brother. On a relieved breath, she stepped back. "I see nay one who resembles Blar."

Sir Petrus walked over, peered out. "Look by the well."

On an unsteady breath, she again moved to the opening, stared at several men standing around the well taking turns drinking from a ladle.

Heart pounding, she slowly scanned each one. At the third fighter, she stilled.

Blar. Laughing at something another man had said.

Relief coursed through her so swiftly that she almost swayed. She'd prayed, had even resorted to thievery to try to save him. Though Sir Petrus thought poorly of her stepbrother, at this moment she was grateful the earl had spared his life.

She turned. "Blar is out there, which proves little more than that, by some miracle, he is alive and has been successful in hiding his disdain for the earl."

The master-at-arms's mouth flattened, but he remained silent.

Cailin crossed to the hidden viewpoint. "Which man is Blar?"

She crossed her arms. "The third from the left at the well."

Cailin peered out. After a long moment, he stepped back, and as his eyes met hers, his expression cool.

For the first time, doubt seeped through Elspet. Shaken, she lowered her arms. Had Blar betrayed her? Had he turned his back on his family, on the bond they'd forged over the years?

She wanted to dismiss her misgivings of a man who was like a brother to her, but a question haunted her. "Sir Petrus, after my escape, do you know if Blar tried to find me?"

"He rode out several times with a band, searching for you."

Proof that he was trying to find her, but because he rode on the earl's orders, the master-at-arms wouldn't see it that way. "Do you know if he ever slipped out to look for me?"

"He did not."

The hardness of his tone set her on edge. "How can you be sure?"

"He is beneath my command. Had he left his post, departed during the night, slipped away from the band, I would have been notified."

Far from the answer she wanted, but she refused to give up hope. "There must be a sound reason for Blar's actions," she insisted. Her stepbrother's loyalty to the earl was surely a ruse as he plotted a way to find her. And once he'd earned the earl's trust, his actions wouldn't be under scrutiny. Then, when he did slip away to search for her, after his brief time as a guard, they would have coin to escape.

* * * *

Cailin met Sir Petrus's gaze, the warning in the older man's eyes assuring him that his mentor's distrust for Blar ran deep. Cailin had known the knight since he was born, and until the day he'd departed, Sir Petrus had done naught without good reason. A point that would weigh heavily in Cailin's decisions.

"We will discuss Blar later," Cailin said at last. "For now, that he is alive and safe is what matters."

Face pale, she nodded.

Sir Petrus glanced toward the covert entry. "I need to return before 'tis noticed I am gone."

"Indeed." Cailin clasped his mentor's hand. Though Father Lamond's suggestion of wearing the monk's garb was excellent, he was thankful they hadn't had to move into the castle and risk being identified. "We will meet here tomorrow at the same time."

His mentor nodded, then slipped into the stable.

Rubbing his jaw, Cailin glanced toward Elspet. She was watching him, her eyes dark with a combination of relief and worry.

Nor could he blame her. She wrestled with the fact that her stepbrother had joined the guard of the noble who'd murdered her mother and Blar's father and despised the notion that his loyalties were in question. 'Twas unsettling indeed.

"Follow me." He lifted the taper and headed down the tunnel. Golden candlelight spilled ahead of them, the air growing staler with each step. He smothered his instinctive reaction to the enclosed space. Since his forced labor on the pirate ship, he'd disliked being confined and would breathe easier once they reached the forest.

Fragments of daylight illuminated the tunnel ahead, and the air grew fresh. They were nearing the exit. His chest lightened and he slowed his steps, glanced over.

Chestnut-brown hair tumbled to frame her face taut with strain, and he ached to draw her to him, to offer comfort.

A foolish thought, nor one he would linger on further. "About your stepbrother—"

"Blar loathes the earl as do I. His loyalty is but a ruse. Once he has earned the earl's trust, I believe he intends to escape and find me."

For her sake, he wanted to believe she was right, but given Sir Petrus's distrust, Cailin had misgivings. "Whether your stepbrother's reason for his loyalty to my uncle is real or false, too much is at stake to take any unnecessary risks. Once I have overthrown my uncle and Tiran Castle is mine, you may speak with Blar."

Anger flashed in her eyes. "Blar is the only family I have. Do you not realize how much he means to me, the risks I took to try to save him?"

"Indeed, because 'twas I who saved you, a debt you repaid by robbing me. Neither," he drawled, ignoring the blush slashing her cheeks, "will I change my mind."

Elspet turned on her heel, stormed toward the castle.

He caught her arm, whirled her to face him.

"Release me!"

"So you can do what?" he demanded, furious that after everything, she'd dare defy him. "Regardless of Blar's loyalty, if you are caught in the castle, you would be arrested."

Beneath the flicker of candlelight, what little remaining color in her face fled, but her voice remained firm. "Blar needs to know that I am alive, am here, and will help him to escape."

The image of her stepbrother laughing with the other fighters far from convinced Cailin that Blar was in imminent danger or was secretly plotting to save her. Given Elspet's anger, reasoning she wouldn't see.

"In time, your stepbrother will know you are safe. However much you dislike the fact, for now 'tis imperative that he remains ignorant of where you are." She opened her mouth to speak; he raised his hand. "I want naught more than to confront my uncle and expose his deceit. However, too many within the castle are loyal to him to make such a reckless move. Once I raise a significant force, we will both have our wishes."

Her mouth tightened, but she didn't argue.

As much as he wanted to let the matter drop, he'd experienced the consequences of her headstrong ways.

"You will swear that you willna try to approach Blar or find another means to inform him of your presence."

Eyes blazing, she jerked free. "You would demand that I swear such?"

"I would." Cailin forced his tone to be hard. "Had you not stolen my sword after you drugged me, I would be more lenient."

"I returned your weapon."

"A broadsword the merchant wouldna have seen and informed my uncle of my presence if you hadna taken it. Swear to me now!"

Emerald eyes glittered. "I have sworn my fealty to you, led you to Father Lamond, and done whatever possible to aid you. That you dinna trust me to have wisdom in my decisions is an insult." She jabbed her finger into his chest. "I am nay a child who needs tending, but a woman—" She jabbed again. "One not afraid to fight."

As she started to shove her finger into his chest for the third time, he caught her wrist and found her pulse racing. Her other hand came up, and he caught that as well.

She was afraid, but she didn't look away. Never had he met a lass as passionate, one who would fight, give all, for someone she loved. What would it be like to have such a woman in his life? In his bed?

Irritated thoughts of her had worked their way into his mind when he should be thinking of naught but his goal of seizing his home, he scowled at her.

She angled her jaw in defiance.

God's blade, what a lass. "You will heed my warning!"

"I have pledged my fealty to you."

Given under duress. He could feel his back teeth grinding. Blast the obstinate woman. He wanted to rail at her, shake her until she saw reason, but with her stubbornness, if he threatened her further, she'd likely dig her heels in deeper.

She opened her mouth to say more.

Out of sheer reaction to smother whatever reckless words she'd spew and shove his ire higher, he claimed her mouth.

Elspet's silky lips stilled against his.

Her mouth was soft, her body warm, and her sensual taste tore through him until his intention to silence her collapsed to need. Like a man parched, he skimmed his hands up to cup her face, teased her with his tongue, teeth, until her body trembled.

On a moan, her lips parted, and he angled her jaw and took the kiss deeper, hauling her against him until her every curve was molded against him.

Images of her naked in his bed screamed through his mind, of touching her, tasting her every inch.

The blare of a distant horn sounded.

Blood pounding hot, Cailin released her, stunned by his actions as he stared at her lips swollen from his kisses, frustrated he wanted more. Blast it, what was he thinking?

Thinking?

No, lost to need, lucid thought had vacated his mind.

Emerald eyes flared as she stepped back. "Is that how you silence women?"

"Nay," he ground out. He took a much-needed step back, his body still humming with desire, her taste still roaring through his every breath. Furious he'd lost control, he glared at her, unsure of who he was angrier with, himself or her.

Irritated at the intensity of how much he wanted her, he tugged up his monk's hood. "Follow me."

* * * *

Cailin headed toward the exit, and Elspet glared at him. Her body still tingled where he'd touched her, his taste still warm on her tongue. Damn him! "Do you think you can kiss me like a barbarian and walk away? Is that what they teach you in when you become a knight?"

He whirled. Beneath the faint light, he stalked toward her, blue eyes darkening like a storm. Wolf's eyes, those of a predator, need churning within. "I have never forced a lady," he said through clenched teeth. "Nor was I the only one taking part in the kiss!"

Emotions tangled in her mind, but fairness insisted upon truth. Whatever else, he was right. What could she say? She hadn't wanted the kiss, but after their heated encounter, now she wanted more.

"Nor," he continued, "does it matter. It meant nothing." He strode toward the exit.

Like a slap to the face, she stared at his retreating form. Though she had been kissed before, never had anyone moved her like Cailin. Move her?

A pathetic name for the heat searing through her every inch, of how for a moment every fiber felt alive, as if his taste and touch was air to breathe.

"That meant nothing to you?" she demanded.

He kept walking.

The bastard. She clenched her fists. Fine. If denial was his strategy, with ease she could keep her distance.

She started after him, realized that in the mayhem of moments before she hadn't sworn to keep away from Blar. She scoffed at his demand. Cailin might be the rightful earl of Dalkirk, but he didn't dictate her life. Nor was she a fool. However much she wanted to trust Blar, now she held doubts.

The quiet scrape of wood had her glancing ahead.

At the tunnel entrance, Cailin shoved the disguised entry open a hand's width, peered out.

The blare of a horn sounded, this time closer.

Fear smothered the ire of moments before. She hurried to his side. "What do you see?"

"'Tis several men from the castle on a hunt."

"At least they are not searching for us."

"I assure you, if they believed we were near, they would abandon their hunt and scour the area in a trice." He grimaced. "Once they are gone, we will ride to the band of Romani hidden in the forest led by Taog MacCarron."

"Why?"

"I believe that I can convince the Romani leader that 'tis to his and his people's benefit to help me overthrow the earl."

She arched a skeptical brow, knowing her friend's ways too well. "He is a powerful man. Why do you think he will back you?"

"Because Taog and his people refused to swear fealty to my uncle."

"The Romani are men who live by their own rules, and who give their trust to few."

"And you know this because…?"

"Over the years, I often traveled with my stepfather to their encampment." She glanced out, keeping an eye on the distant band of knights. "I have made many close friends within their encampment."

Cailin drew his brows together. "Before you awoke this morning, Father Lamond explained that you would know their location."

She nodded. "My stepfather told me a month before where they had moved their camp."

"How did your stepfather know where they would be?"

"There is a tree stump he would go to. Inside, they would leave a rolled-up writ telling them their new location, or replies to questions he had left for them." She paused. "Odd; I never thought how unusual that was until now."

"If they passed missives to your stepfather, they sound far from an unorganized, disreputable band." He frowned. "Do you think they worked in league with your stepfather?"

"I am unsure." Elspet hesitated, remembering the close bond her stepfather had with Taog and his men. Never had she considered their familiarity could mean more, until now. "You think they support King Robert as well?"

"Mayhap. If so, 'twould make it easier to gain their support." Cailin gazed through the opening, then back to her. "The men are gone." He shoved the hidden door open the rest of the way. "Come."

Once he'd sealed the entry and erased any sign of their presence, she followed him through the dense tangle of brush to where he'd secured his horse behind a shield of rocks.

A gust of wind rattled the branches overhead. She glanced at the gray clouds thick with snow. "As long as we arena seen and forced to make a detour, we should make it to the Romani camp before dark."

He mounted, extended his arm toward her. "Then," he said as he lifted her up behind him, "we will ensure that we arena seen." Once she explained in what direction they were heading, he rode from the shielding brush and kicked his destrier into a canter.

The soft thud of hooves upon snow merged with the whip of wind that thankfully covered their tracks. Elspet hung on tight, her body flush against his, a potent reminder of how he'd kissed her until reason had succumbed to desire.

Merciful saints, she didn't need to think about his kiss. More so after he'd pushed her away. Refusing to linger on the hurt, she turned her thoughts to what she'd do once Blar was free.

Her stepfather had close friends at Avalon Castle, on an island off the Western Highlands. She remembered meeting Stephan MacQuistan, Earl of Dunsmore, and his wife, Lady Katherine. Though nobility, regardless that she was untitled, they'd welcomed her with open arms. More, they'd encouraged her to visit in the future. An invitation she would accept. Regardless of Blar's decision on whether to join her, the distance would allow her time to think, to decide what to do with her life, and a way to put Cailin from her mind.

"We are coming to a burn," he called.

She glanced ahead. The sweep of forest angled downward. At the bottom, the rush of water thundered along a twisted path, pummeling boulders blocking its way, roaring past fallen trees cluttered with ice, to sweep out of sight.

"Go right, then follow the flow until you see a thick stand of oak and birch. The Romani will be hidden nearby. My stepfather and I visited a bit more than a fortnight ago. If they have moved, we will look in the stump to see if they have left a missive mentioning their new location."

He nudged his warhorse forward, half-walked, half-slid down the steep incline. "Why did we not check there first?"

"'Twould take a half day's travel, which I had hoped to avoid."

A whinny had him glancing toward the ridge. His body tensed. "Hold on." He kicked his steed into a thick stand of fir. Cailin leaped off the horse, then ran back with a limb thick with needled bristles and erased their tracks before slipping into the dense cover beside her.

Another whinny sounded, then voices. Ahead, a group of knights rode into view as flurries of snow blustered past, laying a silky layer of fresh snow atop which Cailin had erased any sign of their passing.

"'Tis the earl's men," she whispered.

Each second crawled past as the group meandered along the bank, pausing every so often to search their surroundings.

Another gust of wind-tossed snow swirled past.

"Bloody freezing," one of the knights grumbled. "By now, they are hunkered down. If they had left tracks, with the snow falling at a rapid rate, they will be hidden by now."

"Aye," another voice called out. "'Tis a fool's errand to keep searching for them."

The lead rider halted, scoured the area. "'Twill serve us little if we canna see if they rode through here. We will make one more sweep of the area, then return to the castle." He urged his horse into a canter.

"That was close," she whispered.

"As much as I would like to remain hidden, we must leave," Cailin said. "With them scouring the woods, they might stumble upon us."

He guided his horse around a large stand of rocks, following the knights' trail to obscure any sign of their departure. A good distance along their path, he veered closer to the river.

Orange-red smeared the sky as the last of the setting sun faded beneath the horizon as they reached the top of the next ridge. An icy howl of wind screamed past, for a moment blinding him.

"Is Taog's camp much farther?"

"Nay. 'Tis a ways yet."

He scowled at the fading light and drew the horse to a halt. "'Tis too dangerous to continue. We must find shelter before it grows too dark."

She tugged her cape tighter as she scanned the murky landscape. "If the earl's men are nearby, they will have a difficult time seeing us."

"There is—"

Shouts rose as dark shapes charged out of the thick churn of flakes, surrounding them. "Drop your weapons or die!"

Chapter 9

Sword readied as he sat upon his warhorse, Cailin peered through the thick flakes of falling snow toward the warning voice. The soft pad of steps a short distance away in the knee-deep smear of white assuring him that he and Elspet were surrounded. The slide of her dagger against leather scraped from where she sat behind him.

"We are but traveling through," he called out, cursing that he hadn't sought shelter before his uncle's guards had returned and had now placed her life in danger. Blast it, as long as he drew a breath, the bastards wouldn't touch her.

A long moment passed, then a large, fierce-looking man stepped into view. Claymore raised, snow-laced wind whipped against his thick black beard. "Push down your hoods so I can see you!"

Cailin's grip tightened on his broadsword.

Elspet laid her hand on his shoulder. "Wait!"

"Do you know him?" Cailin whispered as he eyed the formidable man.

"Aye." She secured her dagger. "'Tis Taog MacCarron, the man we seek."

Thank God. He sheathed his weapon, then shoved his hood aside.

After securing her blade, Elspet pushed down her hood as well.

The fierce man's eyes shifted to her, widened in surprised, then warmed. "Elspet McReynolds!" Taog boomed, and he sheathed his sword.

"Aye." She jumped down and ran into the huge man's arms.

Irritation slammed Cailin as the burly man enveloped her in a ferocious hug. Nor did he miss the soft rumble of words as the man spoke to her, or the sheer happiness on her face as she gazed up at him.

Elspet had explained that she'd visited the Romani leader's camp many times with her stepfather. Though with how she'd run to him, he was clearly more than her stepfather's trusted friend, but hers.

As if Cailin gave a bloody damn. She could befriend whoever she liked. That she had someone whom she obviously cared for, a feeling 'twould seem the Romani shared, mattered little. Soon the day would come when he was rid of her.

Nor could Cailin overlook the fact that the leader couldn't offer a woman a safe haven, a place where she could raise children and make a home. Life as an outlaw was one on the move, proven by the makeshift tents that were nearly impossible to see beneath the shield of trees.

But that logic far from eased his discontent at how the man folded her within his embrace as if 'twas a common occurrence.

Jaw tight, Cailin dismounted, strode over.

At his approach, with one final hug to the Romani, Elspet stepped back. "Taog, I would like to introduce you to Sir Cailin MacHugh, the rightful Earl of Dalkirk."

Dark eyes narrowed on him. "We were told you died years ago, at sea."

Cailin straightened to his full height. "A lie. One of many told by my uncle in his treacherous plot to claim my title. 'Tis why I am here—" He scanned the armed Romani men who'd moved into view surrounding them, shifted his focus to their leader. "To reclaim my birthright."

Taog crossed his arms over his chest. "A fact that has little to do with me."

Father Lamond had warned him that 'twould be difficult to garner the Romani leader's support, a man with friends, many unscrupulous, but someone who could be trusted. His unsavory life was not by choice but driven by the Earl of Dalkirk labeling him a traitor.

They shared common bonds; in addition to their both supporting King Robert, Gaufrid had nearly destroyed their lives. A fact Cailin prayed would sway the powerful man to his side. "I would like to speak with you in private. First"—he glanced toward Elspet—"I ask that she be given food, and a place to rest."

Taog nodded. "Follow me."

She started after him.

With a frown, Cailin took his mount's reins and walked beside her. "Stay within my sight while we are here."

Surprise flickered in her eyes. "None within Taog's camp would hurt me. I trust these people with my life."

He gave her a hard scowl, keeping watch on the armed men falling back as their leader strode past. "Mayhap, but you are under my protection. Until Tiran Castle is mine, you will heed my warnings."

Another gust blustered past as they followed the leader. Nor did he miss that, in addition to the guards surrounding them, more men who'd been hidden in the woods joined their ranks. Even if they wanted to escape, the opportunity was lost.

Cailin shoved aside the unsettling thoughts as they stepped into a large clearing and focused on their surroundings. A few bows, spears, swords, and other well-crafted weapons were propped near tents, within easy reach. Though the camp was small, he noted that bundles of ties, travois, and other materials were close at hand in case they needed to break camp and flee.

If everything went according to plan, before he departed, as had Sir Angus, he would establish a hiding place to leave messages with Taog.

They made their way around several large rocks and the dense foliage gave way, exposing a much larger cluster of dwellings. Ingenious, he mused, that the outer encampment was designed to convince anyone passing by that it belonged to a small group. More so, at first glance the setting appeared arbitrary, while on closer inspection, he saw that the location of the dwellings allowed the Romani to spot approaching riders long before the intruders were aware of their presence.

Tents with furs shoved inside riddled the area and chests of goods were stacked near the rocks. Flames tangled into the darkening sky from several fires set around the shared dwelling spots, bubbling pots sitting over each one, and scruffy men and a few women sat huddled nearby.

As they moved through the encampment, several people called out to Elspet. Cailin glanced at her, remembered how Father Lamond had explained that she'd visited many times over.

At the center of camp, their leader gestured to her. "Sit, please."

After she complied, she was handed a blanket, and once she'd wrapped it around herself, a bowl of stew.

It pleased Cailin that they'd cared for her first. He met the fierce leader's gaze. "Where can we go to speak privately?"

"We will speak here." Taog glanced at his men before his gaze leveled on Cailin. "There is naught here that we keep from the other."

Nor could he fault him on his method, 'twas one the Templars used as well. The knowledge, wisdom of many shared gave insight into decisions for battle. Cailin nodded and withdrew his sword.

The scrape of steel hissed as the men sitting around them shoved to their feet, their blades drawn.

Fury blazed in Taog's eyes. "A threat?"

"Nay, proof—" Hilt first, Cailin handed the broadsword to their leader "—that I am Cailin MacHugh, the rightful Earl of Dalkirk."

Taog studied the sword. Firelight glinted off the weapon as he raised it for all to see. "The hilt bears the Dalkirk coat of arms." His gaze cut to Cailin before shifting back to his men. "This broadsword disappeared after Cailin supposedly died at sea."

"He looks alive enough to me," one of the men joked.

Laughter rumbled through the group, and a smile touched their leader's mouth. "Aye, it does appear as if he is breathing, and," he said, the humor on his face fading, "his eyes are the same color as his father's." He leveled his gaze on Cailin. "Who took your father's sword from Tiran Castle after your disappearance?"

"A highly respected man," Cailin replied, "and one who, like me, holds naught but distrust for my uncle."

"I would know the man's name," Taog stated.

Cailin shook his head. "He is too important to risk anyone within the earl's ranks discovering his identity."

At the murmurs of dissent, Elspet set her food aside and stood. Slowly, she looked each man in the eye, then lay her hand over her heart. "I can vouch for the man of whom Sir Cailin speaks and swear that Sir Cailin is indeed the rightful Earl of Dalkirk, and an honorable man, one you can trust."

Those within camp gave him hard looks, but he noted some slowly nod their acceptance.

She was a sight to behold, and despite their heated arguments and her stubbornness to heed his will, he couldn't help but feel moved by her passionate recommendation.

"Your reason for coming here is to reclaim your legacy," Taog said, "but doesna explain why you seek us out."

Cailin met his shrewd gaze. "I need men who will swear fealty to me to join my ranks."

Taog arched a skeptical brow as he handed Cailin the broadsword. "You are believing that you can convince us."

He sheathed his blade. "I am."

"Why should we?" the Romani asked.

"To serve justice to a man who would burn hardworking families from their homes—" Cailin allowed the anger at his uncle's treachery to infuse his words, "—and hang Sir Angus McReynolds with a false claim, and pay to have his nephew be murdered."

A slim man cleared his throat. "We heard Sir Angus was caught poaching."

Elspet shoved to her feet. "A lie. You knew my stepfather. He was a man of honor and would rather starve than take what belonged to another." Murmurs rippled through the group in concurrence.

"I never believed the charge," an elderly man near the back piped up.

"Nor I," a young woman sitting next to him said.

"Sir Angus McReynolds might have skirted the law on occasion," Taog said, "but he was a man of honor."

A roar of agreement sounded.

The Romani leader raised his hand, and his people grew silent. He arched a brow at Cailin. "What benefit would it be to us to have you as the Earl of Dalkirk?"

"Because, as Elspet said, I am a man you can trust to be honest and accessible to all," Cailin replied. "I swear to you that I will always listen to your concerns, and I will make judgements in favor of those that best serve the people."

"And choices that line your pockets?" another elder called from the back.

"Nay, 'twas not my father's way, nor is it mine. My uncle is a detestable, ruthless man who cares naught for those beneath him. Once I claim my birthright, I will rule with a fair hand, and the Romani will always be welcome on Dalkirk land, that I swear." He scanned the crowd. "But I need your help."

"Our ranks are not enough to seize Tiran Castle," said a thin, bearded man seated paces away.

"Your aid will lend much to the campaign. I have already spoken with a man at the castle who is now working with those he trusts to build our ranks."

Taog grimaced. "His name."

Cailin hesitated, not wanting to divulge it.

"You ask us to risk our lives for your cause," the leader stated, "we will have his name."

A fair request. Cailin gave a rough exhale. "Sir Petrus Beaton."

"The master-at-arms." Taog raised his brow. "I am impressed. How did you manage to contact him without being seen?"

"There are secret entries into the castle. Ones we will use during the attack." Cailin paused. "Once I leave here, I have several more influential people with whom I will speak to garner further support."

"What if you canna raise a significant enough force to confront your uncle?" a slender woman to the side asked.

Cailin met her gaze squarely. "Failure is not an option. I will not rest until Tiran Castle is back in its rightful hands."

Silence fell upon the group.

And," Cailin said, meeting each person's gaze before continuing, "my loyalty is not to Lord Comyn, but to King Robert Bruce."

Gasps of surprise melded with hums of approval.

An elder with a long white beard stood. "I have never supported the bastard Comyn."

"Nor I," said a woman at his side.

Shouts supporting King Robert filled the air.

Taog stepped beside Cailin. "Those who wish to join Sir Cailin to oust his treacherous uncle and restore the title of the Earl of Dalkirk to its rightful heir and swear their fealty to the Bruce, say aye!"

Ayes filled the air, and the elder who'd asked a question raised her fist in support, a smile widening the slender woman's face.

Cailin glanced at Elspet. Though they had a ways to go, pride filled him at what they'd accomplished.

"'Twould seem," Taog said as he offered Cailin his hand, "that you have our support."

With a nod, Cailin clasped his hand. "I am forever in debt to you and your people."

Taog turned toward the throng and lifted his hands. "'Tis time to celebrate!"

Cheers rose from the group. Someone brought out a lute and another began to sing.

Cailin accepted each person's vow of fealty as he moved through the crowd and thanked them for their trust. A long while later, his mind a whirl with names and a blur of faces, he searched for Elspet.

She sat near the fire, Taog at her side. A sad smile touched her face as her hand rested on the warrior's arm and they spoke in low undertones. What did they discuss so intimately?

Body tensing in what he refused to believe was something as simple as jealousy, Cailin walked over, nodded to the formidable leader, then met her gaze. "You are exhausted from travel. I thought you would be long asleep."

Her face was wan in the soft glow of the fire as though the night's chaotic events—despite their happy conclusion—had caught up with her. He must have looked somewhat fierce as she withdrew her hand from Taog's arm. "'Tis a night to celebrate."

"Aye." He settled beside her and accepted a cup of mead from a nearby man. Cailin took a sip, appreciating the strong, tangy brew, glanced toward Taog, and tried to ignore thinking of him as a rival for Elspet's affections. He had no tie to her, other than a common goal. "My thanks again for your support."

"You convinced my people, though after Elspet's glowing praise, you had mine." He shot her a fond glance, which she returned.

Cailin's fingers tightened on his cup. "I swear you willna regret it."

"Of that I have little doubt." Taog stood. "And I agree, Elspet looks as if she is ready to collapse."

"We had a hard day of travel," Cailin said, "made more so as a short distance from your camp, we had to hide from the earl's men."

The Romani leader grimaced. "I have noticed the increase of rounds by his guards over the past few days. Now I know why. We will speak further in the morning, once you both have slept." He walked to an elder on the opposite side of the fire, sat, and spoke softly.

The elder gave a slow nod.

A wave of tiredness washed over Cailin. Thankful for the Romani's support and that Taog had given them some privacy, he emptied his mug.

* * * *

"Here." Elspet's hand shook from exhaustion as she handed him a steaming mug of stew.

"I thank you." He took a swallow, then another. "'Tis good, but you really should find your bed."

"I will, but being here is…" Painful memories stormed her. Her appetite gone, she set aside her food.

He touched her shoulder. "Elspet—"

A tremor rippled through her. "'Tis difficult being here. The last time I was with my stepfather. His smile… Regardless if I wasna his true daughter, he was always proud of me, and I…" She shook her head. "Never mind, 'tis naught but foolish ramblings."

"'Tis anything but." Cailin lifted her chin, and eyes dark with grief met his. "You had his love, time with him over the years, memories that you will forever hold in your heart. Never forget that."

The tenderness of his words touched her soul, threatened to break her fragile control. "I willna."

He released her, and as if a spell broken, the melding of voices of those around them filled the night, the errant burst of laughter, the somber conversations. Sparks popped from the fire, entwined with the smoke, and drifted into the star-filled sky. Moments later, the tiny flares of red slowly faded to black.

She finished her second cup of ale, pushed to her feet, wove.

A frown lining his brow, Cailin stood and caught her elbow. "I will escort you to our tent."

With the soft haze of drink clouding her mind, she nodded, not trusting herself to speak, too aware of him, of the feelings he stirred inside. They added another layer of confusion onto those of a night filled with bittersweet memories. And yet... his touch had the power to make her forget, something she so dearly wished to do at that moment.

Elspet forced a smile at an elder she passed, trembled as she fought to smother memories of Cailin's kiss.

"You are cold," he said.

Far from it. This man made her feel off balance and ache for him. Nor could she forget the kiss he'd claimed, even if he'd declared that it had meant naught.

Cailin gestured to the tent near a large birch. "This is where Taog said we can sleep."

She stilled. Wanting him, the last thing she needed was to spend more time alone with him. "We?"

Chapter 10

Pulse racing, too aware of him, Elspet narrowed her gaze at Cailin. Though proud of his acceptance by Taog's men, she was besieged by a host of other emotions that left her feeling vulnerable. "I can sleep in one of the women's tents, as I did during my visits with my stepfather." And with her mind skewed by ale, a safe choice.

"If the earl's men attack, I want you nearby, where I can protect you."

Tingles raced up her spine. Within the fall of snow, Elspet scanned the mix of pine, birch, and oak surrounding the camp, where beyond naught but darkness smothered the forest. "Lord Dalkirk would be foolish to try to attack such a large armed band."

Cailin grunted. "If my uncle knew we were here, he would take the risk, more so as his men could surround the camp beneath the cover of night, then at dawn attack."

She wanted to deny his claim, but after her mother and stepfather's murders, she'd witnessed firsthand the lengths to which the noble would go to achieve his objectives. Goals that now included capturing and likely killing them both. "You think the earl and his men are near the camp?"

"I am unsure, but I warned Taog of the possibility."

Elspet again scanned the woods, each shadow prodding her to pause in search of a hidden threat. On a shaky breath, she faced Cailin. "Now what?"

"We try to sleep."

She stared at him in disbelief. "After warning me of a possible attack, I am supposed to sleep?"

"Until my uncle is imprisoned, there is nowhere safe. Here is as good a place as any, more so as the Romani have guards set up around the perimeter of this encampment. Come."

In silence, they moved past several people who nodded to her; she waved her reply. A part of her was thankful Cailin would remain close, not that she'd admit such, more so with fatigue and ale blurring her thoughts.

Her emotions were too raw. She would have preferred to be alone, although given their danger, a foolhardy thought.

After passing another fire, he halted before a tent and lifted the flap, exposing a layer of pine boughs spread out over the ground, a stack of blankets and furs to the right.

Her legs unsteady, she entered.

Cailin stepped in behind her.

In wavers of golden firelight streaming into the tent, she focused her fatigue and drink-blurred thoughts on making a pallet rather than on the fact that they would be sleeping in the same tent. With a shiver at the cold, she slipped beneath the covers, thankful for the soft boughs upon the hard ground, and savored the building warmth. When she could wait no longer, she glanced over.

Half-cloaked in shadows but a hand's length away, he was adjusting a fur over a blanket. She caught the tired lines creasing his face, and the images of a lad too young to deal with such deception made her heart ache. However difficult for her, Cailin struggled against his own challenges: an uncle who'd betrayed him, a man who'd murdered his parents and then had paid a miscreant to ensure he was killed. Against such odds, 'twas a miracle he'd lived.

Lived? No, he'd done far more than that. He'd overcome challenges that would have devastated most and had grown into a formidable warrior to admire. A man who, however much she tried to ignore what he made her feel for him, left her remembering how he'd held her, and the potency of his kiss.

She gave herself a mental shake and instead voiced a question she'd been wanting to ask. "After you escaped from your uncle's hired killer, how did you survive?"

"Go to sleep."

Far from swayed by his stern warning, she rolled to her side, bringing herself closer to him. "You are accomplished with a blade, a proficiency I have rarely seen."

He gave an exasperated sigh. "Skills I learned protecting others during their journey."

At his vague reply, her curiosity grew. "Where have you traveled?"

"Many places."

"Such as?"

"'Tis unimportant."

She tugged the blanket around her and sat up, staring at him in the semidarkness. "Why are you only now returning to Dalkirk?"

With the cover pulled up to his shoulders, Cailin turned, leaving his back to her. "Go to sleep."

Oddly hurt, she lay back, glanced outside, and watched a spark from a nearby fire swirl away into the night. Many still sat around the fires, sharing the events of the day, tales that made some laugh. Sadness swelled inside at memories of her previous visits to Taog's camp, of how she'd enjoyed the stories, and of her stepfather's laughter.

Elspet drew up the covers and closed her eyes, willing sleep to come.

The murmur of prayer had her peering toward Cailin through half-closed lashes. As in the cave, he was whispering the Our Father and, once finished, he again started the Paternoster.

After several repetitions, he made the sign of the cross, then pulled his covers higher. A brief while later, his soft, even breaths assured her that he'd fallen asleep.

A frown crossed her brow. She'd met many knights in her life but never one so devout. Had his uncle's attempt to have him murdered incited his deep spirituality? It made sense, a foundation built on faith that would have guided him through the years since.

Still, it felt as if she was missing something important. She sighed. As if she would discover whatever mystery surrounded Cailin this night, when her mind was skewed by emotions and drink?

The distant voices of those seated around the flames reached her, and a haze slowly enshrouded her mind. Ready for this day to end, she released a slow sigh, closed her eyes, and welcomed the numbing haze of sleep.

* * * *

"Sir Hugh, get back!" a deep voice muttered.

In a groggy haze, Elspet sat up and grabbed her dagger at her side. Vision blurred with sleep, she peered out of the tent and scanned the camp for signs of intruders.

Several fires burned cheerfully in the dark, groups of men gathered around each, but their numbers were fewer, proof that hours had passed since she'd fallen asleep. What had woken her? In the wavering light spilling into their tent from a nearby fire, she glanced toward Cailin, the question dying on her lips.

Face taut, he turned to his side on his pallet, his eyes closed and the furs covering him tossed aside. "I said go!"

Her body relaxed, and she sheathed her dagger. Thank God 'twas not an attack. Yet whatever troubled him was enough to disturb his thoughts even in sleep. He twisted as if fighting invisible warriors.

"Cailin," she softly called.

He mumbled something unintelligible.

Wanting to avoid alerting those outside, she wrapped a blanket around herself, then crawled next to him and carefully drew up his covers.

As her fingers brushed his chest, his hand snapped out, caught hers.

She jerked back; Cailin held tight.

"What are you doing?" he hissed.

"Trying," she said, unable to help but notice the stubble lining his jaw, frustrated he hadn't replied a moment ago, but stirred at the slightest touch, "to pull up your blanket. You were having a nightmare and threw off your covers."

On a sigh, he released her, sat up.

She rubbed her wrist.

Giving himself a visible shake, he ran a hand over his face. "Return to your bed."

Moved by the raw anguish of his words, she remained. "You spoke aloud. Who is Sir Hugh?"

Silence.

"You were warning him to get back. Why?"

"Many years have passed."

Dark grief tangled in his voice, and she shifted closer, wanting to understand, offer the comfort he'd given her. He stiffened but didn't shrug her off. "But his death still haunts you," she said softly.

"It does."

"What happened?"

In the subtle waver of distant firelight, the grief in his eyes was that of a man who'd seen too much death. "He was killed taking an arrow meant for me."

Her chest squeezed. Unsure what to say, understanding too well the heartache of losing someone you cared for, she lay her hand upon his arm. "I am sorry."

"'Twas years ago."

Mayhap, but from his torment, the memory was still raw in his mind. "You were close?"

"He was like a brother to me."

She ached to wrap her arms around him and hold him close, but with the stiff way he sat, he wouldn't welcome her touch right now. "Where were you?"

"In the Holy Land."

On a crusade? "Last night, you said that you had honed your skills protecting those on a journey. That was where you meant, was it not?"

"Aye."

Stories of a massive castle built high upon a plateau overlooking the desert came to mind, along with tales of horselike animals with humps that men rode and could travel for days. "I have never met anyone who has traveled in the Holy Land, only heard tales of those who braved the brutal land and dangerous travel for their faith."

Gaze intense, he watched her for a long moment, but when he spoke his voice seemed far away. "For many, 'tis worth the risk."

"Is that why you were there?"

"One of the reasons."

Excitement raced through her, as if she'd finally unlocked a piece of the mystery of his past. "Last night, after I lay down, before you slept, you whispered the Our Father several times, just as you did when we stayed in the cave."

In the glow of firelight, his face hardened. "You were eavesdropping?"

She shook her head. "Several hand-widths apart, even though you whispered, 'twas difficult not to hear."

He rubbed his hand over his face, then exhaled. "Go back to sleep."

At the sadness in his voice, she touched his arm. "You listened to me in the cave, an offer that I return."

"Elspe—"

"Though we didna start out on the best of terms—" To say the least, she'd deceived him and stolen his sword. "I would like to be your friend, one you can turn to."

"Why?"

She opened her mouth, then closed it, realizing that without her intending it, he'd become important to her.

Very important.

And it wasn't just a physical connection. Her mind and heart were as lured as her body. Astounded, she stared at him. How was this possible in such short a time?

She withdrew her hand, floundered to find an explanation that would satisfy him and bide her time to sort through what she was feeling. "Do you ask why because I am not of noble blood?"

He muttered a soft curse. "I dinna judge a person by their status. Nor," he said, his voice softening, "do I make friends with ease."

"After all we have been through, with my fealty given to King Robert, to you, and the risks I have taken, I would think you know by now that I am a woman to trust."

"You are. There is naught simple about my past."

"What you tell me, I swear I will never share." She hesitated briefly, then blurted out, "I may be foolish to admit this, but you have become important to me in ways beyond the fealty I have sworn you."

His face hardened in the wisps of distant firelight. "'Tis a mistake."

"And mine to make."

"I seek naught more than to reclaim my heritage."

"I know."

As if coming to a decision, he scanned the encampment, then faced her. "What I am about to tell you, you can never share."

Elspet nodded. "I swear it."

"I am a Knight Templar."

"A Templar?" Shock roared through her at the revelation, and she scrambled to discern the ramifications even as she sat back on her heels. "But they were charged with heresy and arrested over a year past."

"Hearsay," he spat. "A lie, as with each charge lodged against us by King Philip."

"Why would France's king utter such horrific falsehoods?" she asked, still floundering beneath the disclosure. She had expected a confession, not this startling revelation. Yet she believed Cailin; he was too honorable to lie. They'd both experienced the brutal backlash of betrayal and had survived.

"For the same reason too many wars have been waged," he spat. "Greed. The king wanted the Templar wealth."

"Merciful saints. So many brave men were arrested and killed."

"They were," he said, his voice ice, "and revenge for our Brothers who were betrayed burns within each Templar who survived."

A gust sent snow blustering past their tent as Elspet listened while he explained how, during the riots in France the previous year, the Templars had sheltered King Philip. After the king debased France's currency to a fraction of its worth, solely to increase his revenue, outrage ignited among his people.

"He was ill advised to believe his subjects would docilely submit their coin," she said.

"Nay, he anticipated their anger, but not the intensity, or that they would pack the streets in rebellion."

Disgust rolled through her at the sovereign's selfish decision. "King Philip was a fool to dare such an extreme measure."

"Not a fool; frantic to replenish his coffers." He slowly exhaled. "A desperate financial state the Knights Templar were unaware of. Even had we known, we had offered him protection over the years, along with the support of our strategic force. None within the Brotherhood would have believed he would betray us, more so when if he had but asked, we could have lent him more money."

She frowned. "More?"

"Aye, Templars have loaned coin to many nobles over the years to ensure their interests were protected, including King Philip. Our trusting the sovereign was a crucial error, one paid for with the blood of many of my Brothers."

Her heart echoed the loathing on his face for France's king, a vile ruler who'd slaughtered devout men guilty of naught but blind faith.

"As King Philip hid in our Paris temple during the uprising," Cailin continued, his voice raw with contempt, "he saw the treasures within the sanctuary and realized if the Brotherhood was removed, 'twould eliminate the huge debt he owed us."

Sickened, she fisted her hands, wishing she could wrap them around the sovereign's despicable neck. "Even if it meant destroying the Templars, knights who had been loyal to him throughout?"

Face grim, he nodded.

"But the riots ceased?"

"Aye, because after he'd concocted his plan to claim the Templar fortune, King Philip rescinded the devaluation, and peace again settled over the realm. He departed the Paris temple. After a brief time, he issued the charges against the Knights Templar from *unidentified claims*, which led to the arrests. Unidentified." His lip curled in disgust. "I, as do the remainder of the Brotherhood, have little doubt the falsehoods were crafted by France's king."

Her hand trembled as she lay it over his. "I am so sorry. 'Tis tragic what those within the Brotherhood have endured." She hesitated, frowned. "But you are here now. How?"

"Prior to the arrests, the Grand Master was warned of King Philip's nefarious intent. Many of the valuables within the Paris temple were transferred to a Templar fleet located in the port of La Rochelle. Most ships headed to Portugal, but five sailed to Scotland." Grim satisfaction glittered in his gaze. "King Philip may have found bits of gold left behind at the

Paris temple, but he will *never* find the sacred treasures the Brotherhood have guarded over the years."

She shook her head. "I would think after the king's despicable actions, Pope Clement V would intervene."

A muscle worked in Cailin's jaw as he thought of the feckless Christian leader. "His Grace wasna selected as pope due to his staunch beliefs or righteous manner, but because he is a man King Philip can manipulate to do his bidding."

She gasped. "France's king would dare threaten the pope? H–how is such a treasonous action possible?"

"Because King Philip is a powerful man, one who will take whatever lethal steps are necessary to achieve his goal."

In the glow of firelight sifting into their tent, Elspet's face paled, and she made the sign of the cross. "God have mercy on those tragically betrayed." Her body trembled, and he laced his fingers with hers and rubbed his thumb against the soft curve of her palm.

Her skin was warm, not hardened with calluses as he would have expected given the trials she had survived as of late. He knew that she, more than most, would understand what he had gone through, which was why he had shared his strife. In truth, it felt good to reveal his past.

An owl hooted in the distance.

Eyes dark with grief met his. "Why did any of the fleet sail north to Scotland?"

A grim smile touched his mouth, faded. "Unknown to most of the Brotherhood, years before, a covert plan had been made with the Bruce to protect the Order's secrets if ever a dire circumstance arose. When Jacques de Molay learned of King Philip's foul plot, he set the plan into action."

"Wait. What does King Robert have to do with the Knights Templar?"

"Had you asked that question two years ago, I would have been confounded by it. But I, as all those who escaped before the arrests began, were informed that Scotland's sovereign was in secret a Knight Templar. As for our sailing to Scotland, King Robert's religious exclusion, along with the Scottish clergy's refusal to acknowledge his excommunication, allowed the Bruce to offer the Brotherhood into his realm with impunity."

She shook her head. "'Tis incredible. Thank God the excommunication allowed you, as many other Templars, the ability to escape, but my heart aches for those betrayed."

"As mine. Over a year has passed since the arrests began, yet I struggle with the loss of so many of my friends, the butchery, and King Philip's betrayal." Grief swamped him as he glanced into the night. A few men still sat around the fires, and he spotted several guards posted where the light reached the forest. Throat raw with emotion, he met her gaze. "By now I was to have returned to the Middle East on crusade, fighting back those who would harm Christians seeking to travel to the Holy Land. Instead, I sit in Scotland with many within the Brotherhood dead, and the bastard king still ruling France."

The shift of clothing sounded, and a hand touched his shoulder.

He stiffened. "I seek nay pity."

"I give you naught but comfort and understanding.".

He wanted to push her away, tell her she far from understood the loss, the hurt, but days before, she'd suffered her own living hell.

Elspet lay her head upon his shoulder. "I thank you for trusting me. Never could I have imagined the horrors you have endured."

"Nor I." Sparks burst from a fire and entwined in smoke, drifted into the night. "After my uncle's deceit, when I joined the Templars, I believed I had found my purpose. Though challenging, 'twas a way of life I loved. The men were like brothers, a family I had never imagined I would have again."

The night bitter with cold, he shifted back and spread out his blanket to include her, moved by how she lay against him with such trust and, without expecting to, finding comfort in her presence.

Another light gust tumbled past.

"Though I regret the horror you have been subjected to, the loss, I am thankful for your return." Elspet lifted her gaze to his, and in the dim wash of light, he saw the sincerity, the tenderness, and the desire that had his blood racing.

Needing to touch her, he stroked her cheek, his emotions torn. "Though I had believed my heritage was forever lost, a part of me is thankful I can right a wrong. The other is ashamed that I think such when so many of the Brotherhood have died."

"There is naught to be ashamed of. Like me, the life you loved was usurped, seized for the sake of power by a man who cared little for those who died, only for his greedy, self-serving goals."

Her strength and understanding beckoned to him, lured him to feel more for her than he'd ever intended. "Mayhap, but I doubt I will ever get past the loss."

"Nor I," she agreed.

Cailin drew her closer. She was proof that there was still good in the world, and hope. 'Twas incredible that, in this mayhem, he'd found a woman like her. More so, considering without his wanting her to, she'd become important to him, a feeling beyond that of keeping her safe. Her confession earlier had forced him to acknowledge the truth, that he wanted her near him, and far away from men who could be his rivals, like Taog. A foolish thought.

One day he would want an heir, but in the future. After he'd reclaimed Tiran Castle, he would rejoin King Robert in his fight to claim Scotland.

As she watched him, her lips parted and his body trembled, aching to touch her. He tried to fight the pull, but as her soft scent of woman and night filled his every breath, reasons to keep his distance fell away. On a groan, Cailin claimed her mouth. He savored her taste, her soft moan, never wanting this moment to end.

Emotions storming him, wanting her more than was right, he broke away, cradled her against his chest.

"What are you thinking?" she whispered.

That I care for you too much, he silently replied, her shaky voice exposing that she, too, had been affected, which helped naught.

He looked out at the encampment, struggling to tamp down the need surging through him. "That at dawn, after I speak with Taog MacCarron and work out several details, we must meet again with the master-at-arms." A safe reply. "We both need to sleep. 'Tis but a few hours until dawn."

"We should."

But he didn't move.

"Cailin, I think—"

He crushed his mouth to hers, damning his actions, aware that he could offer her little, but for this moment, however wrong, he needed her.

Chapter 11

Elspet sank into Cailin's kiss, the gentle seduction, the taste of man and heat. A soft moan rumbled in his throat as his tongue teased her; she pressed her body against his, demanded more.

Desire built as he pulled her into his lap, his hands teasing, caressing, until she was wild with his every touch, could feel the answering reverberations thrumming through his frame.

Never had a man made her want, made her body burn so that logic crumbled beneath need. With him, the barriers fell away and 'twas like drifting on a desire-laden wind where for an instant she felt whole, as if each step of her life had led to this one incredible moment.

His body tensed and he jerked back, shattered the spell she'd fallen under.

Breaths coming fast, he pressed his brow to hers. "I should not have touched you."

Her pulse unsteady, she met his gaze, thrilled at the taut expression on his face, the wildness he fought to control. "I wanted you to kiss me again."

Despite the need etched in his features, he cupped her chin, his touch so tender, her heart ached. Hope ignited that he wanted her for more than this moment, but for...

Her spirits plummeted even as her body burned. She ducked her head, avoiding his gaze. What was she thinking? Passion flaring between them or not, he was a noble, a Knight Templar, a man revered by many, while she had naught but a stepbrother who at this moment she was unsure she could trust.

Elspet started to pull away.

His hold grew firm. "What is wrong?"

Wanting him with her every breath, she shook her head. "You are right, 'tis late and we need to rest."

His intense gaze studied her.

A hard knot formed in her throat for all he made her feel, want, despite their different stations in life. A dangerous thought. One that would lead to naught but heartbreak.

Heartbreak?

No, she cared for him, felt gratitude that he'd agreed to help her free her stepbrother regardless of the lies she'd told him when they'd first met.

Awash in inner turmoil, carefully, she moved away.

"You are upset."

"I am. Not because of the kiss." Even now, its potent effects wove through her body. "That I liked, more than I should."

"As I." Regret darkened his gaze. "But once Tiran Castle is seized, I will be gone."

He'd alluded to his departure from Dalkirk before, but this blunt statement was like a lance through her body. "Why? 'Tis your legacy. Your presence will be needed to address the many wrongs committed by your uncle, and to set things right."

"Which I will attend to. Once matters are settled, I will leave the stronghold's care to those I trust. However much I wish to stay, I have sworn to return to fight with King Robert until all of Scotland is beneath his rule." He paused. "While I am away, as I promised earlier, you will have a place within my castle."

But not with him. His intention was clear, and given her status in society, not unexpected. "I thank you," she said, her words sounding hollow to her own ears. "'Tis generous of you."

He frowned. "You do not want to stay."

And see him return and eventually wed? A shudder rippled through her at the devastating thought. "I am grateful for your generous offer, but I am considering other options as well, including joining the Romani."

She'd said it with forced levity, but he stared at her for a long moment, his face unreadable in the golden shimmers from the fires near their tent. "What is Taog to you?" he demanded suddenly.

"A friend," Elspet replied, confused by his question. "Why?"

"He seems possessive of you."

Was he jealous? Laughable. A handsome, powerful man like Cailin would have little challenge in finding a woman of his own stature. A fact she must never forget. "A close friend."

His mouth tightened, and he gave a curt nod. "Go to sleep."

Perplexed, she slipped between the covers, and with her thoughts and emotions at odds, she lay awake, unable to sleep, for a long while.

* * * *

Smoke from the freshly stoked fires outside the tent twisted in the wind as Cailin knelt beside Elspet. His gaze lingered upon her pale skin framed by her deep, chestnut-brown hair, and how her lashes lay like curved moons upon her cheeks.

A flake of snow swirled inside and landed upon her lips. Lips he'd tasted. Cailin silently cursed. Lulled by the emotions of sharing his past, her understanding, he'd lowered his guard. He tried to smother the memories of the softness of her skin against his, the deep yearning pulsing through his body, failed.

Blast it! He gave her a gentle nudge. "Lass, 'tis time to go."

Sleep-laden lids lifted and emerald-green eyes like water-drenched moss met his. In the haze of slumber, tenderness warmed her gaze, and he was tempted to skim his knuckles across her chin in a soft caress.

Boots crunched on snow as Taog approached. "Is she awake?"

Grimacing, Cailin withdrew his hand. "Aye." The interruption was for the best. He needed to be moving, not remain secluded within the tent and allow his thoughts to linger in dangerous territory.

She gasped as she looked toward the Romani leader. "Why are you here so early?"

"Early?" A smile tugged his mouth. "'Tis long past sunrise."

Lines furrowed her brow as she pushed to a sitting position and glanced outside. "I thought we were to depart before dawn."

"That is what I intended, but there were several things I needed to discuss with Taog before we left. Nor do I mind the few hours' delay. With the hard travel these past few days and your injury, the extra rest served you well."

Her eyes narrowed as she shoved aside the covers. "Nay more than it did you."

Cailin lifted a brow as she jerked on her cape. He'd riled her. Nor could that be helped. He'd made solid progress in the few hours he'd spoken with the band's leader in private. Time in which they'd decided on a place to leave messages for each other, and an occasion he'd used to take a better measure of Taog.

His initial impression proved true. He was a formidable warrior, a fair leader, and a man who cared for those beneath his guard. Though Cailin appreciated the Romani leader's concern about Elspet's welfare, his offer to keep her in the camp and beneath his guard until Cailin seized Tiran Castle was out of the question.

Not that he wanted her by his side, Cailin assured himself. He needed her knowledge of the land and the people as they traveled. Besides, she was safer with him. If that argument was weak, he refused to analyze it further.

* * * *

Falling snow lashed against Cailin's face as he broke through the dense fir skirting the edge of the field. The sun, high in the sky, illuminated the pristine land, the sparkles of light reflecting off the snow-laden land like fairy dust tossed.

Fairy dust indeed. Bemused, he shook his head at the thought. Years had passed since his mother had told him stories of the fey, of how they sprinkled the fields with magic dust seen only on clear, sun-filled winter days. He must be tired indeed to be likening snow to the magical powder.

He glanced to Elspet, riding at his side, took in her stiff posture. "How do you fare?"

Wisps of hair fluttered against her face, she stared straight ahead. "I am fine. We should reach the secret tunnel leading to the castle soon."

Hours ago, he'd chosen to ignore her cool manner, one she'd worn like a cloak since they'd departed camp.

Was she thinking of Taog? Not that he gave a bloody damn if she cared for the Romani leader. 'Twas for the best her interest lay elsewhere. He had vows to keep, not plans for a woman in his life, more so a stubborn lass who, regardless that she'd sworn him fealty, twisted him inside and out.

A rumble sounded in the distance.

With a grimace, he scanned their surroundings as he drew his mount to a halt.

Elspet pulled up at his side, studied the rough landscape, shot him a nervous glance. "'Tis riders."

The thrum grew louder.

"Let us go." Damning the odds that they'd run into his uncle's men, he kicked his mount into a canter. Cailin kept near the firs, where pine needles lay bare and would leave few tracks, wishing he had time to erase any sign of their passing.

As they navigated past a staggered array of large boulders, he caught sight of another group of riders approaching from the west.

"Follow me!" Without a safe option to move into the woods without being seen, he reined hard, guided his destrier between two large stones, wove until they were deep between the huge rocks, then dismounted. "Wait here."

Face pale, she met his gaze. "Where are you going?"

"To erase our tracks."

"'Tis too risky."

"There is nay other choice. If they catch us here without a way to escape, we are dead." His horse snorted as if sensing Cailin's tension. "If I shout for you to go, ride hard to Taog's camp."

Red swept up her cheeks and she withdrew her bow, tapped a quiver secured on her mount. "I willna leave you."

Exasperation and fury shot through him that she'd dare argue. If anything happened to her... Cailin kicked his steed over and caught her mount's reins. "You *will* do what I say!"

Her jaw tightened, a stubborn look he'd grown well familiar with.

"Swear it now!" he snapped.

Green eyes narrowed. "I swear it, but I dinna like it."

* * * *

Elspet's heart pounded as Cailin withdrew his sword, then kicked his horse toward the exit. With each step away, her chest squeezed tight.

What if he died and never came back?

Terror roared through her as he started around a boulder. "Cailin."

He turned.

I love you! Stunned by the words tangled in her throat, she fought for calm. "Damn you, come back to me."

For a moment, something flashed in his eyes, a dark desire that ignited hope that he cared for her more than she'd believed. He gave a curt nod, kicked his destrier forward.

After nocking an arrow in her bow, she glanced skyward, where the sun's brilliant rays flooded the sky. "Please God, keep him safe."

Long moments passed, and with each one, her fear built. Why had she agreed to stay behind? She skimmed her finger over the feathered flight. She wasn't a helpless woman. The blasted, thick, pea-brained idiot. When he returned, she'd...

The soft clop of hooves had her drawing the arrow back.

* * * *

Cailin guided his steed around the rocks toward where Elspet waited, cursing himself for placing her in danger. He should have shortened his talk with Taog, woken her and departed at dawn as originally planned; then they would have arrived at the tunnel hours ago.

As he rounded the last boulder, he saw her relax her hold on the arrow, then lower her bow. Her shoulders sagged.

"You didna have a chance to erase our tracks," she said.

"Nay. By the time I reached the entry, they were too close. If I had tried, I would have been seen. Thankfully, they rode past a good distance away without incident. From where I hid I couldna I tell in which direction they went after they rode out of view."

"Could you hear them speak as they passed?"

"Only bits. They have broken into several groups in hopes of picking up our tracks." He rubbed the back of his neck. "Which, nay doubt, however careful we are, they will find. We need to be long gone before then."

She stowed her bow and arrow, then guided her mount beside his. "We canna ride to the secret entry with the earl's men about; 'tis too dangerous."

"I agree. We will travel north for a ways, then circle back to the cave we stayed in the other night."

"Why not return to Taog's camp?"

He shook his head. "I refuse to risk leaving a trail exposing a connection between us and the Romani." Cailin reined his mount forward. "Let us go."

Snow muted the clack of hooves as they wove through the maze.

At the entry, he paused, searched the surrounding area. Beyond the clearing, snow-drenched hills lay before him, fragmented with jagged walls of sheer rock, smothered with thick, green slashes of fir woven with leafless stocky oaks, ash, and birch.

He glanced over. "We will follow the edge of the rocks, then slip into the forest. Once shielded by the trees, we can ride undetected."

Elspet nodded.

He kicked his steed into a canter.

"Over there!" a man called.

Cailin turned.

Snow flew as a group of knights galloped straight toward them.

God's blade, the guard had left some men behind to keep a lookout! They weren't close enough to the forest to reach it. "Return to the rocks!"

She whirled her mount, dug in her heels.

Broadsword drawn, he rode behind her as she galloped into the narrow opening between the boulders. A short distance inside the maze, they halted. He dismounted, secured a bow and arrows on his back, then started climbing the uneven stones.

"Where are you going?"

"There are only five men headed our way. If I can get a clear shot at the knights when they enter, I should be able to pick them off. I willna be long." With deft movements, taking care given the slippery snow, he scaled the rocks, then lay where he had a clear line of sight but kept himself hidden from their view. He nocked an arrow, waited.

A soft scrape of stone sounded behind him.

He glanced back, muttered a curse as Elspet crawled up beside him.

"I told you to stay there!" he hissed while visions of her taking an enemy arrow flashed in his mind.

She nocked her bow, edged closer. "I willna sit there while you risk your life. And I can shoot as well as most men."

Cailin wanted to throttle her for placing herself in danger but recalled Taog's assuring him that her skill was impressive. He grimaced. Alone, who knew what mayhem she'd get into? At least at his side, he could keep an eye on her.

Cailin glanced down to the rock entry. "I expect the knights to—"

"I saw them ride this way," a deep voice called from close by. "Keep watch, and let me know if you see any sign of them." A man with shoulder-length black hair and a muscled frame cantered into view, a rider in his wake.

Body tense, Cailin drew his arrow back, aimed.

"Wait!" Elspet whispered. "I have seen that man in Taog's camp."

"Are you sure?"

She nodded.

Errant snowflakes drifted past the mounted knight as he halted. Eyes narrowed, he scanned the area. "I think whoever we saw was farther away than we believed and has left," he called behind him.

Two warriors rode past the large rocks to join him, then the last two riders came into view.

Elspet gasped.

Cailin glanced to his side. Her face was deathly white.

"T–the last rider," she whispered. "'Tis Blar!"

Jaw tight, he stared at the rangy man with shoulder-length, straight brown hair he'd seen at Tiran Castle days before, and an unsettling thought crept into his mind. "Your stepbrother is far from the castle."

"He is, but as the master-at-arms said Blar has been riding with the earl's men."

"Mayhap, but does it not seem odd that my uncle would allow a supposed captive not only to join his guard but trust him to accompany them on their rounds?"

"What are you saying?"

After all she'd endured, the last thing Cailin wanted to do was upset her, but the master-at-arms's warning about his distrust for Blar screamed in Cailin's mind, a suspicion he shared. "I believe Blar rides with them more than to protect the castle but to identify you."

Her brows slammed together. "You are wrong." Though doubt wove through Elspet's voice.

"I pray so."

"Ride in the direction in which they were headed," the lead rider ordered, "and see if you can find them. I will search around the rocks. If I spot them, I will sound the alarm."

Blar gestured to the distant entry. "I think Sir Cailin and Elspet went into the breaks in the rocks."

Anger darkened the leader's face. "You think, but you arena sure. The riders we saw were a distance away."

"I know what my stepsister looks like," Blar snapped. "We need to ride closer and look for signs of their passing."

The bow trembled in Elspet's hand. "Why is he challenging the lead rider? Does he not realize if he convinces the guard to come closer they will see our tracks?"

The desperation in her voice shoved Cailin's anger up a notch. Aye, her stepbrother had naught to gain by arguing to ride closer unless he wanted her caught. By the pallor of her face, 'twas something she realized.

The lead rider's face grew hard. "I gave you an order, Blar: go."

"I know what I saw!" Blar glanced at the other men. "I am thinking that he wants the glory of finding my stepsister for himself *and* pocketing the reward."

The others muttered what sounded like their agreement.

"I say we all stay," Blar snarled. "I think my stepsister and Sir Cailin are hiding within the rocks. And Sir James knows it too."

The man called Sir James withdrew his blade. "You will die for that!"

Elspet stumbled to her feet. "Nay!"

Chapter 12

Cailin grabbed her arm to keep her from sliding on top of the boulder; heart pounding, Elspet jerked free, stared down to where her stepbrother sat with the small band of Dalkirk's knights. "Sir James is going to murder Blar!"

"Blast it," Cailin snarled, "get behind me."

"As I suspected," Blar spat, his gaze smug, "Sir Cailin is with my whore of a stepsister."

Whore? The air rushed from her at his foul accusation, and she wanted to retch. How could he say, believe such? "I–I slept with nay man."

Blar grunted. "Rumor is that you open your legs quick enough for any man."

Cailin's arrow flew, sank deep in Blar's arm.

Her stepbrother screamed, and his horse snorted and stepped to one side. A trickle of blood slid from the wound as he glared up at Cailin. "You will die for that!"

"Apologize," Cailin ordered, "or the next one will be in your worthless heart." His gaze cut to the others. "If anyone else moves, 'twill be his last."

"I am sorry," Blar said between clenched teeth.

But he wasn't. Hate spewed from her stepbrother's eyes, a darkness so vile that shivers swept Elspet. How had she never noticed his true feelings for her before? Pain welled in her chest. Foolishly, she'd believed Blar had accepted her into his family, cared for her, and would protect her with his life. 'Twould seem 'twas all a lie.

"Why do you ride with the Earl of Dalkirk's knights?" she demanded.

Blar's mouth tightened; with his good arm, he backed his horse out of arrow range; the others, except for Sir James, followed suit. "Once you come down here, I will explain."

She scoffed. "You must think me a fool. The earl wants me dead, you ride with my enemy, dare call me a whore, and now I am to listen to you?" Her finger wrapped around an arrow, and she wished he was within range. "'Twould seem there is little to explain."

"Always stubborn." He spoke to her as if she were a child. "There is much you dinna understand."

"Like what?" At this moment, she doubted she'd believe anything he ever said again.

Blar scowled at Cailin before turning to her. "This isna the place to talk. What is important is that I have spoken with the earl and he has agreed to forgive you."

She gave a cold laugh, her anger spiking up another notch. "After Dalkirk ordered his men to murder my mother and your father and burn our home, he should be begging us for forgiveness."

Face taut, Blar rubbed his bleeding arm. "You should be thankful that I convinced the earl to spare your life."

"For what, to sleep in his bed?" She narrowed her haze. "I would die first."

"You will rue the day you disobeyed me." Blar started to turn his horse, then glanced toward Sir James with shrewd eyes. "And yet… I am thinking that mayhap 'tis not the coin offered for their capture that draws your interest but that you plot against the earl."

The lead knight's face darkened further. "You dare much."

"Do I?" Blar challenged. "Admit it; you are in league with Sir Petrus."

Fear slid through her. "Merciful saints, why is he speaking of the master-at-arms?" she whispered.

"There can only be one reason," Cailin hissed under his breath. "Someone Sir Petrus spoke with has betrayed him."

Her heart pounded. God, nay!

Blar's sly gaze shifted to the three other knights. "I think the earl will pay us handsomely for this traitor."

Faces hard, the other men nodded.

"Seize him!" Blar shouted.

Sir James unsheathed his sword.

"Bloody hell!" Cailin ran to the edge of the boulder, released his arrow. It sank into the chest of the knight reaching for Sir James.

The attacker tumbled off his horse.

A second knight tried to sneak up behind Sir James.

Heart pounding, Elspet raced to Cailin's side, aimed, and fired.

The second knight clutched the arrow embedded in his chest, collapsed to the ground.

"You will pay for your treachery!" Blar whirled his steed and kicked him into a gallop, the remaining knight on his heels.

As they disappeared around the large stones, throat tight with emotion, Elspet lowered her bow. "Blar is in league with the earl," she whispered, unsure if she was more furious or heartbroken. "I prayed that Blar's reason for joining the earl's guard was to save me." She scoffed, "I was a fool."

"Nay a fool but a woman of deep compassion," Cailin said.

She swallowed hard. "All he ever cared about was himself," she forced out, needing to say the words despite how much they hurt. "The master-at-arms was right; Blar isna a good man." She gasped. "Now that they have discovered that Sir Petrus is loyal to you, we must save him!"

Fury burned in Cailin's eyes. "Aye."

She secured her bow. "As well, Blar's behavior leads me to believe that he was involved with the plot to kill our parents." Sickened, she shook her head. "To be a part of such a vile act... Why? As if it matters now. The important thing is, now we know, and any loyalty I ever had to him is dead."

* * * *

It mattered, but at the moment there was naught Cailin could do about the bastard, though the time to confront Blar would come. He gently squeezed her hand, then focused on the rider below, a sense of familiarity tugging at him. "Sir James, you have made a dangerous enemy this day. When the earl learns that you tried to shield Elspet and me from being found, he will want you dead."

"A risk I was willing to take." The knight nudged his steed forward, paused below them. "Sir Cailin, my full name is Sir James Arbach."

Surprise rippled through him. James Arbach, a man who'd been a friend in his youth. His body relaxed as he acknowledged the man's familiar looks, albeit older. "I remember you."

"'Tis a blessing to see you. You canna imagine my surprise when I heard you were alive."

"Once I had sailed and learned of my uncle's treachery in my youth," Cailin said, "I assure you, I never expected to return."

Sir James shifted in his saddle. "The earl is nasty business."

"He is, one who will be taken care of, that I swear." Cailin paused. "Why did you seek me out?"

"The master-at-arms sent me to find you."

A gust of wind whipped past Cailin as he secured his bow. "Where is he?"

"In the earl's dungeon."

His heart sank. "Wait there, we are coming down." After one last look to ensure none of the earl's men were about, he and Elspet hurried down. A short while later, they rode out and joined Sir James. "What happened?"

"Late yesterday afternoon, after Sir Petrus spoke with me about shifting their alliance to you, another of the knights he talked to betrayed him."

Tension slid through Cailin. "Is he alive?"

"Aye, barely. Though tortured for refusing to answer any of their questions, he told the earl naught." Worry furrowed Sir James's brow. "In our brief conversation in his cell once the guards left, Sir Petrus wanted me to warn you, and explain why he didna appear at your planned meeting. 'Tis why I volunteered to ride with one of the groups of knights to find you."

Cailin grimaced. "I thank you. We will free Sir Petrus."

A pained look crossed his face. "The sooner the better. I dinna think he can survive much longer."

Cailin fisted his hand around his sword, wishing his uncle stood before him. The man's treachery knew no bounds.

"As well, before the master-at-arms was betrayed, in addition to having started meeting with men in the castle he trusts, he sent several messengers to influential men." Sir James glanced toward Elspet. Regret flashed on the knight's face. "I am sorry about your mother and stepfather."

"I–I thank you," she rasped. "I didna know of Blar's treachery."

"Nor I, until he was recently knighted after his arrival at Tiran Castle. Though Blar serves the earl, I assure you, he is loathed by many."

"'Tis easy to despise a man who would turn on his own flesh and blood." Cailin paused, considering the ramifications. "Now that Blar and the other knights know you are loyal to me, they will inform my uncle."

Sir James nodded.

Cailin frowned at the unexpected complication. "Nor can the knights who have shifted their loyalty to me remain at the stronghold. 'Tis too dangerous."

"Indeed, 'tis how I came to my decision this morning," Sir James explained. "The others loyal to you departed the castle beneath the guise of searching for you and Elspet. Once I had warned you, I was to meet with them near the river."

"A good plan. Still, when the knights dinna return to the stronghold, 'twill take little time for my uncle to realize they have betrayed him, label them traitors, and order them killed. As for the meeting with the knights," Cailin said, "'tis one you will keep. Elspet and I will ride with you. After, we will all travel to Taog MacCarron's, where you, as the others, will remain until we make a plan of attack."

Surprise flickered in Sir James's eyes. "The Romani leader isna known for accepting strangers into his camp."

"He isna," Cailin agreed, "but given the situation, there is nay other choice. Also, to avoid the risk of leaving any sign that the Romani are supporting me, we must ensure that any trace of our passage is erased as we travel."

"A fact I will ensure," the knight said.

Satisfied that he'd done all he could do for the moment, Cailin glanced at Elspet. "I promise you, Blar will be dealt with."

She gave a shaky nod. "By my blade."

"Nay. However much you despise him, I refuse to allow his blood to be on your hands."

Her eyes narrowed. "The decision isna yours."

Cailin reined in a retort. Let her believe such. When the time came to deal with Blar, she would learn differently. A cold breeze blustered past as Cailin faced Sir James. "Lead us to where you and the others were to meet."

"Aye."

* * * *

Within the fire's glow spilling into the tent at Taog's camp, the same shelter he and Elspet had used on their previous visit, Cailin secured his dagger.

He exhaled a slow breath, thankful that the meeting with the knights who'd shifted their loyalty to him had gone smoothly.

More of a relief, when their party had arrived at the Romani camp, the knights had been allowed to enter with minimal objection. By now his uncle knew who had betrayed him by their absence.

Elspet tugged on her cloak, then stood. "I am accompanying you to rescue the master-at-arms."

"Nay." Anger flared in her eyes at his response, but in this he refused to yield. "I understand your need to avenge your family, but if you went now, with your emotions driving your every decision, you could be killed."

"You need me."

"Before, your presence was necessary to identify those I needed to speak to. This operation is purely strategic, a tactical mission made more dangerous because 'tis night. For stealth, only Sir James and Taog will accompany me." Cailin secured a final blade in his arsenal of hidden weapons. "Having grown up in the castle, along with the changes to the stronghold since my youth provided by Father Lamond's drawings, I am familiar with the tunnels I need to take to reach the dungeon. Once we rescue Sir Petrus, we will return."

Before she could reply, a commotion in the camp had Cailin glancing up. Their expressions furious, two of the knights from the castle, their weapons drawn, were circling the other.

God's teeth! Cailin stormed to the two men, withdrew his sword, and relieved them of their weapons in a trice. "What in blazes is going on?" he boomed.

Each warrior glared at the other.

Taog walked over and stood beside Cailin.

The shorter of the two swiped blood from his mouth, sneered at the other. "Sir Malcolm..." He shook his head. "Never mind."

Cailin glared at Sir Malcolm. "Why were you fighting?"

Sir Malcolm shrugged. "A difference of opinion."

"I dinna give a damn what the issue is, we are all fortunate to be allowed in the Romani camp," Cailin snarled. "We are all tired, and I refuse to tolerate any disrespect, much less fighting. If I hear a harsh word from either of you, a gripe, I will haul your arses from the camp and leave you for the wolves." He shot both men a warning look. "Understand?"

"Aye," the smaller man replied.

Face taut, Sir Malcolm gave a curt nod.

"Both of you, settle down for the night." Cailin sheathed his broadsword but didn't return their weapons. They'd get them back when they'd calmed. He shook his head in frustration as the men stormed off.

Taog's mouth settled into a grim frown. "I will ensure my men keep a close watch on them while we are gone."

With a look of equal disgust at each man, Sir James walked over. "There is bad blood between them. The fools. With our lives in danger, I would have thought, at least until we are safe, both would have put their differences aside."

Cailin glared at the departing warriors. "If I didna need each man possible in the force to attack my uncle, I would toss them out this night."

"As is your right." Sir James paused. "My horse is ready."

"Mine too," Taog said.

Cailin nodded to them. "I will gather my gear and meet you both at the outskirts of camp." He strode off.

Worry crowded her brow as Elspet fell in beside him as he walked to their tent. "Emotions are high."

"For us all. They are knights and know better." He ducked inside.

"When do you think you will return?"

"If all goes well," Cailin said, retrieving his weapons, then donning his cape, "by late tomorrow."

"Come back to me."

At the quiver of emotion in her voice, Cailin looked over. She had asked this of him before, when he'd doubled back in the maze. Since he was a child, no one had worried for his safety as he'd set out on a dangerous mission or into battle. But here, now, Elspet was someone who cared about him as a friend and, if he were honest, more.

As well, she made him want her as he'd never anticipated and, in truth, made him contemplate a future beyond that of battle.

An ache built in his chest at the ramifications. He was no longer alone, or rather, no longer without someone who'd grown important to him in his life.

How had she broken through his defenses? Was it her stubborn nature that had him watching her in amazement, or her determination to defend those she loved that drew him? Nor could he forget her sweet taste, or how her body trembled beneath his touch.

For the first time in his life, he cursed the day when he would return to fight alongside the Bruce.

Cailin caressed her mouth with his thumb, then—unlike the previous kiss he'd stolen from her in the tunnel—took his time lowering his mouth to hers.

She wrapped her arms around him, and Cailin took the kiss deeper, lost himself in the way she left him strong as well as helpless, as if caught within a magical weave that tangled his every thought until 'twas naught but her.

A wish.

A need.

A necessity as urgent as each breath.

At last he drew back, satisfied to find the pulse at her throat racing beneath his fingers, her mouth slightly parted and her eyes dark with desire.

"I…" What? *I want you for more than a friend?* God's teeth, with the way he'd kissed her, a fool could tell that. If naught for his leaving, with his growing feelings for her, he'd haul Elspet to his bed.

Shaken by his thoughts, he brushed his mouth against hers one last time. "I must go." He strode away.

Taog and Sir James were mounted and awaiting him as he approached. Cailin swung up, glanced toward the tent.

Illuminated within the firelight, Elspet stood at the entry, the soft shimmer of golden light caressing her face.

He kicked his mount into a canter, aware that from this moment, his life had changed.

* * * *

Elspet turned for the eighth time on her pallet, gave up trying to sleep, and sat up. She'd never be able to rest after that kiss and surrounded by worry while he was away.

She scanned her surroundings. Several men sat by the fires, but tonight she noticed extra guards at the perimeter of the camp.

Chills crept up her skin, and she glanced at the cloudy skies. 'Twould make traveling difficult but aid Cailin, Taog, and Sir James—and Sir Petrus, once rescued—from being seen.

Wrapping herself in a blanket, she left the tent and walked to the fire. Several men shifted to make room for her to sit.

She smiled her thanks, then sat and held her hands out before the fire, enjoying the warm flicker of heat.

"I thought you would have been long asleep," Odhran, an elder she'd met before, said.

Elspet gazed into the darkness for a moment, then turned back. "I canna sleep."

"Your worry is understandable. Once Lord Dalkirk discovers a significant number of his men have deserted him to support his nephew, he will be furious." The elder picked up a thick piece of wood, set it on the flames. Sparks shot out, curled up into the rising smoke. "Until now, though the noble had search parties out to capture his nephew and you, he believed that Sir Cailin had meager support and posed little threat."

"With his learning how many of his men have shifted their loyalty to his nephew," she said, her voice tense, "he will do whatever is necessary to ensure that this time, Cailin is dead."

Odhran gave a somber nod.

Something Cailin had left knowing. Yet, with only three men, they could travel fast. She prayed 'twould be enough to keep them safe.

The elder tsked. "Lass, fretting will change naught."

"I know." She unfurled her fingers, picked up a stick, and tossed it into the flames. Another burst of sparks shot into the night.

"I tell you, he is gone," an angry voice charged.

Shoving to her feet, Elspet turned and found the person speaking was the smaller man who'd gotten into the skirmish earlier.

Two of Taog's men hauled the knight forward before the Romani leader's men at the fire. "Tell them," the larger of the two ordered.

Anger filled the younger knight's eyes, and a streak of blood smeared his brow. "I was going to." He jerked his arm away. "'Tis Sir Malcolm. I was gathering firewood when I saw him making to slip away. I tried to stop him, but he hit me over the head with a piece of wood. Once I came to, I hurried back to tell you as quickly as I could."

She fought the rising panic. "Where is he going?"

Worry filled the young knight's eyes. "To Tiran Castle to warn the earl that Sir Cailin and two others are sneaking into the castle to free the master-at-arms."

Heart pounding, she stood, turned to the senior man, one of the two who had dragged the young knight forward. "We must warn Sir Cailin, Taog, and Sir James!"

"We canna catch up to them now," the large Romani warrior said grimly, "but mayhap we can capture Sir Malcolm before he reaches the castle."

Fear tore through Elspet as she nodded, and she prayed he was right. "I will meet you at my horse."

The Romani warrior moved before her, his size leaving her within his shadow. "I am under orders. You will remain here, where you will be protected."

He shouted out commands, overriding her protests, and within moments several riders galloped from the camp.

Chapter 13

The foul stench of blood and death permeated the secret tunnel, the air raw with the moans of the injured as Cailin lifted a small torch and moved forward behind the dungeon walls. "Can you see Sir Petrus through any of the hidden peepholes?"

"Nay," Taog whispered behind him.

"Nor I," Sir James said a few paces away. "They must have moved him."

The ominous drip of water plopped from above, and Cailin pushed on. Within the meager light, through the thin slits in the stone, he made out the smaller cells, each holding several men. "Blast it, I had hoped to be long gone from Tiran Castle by now."

"We would have been," Taog agreed, "if we hadna lost time digging out the secret entry."

"A move I should have expected my uncle to make, one nay doubt he ordered since learning of my return to Dalkirk land." He shook his head at his lack of forethought. "'Twas sheer luck Gaufrid hadna sealed that branch of the tunnel when Elspet and I visited the stronghold. God help us if he discovers we are here."

Cailin made to step forward, then paused. In a cell along the far wall, an elder lay sprawled on the floor asleep, his gray hair tangled with smears of blood and dirt. His gaunt features evidence of his lack of food, his filthy garb of neglect.

Thoughts of his father flickered to Cailin's mind. If he'd lived, he would have been about the same age. God's blade, what had the man done to earn such despicable treatment?

He squinted through the dim light at the other prisoners locked within the surrounding cells. Their garb, though plain, was in good repair, and a pitcher of water was available, along with extra blankets in each corner. A stark contrast to the elder's empty cell. 'Twas as if the old man had earned his uncle's personal censure. Whatever the reason, no one deserved to live in such squalor. Once he seized Tiran Castle, he'd find out the crime committed. If but a petty charge, which Cailin suspected, knowing Gaufrid, he'd ensure this elder was released.

"I see Sir Petrus is in the last cell," Sir James whispered, having moved ahead.

Cailin crept to where the knight stood, secured his candle into an indentation in the wall. His jaw tightened as he took in the torchlit scene.

Within the wash of light, the master-at-arms was shackled to the wall. Blood matted his hair, and swollen cuts and bruises marred his muscled body. Only a vile scoundrel would subject anyone to such torture.

"Do you see any guards?" Cailin whispered, his voice shaking with fury.

"Nay." Taog shook his head with disgust. "'Tis not fit for an animal."

"Indeed."

"I see nay guards either," Sir James said.

After one more glance around, Cailin grabbed the extra keys to the cells and shackles hanging on a nearby hook known only to him, his mother, and father, then moved to the wall on the other side of the master-at-arms's cell. He pressed his finger in an indentation, pushed. A slight grating sounded as the stone shifted.

Paces away, Sir Petrus remained limp, his eyes closed.

Cailin stormed over, wrestled open the shackles; Taog and Sir James caught his body as the knight collapsed.

After a quick inspection, Taog met Cailin's gaze. "He is alive."

"Barely." Cailin returned the keys to their hiding place. "We must hurry before the guards return and find him gone."

The distant bongs of the church bell melded with the soft scuff of steps as they made their way along the secret tunnel.

As they neared the stable, shouts from outside the thick walls made them pause.

Mouth grim, Taog glanced at Cailin. "Do you think the guards have discovered Sir Petrus is gone?"

"I pray not. Stay here." Cailin hurried to the slits in the stable and scanned the bailey.

In the torchlight, a lone rider dismounted as other knights ran toward him.

"God's teeth," Cailin hissed, "'tis Sir Malcolm."

"What is he doing here?" Taog asked as he held the master-at-arms propped between him and Sir James.

"'Twould seem," Cailin spat, "his vow of fealty was naught but a ruse." The men surrounding the rider parted as his uncle strode toward them. Cailin's eyes narrowed as he watched Sir Malcolm's animated figure while he spoke to the earl.

Gaufrid nodded, then began shouting commands. His knights ran toward the stable.

"What is happening?" Sir James asked.

"I couldna hear what Sir Malcolm said, but my uncle has ordered his men to prepare to ride, which could only mean one thing."

Taog swore. "The bastard told Dalkirk the location of my camp. Nay doubt he also revealed that the knights who'd abandoned him were there, along with you and Elspet."

"Aye," Cailin agreed, meeting the Romani's gaze, the fury there matching his. "We must alert them."

"By now, my men will have discovered Sir Malcolm's absence," Taog said, "and have sent out men in search of him."

"Except they dinna know that he isna missing but a traitor." Cailin hurried over to Taog. "Ride back and warn the camp. Sir James and I will follow with Sir Petrus."

The Romani's brows slammed together. "I refuse to leave you—"

"Our people must be warned. Either you go or Sir James. Choose!"

Eyes hard, Taog glared at Cailin. "I will go, but by God, take care."

Cailin gave a curt nod, then stepped next to the master-at-arms and took his weight from Taog. "Godspeed."

After lighting a taper, the Romani leader hurried off.

Knights' voices inside the stable grew louder.

Cailin placed his finger over his lips. "Can you hold him alone for a moment?"

Sir James nodded.

He shifted the weight of the prone man to the knight; Sir Petrus made the slightest of groans. A moment later, Cailin crept to where he could look out.

"'Tis foolhardy traveling in the dead of night," a knight entering the stable grumbled.

"Aye," the man at his side agreed. "Sir Malcolm told the earl that he slipped away. Those at the Romani camp willna likely discover him gone till morning. A fool could see that if we leave at first light, we would still have time to surround the camp and surprise them."

Blast it, he must buy Taog time to warn Elspet and the others at the camp. Cailin crept back to Sir James, who'd shifted and propped Sir Petrus's unconscious body against a wall.

"They are preparing to attack the Romani camp, as we feared," Cailin said. "I am going to create a diversion to delay their departure."

On a groan, the master-at-arms's eyelids flickered open, and he gave a rough cough. Pain-filled eyes held Cailin's. "I—" His entire body shook. "I–can help."

That Cailin doubted. "If you can walk when we depart, 'twill help us immensely."

"I can. The bastard willna keep me down," his mentor rasped. "Y–you mentioned a diversion. What are you going to do?"

He took another candle from a nearby indentation, lit it, and handed the taper to Sir James. "I am going to start a fire in the stable. You and Sir James head down the tunnel. I will catch up with you."

"Aye." After wedging his shoulder beneath Sir Petrus's arm, a candle in his free hand, wavers of yellow illuminated the blackness as Sir James helped him hobble into the shaft.

Cailin peered through the slit, thankful to find only two guards near the secret exit. He crept into the stable and to the first knight, then slammed the hilt of his dagger against his head.

With a grunt, the warrior dropped to the hay.

The horse shifted, but thankfully, the other knight, three stalls down, was securing the girth on the saddle, his back to Cailin. Moments later, Cailin knocked out the second man and hauled both guards into the shadows of the bailey. After a quick glance around, thankful no other knights had entered, he freed the horses, then set the hay ablaze.

Squeals and snorts filled the air as smoke began to billow from the stable. A stallion bolted for the bailey; the rest followed.

Shouts filled the air as Cailin slipped inside the secret tunnel. Taper in hand, he hurried down the blackened passageway to catch up with Sir James and Sir Petrus, and prayed they'd reach camp to warn the others before the earl's men attacked.

* * * *

Positioned behind a large rock, Elspet scanned the dense stand of trees, searching for any sign of movement as she and Taog's men hid in the woods surrounding the encampment.

Sunlight highlighted errant flakes of snow whirling to the ground like shimmers of hope. Dull thuds rang out as a woodpecker tapped on a nearby oak while several doves sat upon a barren limb and a squirrel chased another through the tangle of branches.

At any other time, she would have appreciated the beauty, lingered on how the soft sheen of white coated the landscape in a pristine glow, but with each hour passing since Taog's return at first light, her worry grew.

Where were Cailin, Sir James, and Sir Petrus? Had they been forced to hide en route? Traveling with an injured man would slow them, evading the earl's guard more so. Please God, let them have safely escaped the castle.

"I see nay sign of anyone," Taog said at her side.

"Nor I. They should be here by now. Do you think they were caught?" Elspet asked, voicing her worst fear.

"Nay," Taog said. "Cailin is too smart. If he sensed danger, they would have hidden until the earl's guard had passed."

The truth, 'twas foolish to worry. Cailin was a Knight Templar, trained above most, with skills he would use to ensure that he and the others were safe. If anything, she should be thankful a man of such caliber would soon rule Dalkirk. He was intelligent, fair, and did naught without sound reason.

Memories of his kiss, the tenderness of his touch, sifted through her mind as she scoured the sweep of trees. An ache built in her chest at how within days he'd become important to her, more than she could have ever imagined. It should be impossible, but however foolish, she wanted more with him, wanted...

Forever.

Elspet struggled to catch her breath. Merciful saints, she loved him!

With the meager time they'd known the other, it should be unfathomable, but with every beat of her heart, and however much she'd tried to control her growing feelings before, she could no longer deny something that resonated straight down to her soul.

The joy of the realization faded beneath the memory of everything that stood in their path. More so as they had many hurdles to overcome before their mission was successful. And though he cared for her, would he ever want more?

Once he seized Tiran Castle, he would regain his rightful position as Earl of Dalkirk, while she had naught but the clothes on her back. Aye, he'd offered her shelter and had kissed her with passion, both a far cry from a promise of love.

Elspet shook her head at herself for mulling over her feelings like an empty-headed lass. Though she loved Cailin, if he never wanted more than what they had, however much it would hurt, she'd go on, find something that mattered to immerse herself into.

But it couldn't be in Dalkirk.

In time he would be required to find a woman of noble stature to bear him an heir, but thoughts of him with another broke her heart.

Mayhap she would—

"I see movement on the northern outskirts of camp," a man called a distance away.

Smothering her dismal thoughts, Elspet focused on the barren oaks, their limbs rattling in the wind like bony fingers reaching skyward, with a few stubborn leaves clinging to errant branches, long since faded to a dreary brown.

Between the weathered trunks, flashes of riders came into view.

Heart pounding, she nocked her bow, prayed it was Cailin and the others.

Masked within the shadows, a horse and rider came into view, followed by a large man slumped over his mount's hindquarters.

They rode into the sunlight, and she lowered the bow and sheathed her arrow. "'Tis Sir Cailin, Sir James, and Sir Petrus!"

Cheers rose and the men surrounded the small party as they rode into camp.

Face weary, Cailin halted his destrier, swung down, and reached up for Sir Petrus.

"Let me help you," Taog said as he stepped next to him.

The master-at-arms grunted as he was lifted down, then he slumped over.

"He has passed out," Taog said.

Cailin grimaced. "With how badly he had been beaten, 'tis a miracle he is still alive." He turned, and his eyes met hers.

Beyond the exhaustion, the tenderness in his gaze had Elspet wanting to run to him, needing his touch and, however foolish, filled with hope that a future for them existed. Though before the warriors, she refused to offer him less than the respect he deserved.

Worry had her glancing toward the forest before moving to his side. "Thank God you have returned safely. Taog warned us that you had seen Sir Malcolm."

Cailin nodded. "We were unsure if you knew that the knight had betrayed us."

"They knew," the Romani leader said as he joined them. "I met my men halfway back, and during the ride to camp they told me what had happened. While we awaited your return, I used our combined forces to set up a defense around the camp. Also, I positioned runners a distance away to keep watch for any sign of Dalkirk's men."

A shiver swept through Elspet. "You believe the earl will attack this day?"

Cailin gave a somber nod. "Now that my uncle knows where I am, he wants to kill me and my loyal supporters before I can raise a significant force."

Nausea welled in her throat.

"One of our scouts is returning!" a perimeter guard shouted.

A rider broke through the brush. A layer of froth covered his steed as he drew him to a halt. "The earl leads at least three hundred armed men and they are headed this way!"

Cailin muttered a soft curse. They were outnumbered by at least seven to one. "How far away are they?"

"An hour, two at most," the rider replied.

Taog glanced toward Cailin. "Go. A warm meal and rest will serve you well before the soldiers arrive."

Cailin glanced toward where the master-at-arms was being taken, then shook his head. "We have no time to waste. I know a few strategies that could help make a difference."

"Explain," Taog said.

Elspet listened and was impressed by the procedures Cailin laid out, many she'd never heard of. Templar techniques, no doubt.

Once he was through, Cailin glanced around. "Any questions?"

Appreciation in his eyes, Taog shook his head. "Nay. These tactics will give the earl and his men more than they bargained for, and us a chance."

"They will," Cailin agreed. "I will check on Sir Petrus, then oversee the preparations."

"I will have the men start felling small trees." Taog departed.

Face taut, Cailin strode to where two men were settling Sir Petrus inside a tent.

Elspet walked beside him, impressed by his control. Instead of allowing fury at the brutality served to the master-at-arms to guide him, he focused on a plan that would equal the odds, if not give them an edge against the earl's forces. How many men would have reacted with such precision, such control?

Strong-scented herbs filled the air as they reached the tent. Inside, an elderly woman dipped a cloth into an herbal concoction, then cleaned each cut with care.

A dark frown on his face, Cailin entered and knelt beside the healer.

The elder tended to the next wound, dipped the cloth into the mixture, then looked up, her eyes grave. "I canna say if he will live through the day, but I swear to you, I will do all I can."

Cailin nodded. "I thank you." He placed his hand on the master-at-arms's shoulder, closed his eyes, then his lips moved in silent prayer.

Kneeling, Elspet added her own entreaty to God that Sir Petrus lived. After making the sign of the cross, Cailin departed. Throat thick with emotion, she fell into step beside him as he strode toward the large rocks where many of Taog's men were taking position with numerous weapons.

"When the earl attacks, I want you to stay near me." Eyes dark with concern met hers. "If I could spare you the horrors of battle, I would."

She shook her head at his misplaced sense of responsibility for her. "None of this is your fault. Any blame for those who will be harmed lies at your uncle's feet. Nor does he care who dies as long as he remains in power."

Cailin's mouth tightened. "The truth, but it doesna change that you, as the other women in camp, are in danger. If there was somewhere I could have you all hide, I would."

"There isna. Nor would I be asking for shelter when each person is needed to defend the camp."

Deep lines carved his brow. For a breathless moment, she thought he might kiss her, but the instant passed.

Jaw tight, Cailin halted where men stood awaiting instructions and began shouting orders. Some men began digging pits, while others sharpened stakes and jammed them into the ground to build a palisade.

Elspet was amazed at how, when one job was completed, without hesitation, Cailin moved men to another, each task adding another layer of defense.

When she'd first heard the news of the pending attack, of the number of men led by the earl, she'd feared they had little chance. Now, as she scanned the camp that in a short time had been transformed to a makeshift fortress, hope flickered inside.

Wiping the sweat from his brow, Cailin walked over to where she was piling stones to use in the catapult. He shot her a fierce scowl. "Once the battle begins, if I tell you to do something, do it!"

If she'd seen only anger in his eyes, the hard rebuttal on her tongue would have been unleashed without hesitation, but she saw the fear, the concern, because he cared for her. "I will."

With each passing moment, amid the shouts, orders, and curses, she fought the growing dread. However brutal the attack on her home almost a fortnight ago, she sensed that 'twas naught compared to the assault the earl planned this day.

But this time the bastard wouldna win. Elspet wiped her brow, returned to her task. Whatever she needed to do to give Cailin success she would.

A grim smile touched her mouth. And the earl would soon learn that he far from faced a haphazard band, but a well-armed force.

* * * *

An arrow nocked in his bow, beneath the crystal-clear skies, Cailin stared at the swath of forest littered with towering rocks as the earl's well-armed knights rode into view, followed by endless rows of foot soldiers.

As he'd expected, Gaufrid's men had surrounded the encampment and were now closing in; his uncle wanted to ensure that no one escaped, that all who'd sworn fealty to Cailin would die.

He glared at the man he'd once believed loved him, a man who was the only family he still had. But now he knew the truth, something his uncle would regret.

A grim smile touched his mouth as he glanced at the various weapons the Romani, the knights, and he and Elspet had prepared this day. Trebuchets lay strategically placed, pits with sharpened sticks at the bottom covered with sticks and brush were cleverly positioned, and hot oil was boiling in cauldrons along with numerous piles of stones stacked by each siege engine awaiting use.

His uncle stopped at the edge of the forest, raised his hand. His knights halted. "Sir Cailin," he shouted, "if you and Elspet give yourselves up, my men and I will leave the camp untouched."

Taog grunted at Cailin's side. "A lie."

"Aye," Cailin agreed. "The bastard wants us all dead."

"Sir Cailin, if you dinna cede willingly," his uncle continued, "you give me no choice but to attack."

"Sir Cailin? You mean the rightful Earl of Dalkirk," Cailin called. "If you look around, you will see that you are far from in a position to offer threats."

A scowl marred his uncle's face as he glared at the siege engines before turning back to him. "You are greatly outnumbered. Are you so selfish that you would sacrifice the lives of innocent men and women?"

"Selfish? A rich claim when 'twas you who murdered my father and mother," Cailin shouted, "and paid to have me killed."

"'Tis lies," his uncle called back. "Your parents' deaths were an accident."

"A witness informed me otherwise," Cailin stated, his voice ice. "And before the captain you hired to kill me sold me to pirates, he admitted your treachery. The only thing you care about is ensuring that I am dead so you can keep my legacy."

Rage mottled his uncle's face. "I am deeply wounded that you would believe such mistruths. You are my nephew, my only family, and I am willing to help you."

"You know not the meaning of family," Cailin spat. "Save your lies for someone who believes you. I never will."

"Then you leave me no choice." Expression fierce, the earl raised his hand, scanned his men lining the camp. "Kill them all!"

Chapter 14

The screams of men, the stench of burning flesh, and the clash of blades filled the air. Each volley of the catapults from the Romani camp splintered the Earl of Dalkirk's ranks, as they had since the initial attack hours before, forcing his men to fall back and regroup.

In Gaufrid's calculated attack, he'd omitted one critical factor: that he would encounter formidable and organized resistance.

Elspet and several other women lifted another pile of stones into the pouch of the trebuchet. Once full, they hurried back; Elspet jerked the strap free.

The counterweight dropped and the sling hurled the load.

Pain-filled screams sounded from the enemy ranks as the wall of attackers again parted.

Three more volleys in quick succession drove the foot soldiers to withdraw from bow range.

Cailin glanced toward the setting sun. Bedamned, by now he'd hoped to have crushed his uncle's invasion. But with his uncle's forces having destroyed two of their siege engines, his combined forces with Taog were losing ground. His uncle boomed orders with twisted glee.

Between the screams and shouts, the earl's men formed a solid line around the camp in preparation for another charge.

Dread crawled up Cailin's spine as he nocked another arrow. With most of their defenses destroyed and their piles of stones to throw in the trebuchet down to a single rock, they couldn't turn back the next attack.

Face pale, Elspet shoved the last stone into the siege engine's pouch, then met his gaze. "We have naught more to throw. What are we going to do?"

He opened his mouth, closed it, faced with the horrendous reality that in the next few moments when his uncle's troops stormed the camp, many people would die.

Cailin didn't care about himself, but he did care that Elspet, Taog and his people, and the knights who'd recently sworn fealty to him would suffer for his uncle's twisted need for power.

"We are going to fight." He muttered a curse. "Never did I mean to involve you in this."

"After what the earl did to my family," Elspet withdrew her sword, "'tis my fight as well. Though you have sought to protect me, I willna hide behind you or any man but seek my own justice."

Humbled, he nodded. Mouth grim, he met Taog's gaze, worry lining the leader's brow, but resolve as well. "Let us give the bastard more than he bargained for," Cailin called.

Taog raised his sword. "Aye!"

The Romani people cheered.

In the face of impossible odds, unsure whether this would be their end, Cailin looked at Elspet, and his heart wrenched. Never had he imagined that he would find a woman he wanted so much, one who touched him as no other. His emotions in turmoil, giving into his heart's demand, he strode to Elspet, caught her mouth in a fierce kiss, hot with need, demanding with a fierce desperation. "I wanted more for you, I wanted—"

"Charge!" his uncle screamed from behind his ranks. The roar of men and the whinny of horses filled the air.

With brutal precision, his uncle's foot soldiers cut through the stakes of the palisade, then engaged the outer guard, steadily moving forward.

"Stay beside me, Elspet!" Cailin ordered as he secured his bow and arrow and withdrew his broadsword, fighting exhaustion and damning that once surrounded 'twould be but a matter of time until the inevitable.

"I love you, Cailin!" she blurted out.

Stunned by Elspet's words, the emptiness in his heart since losing his parents eased. Never had he imagined he would find a woman he'd want in his life, much less one who loved him. What he wouldn't give for another day, more time to spend with her.

A stocky knight rushed him.

Cailin bunched his arms, dropped him in a single blow.

From the side, three men stormed past Taog's men and headed straight toward Elspet.

"Watch out!" Cailin yelled as he lunged forward, driving his sword deep into the lead knight's chest, slashed his dagger across the other warrior's throat, then whirled to face the final assailant.

The fighter's blade was driving toward Cailin's heart. Bracing his feet, Cailin angled his broadsword to block the swing. Forged steel scraped with an angry hiss. Teeth clenched, he twisted his sword free, drove it into the attacker. He glanced toward Elspet.

She ducked as a large knight charged, plunged her dagger into his chest as he rushed past, then yanked her blade free.

The warrior wove, toppled to the ground.

The blur of movement to his side had Cailin whirling to meet the next challenger.

As the new combatant raised his broadsword, a large man battling Taog collapsed against Cailin, throwing him off balance.

Cailin's swing missed; his uncle's knight's blade sliced through his thigh.

Gritting his teeth against the pain, Cailin rolled, pushed to his feet, drove his sword deep into his attacker.

A look of pure shock widened the man's eyes as he dropped into a lifeless heap.

Cailin ignored the blood flowing down his leg, turned to fend off several warriors charging him. His entire body trembled with exhaustion as he raised his arm for the next swing. If he would die, by God he'd take as many of the bastards he could with him!

A horn sounded.

The thunder of men's shouts rose above the clash of battle.

Cailin's heart sank. God's blade, more men; they were doomed.

No, he refused to quit, would fight until his last breath. Struggling against the pain, he disposed of the next assailant, whirled toward the fresh influx of troops.

Stilled.

A fierce-looking man holding King Robert's banner led the sizable force into the fray.

Rónán!

A fresh surge of energy filled Cailin. The Bruce had made good his pledge that, if possible, he would send a fighting force, one that would rout his uncle's men.

"'Tis Rónán O'Connor, a friend, who is here to aid us!" Cailin shouted.

Stunned relief swept Taog and his people's dirt- and blood-streaked faces as in a steady wave, the new combatants cut through Dalkirk's men.

Body trembling, Elspet lowered her sword. "Thank God."

In the mill of horses and retreating fighters, face flushed with outrage, his uncle raised his sword at Cailin. "'Tis far from over! I will be back. Next time my forces will be united with the Earl of Odhran's!" He whirled his mount and fled into the woods, his men on his heels.

Cheers rose within the Romani camp.

With a weary smile, Taog wiped his blade, then sheathed his sword. "'Tis a prayer answered."

"Aye," Cailin agreed, "but my uncle's threat to combine his forces with the Earl of Odhran's is a union we canna allow."

"How can we stop him?" Taog asked.

"We must lay siege to Tiran Castle and prevent him from sending a messenger to Odhran. Gather any of your men who are able and tell them to prepare to ride."

The Romani leader nodded.

"Rónán!" Cailin waved his friend over as he hobbled beside Elspet.

"Thank God you are—" She gasped as she took in his gash. "Your wound needs attention."

His injury throbbed. "I will tend to it, but for now, 'tis imperative that we reach Tiran Castle."

Hoofbeats thrummed over the snow-covered ground as Rónán broke away from his knights and cantered over. He drew his steed to a halt a few paces away. Curiosity flickered in his gaze as he glanced at Elspet, then he turned to Cailin, scowled at the large wound on his thigh. "God's truth, 'tis deep."

Cailin grunted, tore a strip of cloth from a dead fighter's garb, wrapped the wound tight. "It would be bloody worse had you not arrived when you did. Nor can we linger. We must surround Tiran Castle before my uncle can send out messengers seeking aid."

His friend gave a curt nod. "My men and I will join your ranks." He cantered to where the Romani warriors were waiting.

Bracing himself against the pain, Cailin mounted, then paused as he found Elspet frowning at Rónán. "What is it?"

"'Tis the Irishman I saw visit my stepfather," she said, "the one you said was like a brother to you."

"Aye. As your stepfather was loyal to King Robert, nay doubt Rónán's visits involved duties from the king." Cailin shifted, trying to alleviate some of the pain without success. "Hurry, we must leave."

She frowned at his wounded leg, then mounted her horse.

Cailin kicked his destrier into a canter, and she fell in behind him.

* * * *

From the tree line surrounding Tiran Castle, Cailin studied the stronghold a moment before facing Elspet. "Stay with Taog and his men while I speak with my uncle. If he is wise, once he realizes that he has no hope of waiting us out, he will surrender."

Her eyes darkened with worry. "You believe he will?"

"Nay, but I must try." He cantered to where Rónán awaited him, then they rode to the fortress, Cailin holding a white flag high.

Streaks of red and orange cut the sky as Cailin halted before the portcullis of his home, the memories of his youth, of the happiness there smothered by Gaufrid's betrayal. He glared at his uncle standing upon the wall walk, peering down. "Cede and I will show you leniency!" he shouted up.

"'Tis my home!"

"One gained through treachery."

"'Twas nay wrongdoing," Gaufrid snapped. "I received news you died."

Cailin scoffed. "You paid the captain of the ship to kill me."

His uncle's face darkened with outrage. "A lie!"

"If 'twas a lie," Cailin said, disgusted at how his uncle spewed mistruths without compunction, "when you learned that I had returned to Dalkirk lands, you wouldna have sent troops to capture me but would have welcomed me into my home."

"My orders were given out of concern. Nor will I tolerate your twisting my actions into something nefarious." He angled his head in a regal tilt. "Had your purpose upon your return to Dalkirk land been honorable, you would have ridden straight to Tiran Castle and we could have resolved your false beliefs. Instead, you dared to malign my character, a slander I willna tolerate. Once," he drawled with loathing, "I would have welcomed you, but nay longer. You are nay blood of mine. Begone!"

"You, as I, know the truth. Hear me: You will yield what is mine by grace *or* through force."

"An empty threat."

"Indeed?" he said, his voice dry. Cailin glanced around him for emphasis. "With the castle surrounded, none can leave, and your supplies will run out within a month."

A cold smile touched his uncle's lips. "Lay siege if you wish, but en route to the stronghold, I sent runners with missives for reinforcements to the Earl of Odhran, along with several other powerful lords."

Blast it! Still, regardless of whether his uncle's claim was true, he refused to give up. "You have made your decision, one you will regret." Cailin cast the white flag to the ground and cantered toward the tree line.

Rónán fell in beside him. "That went well."

"I expected nay less." Nor would he linger on circumstances he couldna change. Elspet's claim of love during the attack came to mind, and his chest tightened with emotion. "Upon our return, I will introduce you to a woman who has become important to me, one I trust with my life."

His friend's brow raised. "The lass I saw beside you when I first arrived in the Romani camp?"

"Aye. Had I not been in such a hurry to surround Tiran Castle, I would have introduced you then."

"She is a beautiful woman. I can see why she's captured your interest."

"She is, but she is intelligent and determined as well." He guided his horse up the incline. "Her stepfather was Sir Angus McReynolds. On your last visit, she was hidden and saw your meeting with him."

"I knew Angus had a family, but I never met them." He frowned. "Wait, you said he *was* her stepfather."

A gust whipped past. "Aye. Angus, and his wife, were murdered by my uncle's hand."

Fury flashed in his friend's eyes. "The bastard."

"That and more." In short, Cailin explained what had happened. Moments later, he guided his destrier to where Taog and Elspet waited, then swung to the ground.

Rónán followed suit.

Pride filled Cailin as he moved beside Elspet, damning that they hadn't had time alone since the battle. "Sir Rónán, may I introduce to you Elspet McReynolds, whom I hold in high regard."

His friend bowed. "'Tis an honor meeting you. My deepest regret on the loss of your stepfather and mother. Though I never had the honor of meeting your mother, your stepfather will be greatly missed."

A flicker of pain streaked through the exhaustion on her face, and she exhaled a trembling breath. "I thank you."

"As well," Rónán said, "Cailin informed me that you saw me on my last visit to meet with Angus. I regret that we did not meet then."

A blush swept up her cheeks and she cleared her throat. "As I."

Cailin nodded to the Romani leader. "Taog, this is my good friend, Sir Rónán."

Taog nodded to the knight. "You saved our hides."

"I am thankful my men and I arrived in time."

"How did you know that we were in danger?" the Romani leader asked.

"I spoke with King Robert before I came to Dalkirk," Cailin explained. "The Bruce promised if men returned, he would send them. The chances were slight, so I didna mention the possibility." He glanced around, noted the numerous injuries. "There is much more to speak of, a conversation we will continue once all of the wounded have been cared for."

"Starting," Elspet said, her voice firm, "with you."

"Once those with serious wounds are seen to," Cailin stated, "I will tend to my own, but not before."

Elspet's brow furrowed. "And you call me stubborn? You are two times as stubborn as the orneriest boar."

Rónán's mouth tilted in a smile. "He is indeed."

* * * *

Seated near Cailin, Elspet shifted for a better view of his wound. Wiping the sweat from her brow, she glanced at several people treating the last remaining injured and recalled those who hadn't survived.

She cursed the unnecessary deaths, all because of the Earl of Dalkirk's greed. Thank God their losses were few. Still, each one tore at her heart.

"Dinna move," Elspet warned him as she cut away the jagged material wrapped around the wound on his thigh, exposing the angry gash. She took a steadying breath and cursed his persistent refusal to treat his injury before now. Merciful saints, a bit to the left and he would have bled to death. Not that he was doing well now.

"'Twill have to be cauterized," Rónán said, his voice grim. "I have already put my blade in the fire."

"I thank you." She frowned at Cailin. "You should have let me tend to you earlier."

Face streaked with pain, he shook his head. "Others... others needed help far more than I."

She glared at him before cleaning the deep gash, terrified by the amount of blood he'd lost. Once done, she sat back. "Sir Rónán and Taog, hold him while I seal the wound."

Rónán shook his head. "Go wait at the fire until we are done; 'tis not what a lass should see."

On a muttered curse, Elspet retrieved the heated dagger, leveled her gaze on him. "I said hold him!"

The formidable knight studied her for a long moment, then gave a curt nod. Rónán held a strip of leather up to Cailin's mouth. "Clench this in your teeth."

Cailin complied.

Rónán moved behind Cailin and caught his shoulders.

Taog pinned down his injured leg.

The glowing red blade trembled in her hand as she met Cailin's eyes. "I am sorry."

"Do it," Cailin growled.

With a silent prayer, she pressed the flat of the dagger against his wound. Heated metal hissed against the skin. On a strangled groan, Cailin collapsed.

Rónán gently lay him down. "Thank God he passed out. I prayed he would, but at times he can be a bit stubborn."

"Indeed," she agreed, her stomach still churning at the pain she'd dealt Cailin. Several men passed by carrying posts and rolled-up blankets as she lifted the blade, relieved that the bleeding had stopped. "As, 'twould seem, are his friends."

A smile touched Rónán's mouth.

"The bloody fool," Taog snapped. "He should have been tended to long ago."

Rónán sat back. "He should have, but Cailin puts others before himself."

"He does." Taog paused. "Once he becomes earl, he will bring much-needed stability, pride, and common sense to Dalkirk lands."

Pride filled her. "He will."

"I will help Elspet finish here," Rónán said.

The Romani leader scanned the encampment, gave a weary nod, then headed toward where several men were setting up tents.

Elspet applied the herbal mixture the healer had given her earlier.

"Let me help you." Rónán said, lifting Cailin's thigh when she began wrapping the bandage around the gash.

"I thank you," she said, curious about the man, too aware of the questions in his eyes. And why wouldn't he have them, given the ease of conversation between himself and Cailin, and with Cailin's claim that he was like a brother.

She continued to wind the bandage around his leg. From Rónán's closeness with the king, his confidence, his muscled frame, and the way he'd handled his weapon with mastery, she suspected he was a Knight Templar as well.

"Are you all right?" Rónán asked.

"Aye." As much as possible, given the situation. But days ago, she was living a simple yet happy life in which the highlight of any day was whether the earl and his men rode by.

Now, the Earl of Dalkirk wanted her dead, she was hiding out with Taog and his men, and she was in love with Cailin, the rightful heir of Tiran Castle, a Knight Templar.

Once she'd secured the bandage, she sat back. "I pray he doesna become fevered."

"We will keep a close watch on him. As the injury isna severe, knowing him, he will be back on his feet tomorrow."

"Not severe?" She slammed her brows together, tossed the extra cloth aside. "But a breath to the left and he would have died!" Which terrified her the most. In the horror of recent events, that she had found a man like Cailin, fallen in love with him, left her astounded. She refused to consider a life ahead without him.

"But he isna dead."

"'Tis not a game!" Emotions tumbling upon the others as she started to shove to her feet.

Rónán's hand caught her arm. "Far from it," he said, his voice deadly serious. "Nor do I, or those we fight alongside, take any day given for granted."

After a glance to ensure that no one was close enough to hear her, she knelt beside him. "You speak of the Knights Templar."

Surprise flickered in his eyes for a second before he shielded the expression. He removed his hand, frowned at Cailin.

"Aye, he told me about the Brotherhood and its secret dissolution, but," she said as grayish-green eyes lifted to hers, "no one else here knows."

With a thoughtful look, he cleaned his dagger, secured it. "When I first arrived, he said you were important to him."

She angled her jaw. "I love him."

"I see." A smile tugged at the corner of his mouth. "Does he know?"

"Aye."

He gave a slow nod as two women carrying baskets passed by. "You were childhood friends, then."

Though handsome, and his voice edged with a brogue that would woo many a woman, loving Cailin, she wasn't swayed by his innate charm. "Nay, in my youth I only saw him from a distance."

"Yet in but a handful of days," he drawled, "he not only grew to trust and care for you but disclosed he was a Templar. I would be interested in hearing how you met."

Heat touched her face at how she'd deceived Cailin. She soaped her hands, rubbed hard. "'Tis difficult to explain."

He chuckled, a deep, warm sound, easing the tension thrumming through her. "Lass, I would be disappointed if it wasna."

She hesitated to admit the details. Why? This was Cailin's trusted friend, one of the Brotherhood. Cailin would tell him, of that she had no doubt. "I robbed him in the woods when he was in search of my stepfather."

Rónán's mouth fell open in disbelief. "You jest."

Taking a deep breath, keeping her voice low, Elspet explained.

"I am embarrassed to admit that after I had stolen his broadsword, he forgave me," she said, "more than that, he agreed to help me learn whether my stepbrother still lived. Cailin is an honorable man, more than most."

"He is." Rónán shook his head. "If you or Cailin hadna told me of these events, I never would have believed them possible. I can only imagine the look on his face when he awoke and his broadsword was gone."

"Nay doubt 'twas fierce, but I was desperate. Still, I assure you, it took every ounce of courage I had to dare to face him after my deceit."

"But you did," he said, his voice solemn. "Something that, however furious he was, earned his respect."

A smile touched her lips. "That I doubt. He was ready to toss me out on my ear. Only my convincing him that I could help him regain his legacy saved his turning me away."

"It would." He paused. "You mentioned Cailin was looking for your stepfather. Why?"

"Because King Robert told him that he would lead Cailin to Father Lamond."

"Though true," Rónán drawled, "nay doubt the Bruce was aware that Angus had a beautiful and intelligent stepdaughter."

Flustered by his praise, she frowned. "I have nay idea of the king's knowledge of my family. Though I dinna see what my appearance has to do with anything."

Humor touched his gaze. "You wouldna. 'Tis something Cailin can explain."

Cailin groaned.

Elspet turned to Cailin, her reply to Rónán falling away.

Blue eyes raw with pain flickered open.

"Glad to see that you decided to join us," Rónán said.

* * * *

Cailin grimaced, the pain rolling through him making each breath hurt. The scent of cooking meat filled the air as he glanced around, noticed numerous tents were standing, while men were now repairing shelters damaged during the attack.

"How long was I asleep?" Cailin asked.

"Long enough for Elspet to explain how you met."

At the humor in Rónán's voice, Cailin glanced toward her. "'Twas an unusual event."

She cleared her throat. "You must be hungry. I will bring you something to eat." With a nod at Rónán, she stood and headed toward a cook fire fragrant with the scent of simmering meat and herbs.

Once she departed, Cailin shifted his gaze to his friend. "I prayed that King Robert would send troops, but with his being unsure whether any warriors would return to his camp in time, I couldna count on any reinforcements. I thank God you arrived when you did."

Somber, his friend nodded. "I am thankful we reached you in time. When I returned from taking a missive to Stephan MacQuistan at Avalon Castle, the Bruce explained the situation, then placed me in charge of a contingent and sent me to aid you."

It seemed a very long time since he, Stephan, Rónán, and the others of the Brotherhood had fled France with Templar treasures when less than two years had passed. But until he drew his last breath, the foul memory of the French king's betrayal would never fade.

"'Twould seem that King Robert's matchmaking has found another mark."

His friend's teasing pulled Cailin from the dark place in his mind. "A ridiculous notion. If anything, I would advise you to keep your concern for yourself. Nay doubt you are in King Robert's sights."

He chuckled. "That I seriously doubt. After watching you, Stephan, Thomas, and Aiden, I well know to beware the king's romantic interventions."

"We will see, my friend," Cailin said, "we will see."

"Oh nay," Rónán said with a laugh. "You are not dismissing the subject. Dinna you find it interesting that the Bruce sent you to a man who has a beautiful and intelligent daughter?"

"Pure circumstance." But his friend's words gave him pause. Never had he believed he would become entangled in the Bruce's matchmaking endeavors, but had he?

"Elspet said she loves you. From watching the two of you together, I believe 'tis a feeling you share."

"She is important to me, but love her? I dinna believe 'tis possible. Too much lies before me to consider a life with a woman or a family."

Though she made him want what he'd never considered before. Cailin shifted, winced at the shot of pain. 'Twas foolish to allow those needs in his life when naught lay before him but war. Notions of family were for those who had the luxury of preparing land to till, not for battle. Once all of Scotland lay beneath King Robert's control and the day came to wed, if the king was involved, 'twould be to dictate whom he married.

But, because Rónán was his friend, Cailin would explain. "Regardless of what Elspet makes me feel, if she knew how much I cared for her and I were to die, 'twould break her heart."

Rónán scoffed. "With her in love with you, if anything happens to you, her heart will be broken regardless. Telling her how you feel now, in the end, will spare her naught."

Irritated that his friend could be right, he scowled. "And you are an expert because?"

His smile widening, Rónán held up his hands. "'Tis obvious, but then, my mind isna skewed by thoughts of a woman in my bed."

Refusing to linger on the topic, Cailin scanned the distant castle, noted the guards making rounds on the wall walk. Inside, no doubt his uncle awaited reinforcements and prepared for war.

On a rough sigh, he glanced skyward. Clouds slowly drifted past, their thick puffs blocking out the sun before moving on and streaks of golden sunlight again illuminated the land.

"Until your arrival, I far from had enough men to attack the stronghold. Now, with my uncle's losses, I believe the siege will secure his surrender."

"Unless reinforcements arrive."

"Aye." He curled his hand into a fist. "Blast it, I canna allow him to gain any lord's support!"

"What can you do?"

He scoured his mind for any answer, then an idea came to mind. "My uncle mentioned the Earl of Odhran. He is the closest noble who could offer him support and is but a two-day ride. More important, he was a close friend of my father. Though his runner has already set out, if I can reach the earl, regardless if he is en route, I believe I can convince him to join ranks with me."

Rónán's eyes narrowed. "God in heaven, with your leg injured, you canna be thinking of making such a hard ride."

"I—" he gritted his teeth against the pain as he shifted—"had little trouble riding here."

His friend scoffed. "There is a big difference between a few hours' travel to lay siege to Tiran Castle and a hard, two-day ride."

"Mayhap, but I have little choice. If my uncle receives reinforcements, he will ensure that we all die."

Chapter 15

Hints of purple lingered in the western sky, an ode to the upcoming night. At best, they had another hour of daylight. Fighting to wash away the memories of battle all too clear, Elspet drew a deep, cleansing breath of the chilly, pine-scented air.

"Though Tiran Castle is now surrounded and my uncle's ability to attack is contained," Cailin said, a scowl in his voice, "I would have preferred that you had remained with Rónán rather than ride with me to Syridan Castle."

Muscles aching, she glanced over. Snow littered Cailin's red hair as he guided his destrier through a narrow stand of trees. "As I explained at camp, with my stepfather a close friend of the Earl of Odhran and his favoring me, if there are any issues, my presence will help him to shift his support to your cause."

"There willna be problems."

The defiance in his tone reminded her of how stubborn he could be. "Had you been sure, you wouldna have allowed me to ride with you."

A muscle worked in his jaw.

"Do you think your uncle's runner has arrived at Syridan Castle?"

He shook his head. "With the heavy snow throughout the day, I believe the earliest he will arrive is tomorrow. Even at our hard pace, at best 'twill take two more days to reach the stronghold."

Limbs rattled overhead beneath a strong gust, and errant brown leaves tumbled across the blanket of white marred by stones breaking through.

On a shiver, she tugged her cape tighter and guided her mount around a fallen oak. "What if we encounter the Earl of Odhran's men heading toward Tiran Castle?"

Cailin's mount snorted as he forged his way up a steep incline. "A possibility I doubt. Even if Odhran gives my uncle his support, it should take a large force several days to ready their arms and prepare to ride."

"What if the earl refuses to recognize that you are the rightful Earl of Dalkirk?" she asked, voicing her worst fear.

"If we canna gain Odhran, or any other lord's support, we will fight with the troops we have."

Memories of Cailin and Rónán's discussion with Taog about various tactics to consider in seizing Tiran Castle last night came to mind. Though she'd listened to bards tell tales of battle, she wasn't familiar with the various techniques in laying siege.

"'Tis amazing that a fire in the secret tunnel beneath a castle wall will cause the fortification to fail," she said.

"'Tis a maneuver the Templars have used with great success. Once the wall collapses, in the ensuing mayhem, we storm the castle. With the benefit of surprise and my uncle's troops severely depleted, even if by some chance reinforcements arrive, we have a chance to seize the stronghold."

But he couldn't be sure. Nor did she want to consider the risks, or how many more men could die. She noticed him shift in his saddle. "How does your leg fare?"

"'Tis better."

That, she doubted. "'Twould have been best to have rested another day before starting the journey, but Rónán warned me that you wouldna be swayed."

Cailin grunted. "I assure you, he has seen me in much worse condition."

That he could make light of the seriousness of his wound amazed her. Most men would have been abed for a week or more. But then, Cailin wasn't most. He favored his leg when he walked, little more.

Curious to know more about him, she guided her mount a bit closer. "Where did you and Rónán meet?"

"During a battle in the Holy Land, he saved my life. We have been friends since."

A gust of wind swirled around them. "Rónán never mentioned that."

"He wouldna. Though a fierce warrior, he is a proud and humble man."

After speaking with Rónán, and given his actions since they'd met, that she believed. She smiled, thinking of his smooth, lyrical brogue. "How did an Irishman come to join the Brotherhood?"

"An orphan, he was taken in by a brutal man who beat him regularly and made him work from dawn 'til dusk. At the age of seven, barely surviving a severe thrashing and believing the next would kill him, he fled." Cailin shoved through a stand of fir, then guided his mount down a steep incline, a tumble of loose snow rolling ahead of them. "With the man having sworn to kill him if he ever tried to bolt, Rónán kept in hiding for months. He never looked back or told anyone."

Her heart went out to Rónán. "'Tis sad, knowing he never knew the love of a family."

"He found a bond of brotherhood with the Templars."

Mayhap, but kinship with men trained to fight was not the same as having a mother and father or memories of family. "Do you think one day he will return to confront the scoundrel?"

He shrugged. "Even if Rónán returned, with the years passed, the cur who took him in is probably dead."

"How did Rónán live before he joined the Brotherhood?"

"For several years, by his wits, doing whatever he had to in order to survive; then he joined the galloglass. 'Twas while he was with them that he met several Knights Templar. Impressed by their discipline, code of honor, and fighting skills, Rónán departed with them and later swore his oath to the Brotherhood."

"Incredible. After all he endured, he could easily have gone down a darker path."

"He could have."

"A fate you could have chosen as well." That Cailin had not was a miracle, which made her heart fill with admiration and love for all he had conquered.

He shrugged. "I did naught but survive."

"Nay," she said, her voice softening, "like Rónán you persevered, overcame what would have overwhelmed most."

Another gust of wind skimmed past. Flakes of wind-driven snow spiraled between them, then gently sifted to the ground.

Cailin's eyes lifted to hers, his gaze intense.

Warmth tingled up her skin, and his eyes darkened in response, and she believed the dreadful memories of the battle had faded. With one look he could do that: steal away her fears, the horrors of her day, and make her feel safe, wanted, desired.

How would a life with him be? Days filled with hard work, but friendship and laughter. Then there would be the nights. What would it feel like to be in his arms, to give herself to him completely?

Despite the cold, warmth surged through her at thoughts of his touch, of his muscled body against hers, and of his mouth skimming over her skin. Elspet wished they weren't on a journey driven by strife, that they could find a place where they could spend days together and more.

A dream.

Or was it?

Her mind racing with possibilities, she glanced at the sinking sun. They had this night. Though only hours, 'twas time when they would be alone.

A while later, with their horses tended to, Elspet sat before the fire in their makeshift camp. The sharp smell of freshly split wood entwined with the char of smoke as she watched Cailin's muscles flex as he chopped kindling.

So much had changed since they'd last stayed in a similar setting. Then, he'd viewed her as a woman he was unsure he could trust, and she'd been desperate to convince him to help her.

Wood clattered paces away as he set down a pile. He set several sticks into the fire. "That should hold us until the morning."

"Aye." Elspet handed him an oatcake, then ate her own. As she watched him eat, her thoughts strayed to when she'd told him that she'd loved him before the battle. But since they'd departed the Romani camp, he'd mentioned naught of her confession, much less his feelings for her.

As a child, she'd dreamed of a lord one day coming to sweep her away, but too well she knew those were the fantasies of youth, of those innocent to the treachery of life.

If she wasn't careful, she could let herself drown in all the betrayals they'd each been dealt. His uncle. Her stepbrother. And the resulting aftermath. The gory battles.

"How can you sleep after a battle?" She rubbed her brow. "Dinna the horrific images haunt your mind?"

* * * *

Cailin hesitated as he noted her visible distress. He picked up a piece of wood, tossed it into the flames, understanding her struggles with the violence she'd faced this day, of how during the battle she'd taken several lives. A burst of sparks swirled up within the smoke. How could he explain the details of his past and her present in a way to help her overcome her concern? He settled on a simple version of the truth and prayed it brought her a sliver of comfort.

"For a while, every time you close your eyes, the skirmish plays over in your mind, the blood, the screams, and what you could have done differently to save a friend's life or push the enemy back." He met her gaze. "Out of sheer exhaustion, you sleep. After, you prepare for the next clash, but a part of you withdraws where you engage with a focus only on the goals of the battle, not that men are dying beneath your blade."

She drew up her legs and rested her chin on her knees. "Do the memories ever disappear?"

"They fade, but they are always inside you."

"Oh."

The anguish in that single word had him reaching out and cupping her chin. "You did what you had to do. Your skill, determination, saved many lives."

"But because of me," she whispered, "several men are dead."

"Warriors who would have killed you if given the chance."

She closed her eyes for a long moment, then opened them again, the anger and frustration there easy to read. "I despise war."

"As I, but 'tis a necessity against those who immerse their lives in evil, concern themselves with the accumulation of wealth and power above all else."

"Indeed." She released a rough exhale. "'Tis sad, knowing there will always be conflict, that regardless of how one man fights for power, another plots with the same intent."

"Mayhap, but beyond those consumed by the need to control, there are many more who care, who touch lives and assure others that good remains in the world. Like you."

Her lips parted slightly. "I...I have done little."

"Nay," he said, his gaze tender, "you have done much. You fight for those for whom you care, and take time to help those less fortunate."

Elspet arched a brow. "And you know this because...?"

He swept his thumb along her lower lip, the silken slide luring him to kiss her. Foolish thoughts given the feelings she inspired, dangerous ones he had no business lingering upon. "Taog told me. And I have seen with my own eyes your conviction."

"Oh..."

Her claim that she loved Cailin kindled in his mind. He wondered what she'd say if, with imminent danger behind them, he asked her if she'd meant her admission.

If she confirmed her declaration, how would he reply?

With his life as a Templar, he'd never considered a woman in his life, but as of late, thoughts of Elspet invaded his mind and made him wonder what life would be like for them together as husband and wife. As now, with her body a hand's breadth from his, her emerald eyes watching him with a mixture of confusion and desire.

He wondered if she realized how much he wanted her, how tempted he was to skim his hand along the soft column of her neck, to pause upon the erratic pulse beating at the base.

"Cailin, I—"

His intent to keep her at a distance faded beneath memories of the silky slide of her taste, and he claimed her mouth, her soft gasp, then acceptance, emboldening him further.

Beneath his heated kiss, she took, gave, demanded more.

Blood pounding hot, Cailin drew back, cupped her face in his, the tenderness there, the desire, almost dropping him to his knees.

Her lips swollen from his kiss, confusion flickered in Elspet's eyes.

Though he wanted her, 'twas wrong. He released her. "Sleep. We have a hard day of travel tomorrow."

Her hand caught his. "When I confessed that I loved you, I meant what I said. Though 'tis wrong to admit such," she breathed, "I want you as well."

His body hardened, her soft scent of woman and earth luring him to accept what she offered. Through sheer will, he withdrew from her touch, wanting only to stay. "I canna give you what you seek."

Hurt streaked across her face, and he damned that he'd caused it. "Then why do you kiss me as if you want more?"

He should walk away, leave her alone, but however dangerous, finding he needed to share what she made him feel. "Because I want you more than 'tis right. Nor had I expected to find someone like you. Someone who makes me care more than I had ever imagined."

Hope ignited in her eyes. "I know you must leave once you have reclaimed your home to fight for King Robert, but once the battles are over, you will return."

Warmth seeped through him at the hope in her voice. Until recently, he'd never allowed himself to consider a future of more than the next conflict. After spending time with her, he found himself wanting a family, a child to leave a legacy.

Coldness invaded his heart. Too well he knew that naught could be guaranteed in battle, but blast it, he wanted her in his life.

Torn, he took her hand, a storm of feelings swamping him until his chest tightened against his struggles. "Though I must leave once Tiran Castle is mine, I ask that you wait for me."

Warmth filled her eyes. "And I ask that you wait for me. That you invite no other into your bed."

The audacity of her entreaty caught him off guard. He arched a brow. "Few women would dare to make such a bold request."

A smile touched her mouth. "Few women would dare rob a knight of his sword, then seek him out to ask forgiveness or to help her with her cause."

The tension pouring through him eased. He chuckled. "Indeed."

"Nor have you replied to my request."

"I havena." He pressed a soft kiss upon her lips. "Until I return, there will be nay one else but you."

She nodded. "I swear the same."

Cailin drew her against him, and for the first time in his life felt complete. Why?

He didna love her.

She intrigued him, made him want. With her beauty, intelligence, and a body that would make any man ache for her, 'twas expected. But love?

Unsure how to explain the needs she inspired, the sense of destiny, he shoved aside his musings and focused on her, on this moment. He brushed away a swath of hair from her cheek, paused on the finely braided strip of leather around her neck. Though he'd noticed this before, with his mind focused on the mayhem, he'd dismissed any further thought. Now, a sense of familiarity nagged at him.

He slid his finger beneath the cord, lifted. A silver-forged Celtic cross hung before him, a ruby embedded at the center. Heart pounding, he stared in disbelief, lifted his gaze. "Where did you get this?" he demanded.

Confused eyes searched his. "My mother found the necklace in the woods when she and my stepfather were traveling and she gave it to me." She frowned. "Why do you ask?"

Because," he rasped, "it belonged to my mother. 'Twas lost the day she died in the hunting accident." His throat tightened with emotion as he swept his thumb over the gemstone. "Never did I believe I would see it again."

The years rushed past as he remembered being a young lad watching his mother brush her hair, drawn to the finely crafted cross around her neck. Of how she'd explained that the necklace was an heirloom, one that she would pass down to the woman he married.

She withdrew the cross from his fingers, drawing him from his memories, and started to lift it over her head.

Something within Cailin made him still her hand. Though she thought her being given his mother's cross was due to circumstance, he believed 'twas his mother's silent blessing that Elspet was the woman for him. "Nay, wear it, 'tis fitting you would have it."

"Are you sure?"

His doubts of moments before faded. "Aye." Cailin cupped her chin, again brushed his mouth over hers with a lazy slide, her sigh, a soft moan, burning through his body straight to his groin.

* * * *

At his kiss, heat scalded Elspet until her every thought was of this moment. Though Cailin hadna said he loved her, he wanted her, and had promised to come back to her as well.

A vow few men would have given a woman unless he cared.

Savoring his touch, she arched her neck, moaned as his lips skimmed along her jaw, then down the sensitive skin of her neck.

She pressed her body against his. "I want you."

On an unsteady breath, he lifted his head, the desire in his eyes making her shudder with need. His breath unsteady, he lay his brow against hers. "And I want you as well, but you deserve more than my taking you in a moment of lust."

Hurt, she moved back, searched his eyes. "Is that what our making love would be to you, lust?"

"Nay. What you make me feel, need is…"

"What?"

He brushed away wisps of hair that had fallen against her cheek. "You have never been with a man, have you?"

She ignored her bruised hope that he'd say that he loved her. For now, that he cared for her deeply would be enough. "Nay, but neither have I been in love before."

"Elspet, listen to me. However much I want you, I canna promise that I will return from battle."

"I know." She reached up, loosened the ties of her gown, allowed it to billow to the ground, exposing the thin shift beneath.

His throat worked and his eyes darkened as he raked her body with his gaze. "God in heaven."

Aware she was taking a huge risk but needing him, aching to feel his touch, and wanting to share with him the most intimate of moments, she pushed the first strap off her shoulder. Elspet moved to the second strip of cloth.

His fingers stilled hers. "Let me."

Pulse racing, her body burned as his sultry gaze seared into hers as he slid the cloth down, then cupped her breast.

Body tightening, she gasped as he brushed his finger over the rigid tip, gasped as he leaned down and suckled, teasing until she lost herself in his every caress.

Her body trembling, he lay her upon the pallet they'd made earlier. Bathed in the warmth of the fire paces away, with soft, gentle caresses, he explored her every curve, and 'twas as if she was floating, her world naught but sensation and whispers of need.

With his every touch, desire built, and when he edged lower, released the few ties to bare her to his view, she didna feel shame but joy.

She'd wondered how she'd feel beneath a man's intimate touch, if she'd be overcome with nerves or shy. But with Cailin she felt empowered, as if this was the moment, the man she'd waited for her entire life.

Naked before him, with his hands stroking her as his mouth paid homage to her every curve, she relished the bursts of sensation his touch ignited, the care he took to ensure her pleasure. Anxious to feel his body against hers, she loosened the ties of his garb.

On a groan, he tossed off his clothes. Naked, his breathing unsteady, he met her gaze. "Are you sure?"

"More than anything."

"I never intended to make love with you," he confessed. "Intimacy goes against my Templar teachings."

"I know," she said, understanding his conflict. "But the Brotherhood is dissolved, and your life is your own." She pressed soft kisses over his mouth, mimicked his action in sliding her lips down the thick muscle of his throat. "Make love with me, Cailin. I am not a foolish lass but a woman who loves you. Give me this night, memories to keep until you return."

Face strained, he nodded. "If I have to crawl, I will come back to you, that I swear." He kissed her, hot, hard, his hands driving her mad as his mouth demanded more.

* * * *

Slowly, Cailin worked his way over her body, learning what she enjoyed, lingering, then moving lower. Her sweet taste filled him, and he lost himself in the moment.

Given his Templar teachings, though he'd tried to convince himself 'twas wrong to make love with Elspet, she felt right in his arms.

He kissed his way along the flat of her stomach, then edged lower, loving her response, the way she arched as he parted her and exposed her moistness to his view.

Taking his time, he touched, teased her, savoring her soft cries of pleasure. As she began to tremble, aware she was close to the edge, he straddled her and pressed his hard length against her wetness. "I..." Stunned by the words that formed on his tongue, Cailin stilled, overwhelmed by emotion.

Eyes dark with need, Elspet surged forward.

Cailin's mind blurred, the startling words tangled in his mind as he sank deep into her slick warmth. She cried out as he tore the thin barrier of her innocence, and he stilled, his breaths coming fast. His body demanded that he take, but he held. Regardless of how much he suffered, he would give her the time she needed, give her the tenderness she deserved.

He caressed her cheek. "I am sorry for the pain."

Sweat glistened upon her face and happiness filled her eyes. "Dinna be. This, us, 'tis beautiful."

Wanting her to forget the hurt, he claimed her mouth as he caressed her breasts. When she shifted restlessly beneath him, he began to move. With each stroke, she rose to meet him, and he lost himself to all but her, how her body welcomed his. As her silky wetness tightened around him, she came apart. Heat surging through him, Cailin followed.

His mind a pleasurable blur, Cailin rolled to his side and drew her with him, needing to hold her, wanting this moment to last forever.

Chapter 16

The soft crackle of fire slipped into the haze of Elspet's sleep. She shifted, grimacing at the soreness of her body, then smiled at the memories of the hours through the night when she and Cailin had made love, of his tenderness, of his every touch.

Emotion tightened her throat as she withdrew the necklace from beneath her shift, stared at the silver Celtic cross with a ruby at the center.

His mother's.

Yet Cailin had pressed her to keep what was obviously important to him. Humbled, she stroked her finger over the forged cross. Never had she believed she'd find such happiness. Against an unlikely start, he'd won her heart. Warmth filled her as she turned over to face him.

The pallet next to her lay empty.

She listened for a moment.

At a soft nicker, she glanced toward the place where they'd hidden the horses deeper in the cave. After a slow, languorous stretch, she dressed, then headed to where torchlight flickered from the smaller cavern.

She rounded the corner. Illuminated within the soft wavering light, Cailin tightened the cinch.

Elspet savored the play of his muscles, and her body tingled. They needed to leave, but mayhap she could convince him to tarry for a short while.

Loosening the ties of her shift, Elspet walked over, wrapped her arms around him, and pressed her body against his back. "I was hoping to awaken in your arms."

He stiffened.

Unease trickled through her, but she dismissed it. With the hard travel ahead, he was tense about the upcoming day.

Cailin turned, caught her wrists, and drew them away.

His taut expression set her on edge. Merciful saints, something had happened, the reason he was awake. "What is wrong?"

"You could be with child."

She blinked. Of all the things she'd anticipated him saying—that he'd heard men searching for them nearby, that his mount or hers had gone lame—never had she considered this. Nor, after their words last night, did his concern make sense. "I could be, but one night far from assures such."

He didn't react to her comment, nor exhibit the tenderness she wanted to see given the intimacy they'd shared. A flicker of doubt speared her.

He would want their babe, wouldn't he?

Of course he would.

He'd asked her to wait for him, had wanted her to keep his mother's cross, so why was he so concerned by the possibility that she might carry his child?

"Once I seize Tiran Castle," he said, his voice firm, "we will wed."

Duty, not that he loved her, wanted her, found joy that their passion would gift them with a son or a daughter, but an obligation.

Had she read too much into last night? He'd warned her that he could make no promises, but she'd assured him that she didn't care, had pushed him until he'd taken what she'd freely offered. Yet regardless of what she'd said, a part of her had wanted him to realize what he felt for her was more than caring deeply but love.

Foolish thoughts. Those were her dreams, not his.

Hurt, angry at herself for becoming caught up in dreams and longings, she stepped back, and secured the ties of her shift. "I didna make love with you to trap you into marriage."

"Nor did I intend to imply 'twas your plan. I care for you. 'Tis that our child willna be a bastard."

Her temper threatened to spike. Elspet wanted to rail at him that she didn't give a damn what others thought. Odd; all her life she'd dreamed of a nobleman sweeping her off her feet, but now she realized that naught mattered without love, nor would she settle for less.

"If we discover that I am with child, we will discuss it further. For now, I willna marry you."

Blue eyes narrowed. "You will."

"I will not, and I think by now you would have learned that I willna allow you, or anyone, to force me. I ride, I fight, I make love. My choices."

"Being an unwed mother is not a choice."

She tilted her chin. "Nay more than being an unwilling bride."

His jaw clenched and his mouth opened, but he didn't speak. At last, he said, "This is not the time for a proper conversation."

Her heart breaking, she glanced toward the entry, where the first rays of light streaked across the sky. "'Tis time to go." She walked to where they'd stored their belongings near the fire and began packing the few items they'd brought.

* * * *

Wind-tossed branches overhead fractured the midday sunlight streaming through the forest, creating smears of blackness upon the pristine blanket of white. Cailin wove his mount between dense brush littered with dead leaves clinging to the branches, then up a steep incline. At the top, he glanced at Elspet.

Face set, she stared straight ahead, a remote look she'd worn since their discussion in the cave two days past.

After telling her that he cared for her the evening before, he'd expected her to be pleased with his offer of marriage, that he'd want their child to not be a bastard. She had no family except for her despicable stepbrother, and no coin.

Why hadn't she agreed and made this simple? Then, when he departed to rejoin the Bruce, she would have been safe at Tiran Castle, and he could have focused on serving their king until his return.

Blast it, this whole disaster was his fault. Never should he have touched her. Regardless if she'd wanted him and had asked for no promises, or that he'd foolishly allowed himself to believe that her having his mother's cross was a sign of her blessing, neither removed the fact that his taking Elspet's innocence had made her his responsibility.

Frowning, he scanned the surrounding bens, guiding his destrier around a large drift at the base of a sheer cliff.

A hawk screeched overhead. The fierce predator glided upon the currents over the trees.

Mayhap he should try to engage in conversation? He grimaced. As if she'd replied to any of his questions with more than three words since they'd departed the cave. In time, she would calm; then he'd convince her that his plan held merit.

A blast of wind rich with the scent of pine swept past him as he topped the next ridge.

Beneath the afternoon sun, seated at the edge of a lock, stood Syridan Castle. A massive fortress, its defenses a formidable challenge for the best-trained troops. Men moved along the wall walk, and the distant clash of blades rang out.

In silence, Elspet drew her steed up beside him.

"Regardless of whether the messenger has departed for the next lord he is sent to meet with, I will convince the Earl of Odhran to support me. As well, once Tiran Castle is mine, we will speak of our future."

Her head turned toward him. Emerald eyes narrowed. "There is naught more to say."

There was, but if there was one thing he had learned over the years, it was when to choose his battles. Cailin kicked his horse into a canter, Elspet followed.

As they halted before the gatehouse, a guard on the wall walk peered over. "Who goes there?"

"Sir Cailin MacHugh," he called up. "I come bearing news of importance and must speak with the Earl of Odhran immediately."

"And the lass?"

"Elspet McReynolds," she replied, "a friend of the earl."

The guard strode from view, and the rushed murmur of voices reached him.

The thud of the portcullis rang out, then the iron gate clunked up.

"Whatever happens, stay near me," Cailin whispered. He guided his destrier into the gatehouse. As they entered the bailey, he spotted a stern, dignified-looking man standing on the top step of the keep, staring at him.

Knights trained in the lists, and others were in the stables, preparing to mount their steeds, while other men, their swords sheathed, headed toward the gatehouse.

Cailin nodded to the first man as the troops moved past, then turned back to the single man on the step. "He must be the welcoming party. I had hoped 'twould be the earl." He glanced toward the pole above the keep, where the earl's flag, announcing he was in residence, was hung, stilled. "God's teeth!"

"What is wrong?" she asked.

"There is nay standard flying!" Bedamned, so caught up in his frustration at Elspet, he hadna looked. He glanced toward the guard who'd passed moments before, noticed they'd begun to fan out behind him. God's blade, 'twas a trap.

"Elspet, dinna ask questions," Cailin said, praying it wasn't too late to escape. "On the count of three, whirl your horse and ride out of the gatehouse as fast as you can. One. Two—"

"Halt or die," a deep voice warned behind them.

The destrier shifted beneath Cailin, as if sensing his disquiet. He edged his warhorse closer to Elspet. If an avenue to slip out presented itself, he'd haul her over and ride.

The warrior's brows slammed together. "You are under arrest."

Cailin spotted a man half-hidden, cowering near the keep's entry and bearing his uncle's colors. The runner no doubt. "On what charge?"

"Sedition against the Earl of Dalkirk!" The warrior nodded to his men. "Seize him!"

The surrounding guards charged; one grabbed Cailin's sword arm, while several others caught his legs and jerked him from his mount.

"Cailin!" Elspet screamed.

He ignored the shot of pain from his wounded leg, drove his fist into one of the knight's jaws, and his boot into another's chest. Several men hauled him down, blocking his view of Elspet. He twisted to break free.

"This will bloody stop your fighting," a deep voice snapped.

A boot slammed against the back of Cailin's head, and blackness consumed him.

* * * *

The drip of water echoed from a distance, and a foul stench permeated Elspet's every breath as she stared between the bars at Cailin sprawled upon the floor in the cell across from hers in the dungeon.

Since they'd shoved him inside yesterday, he hadn't moved. Please God, let him be alive.

After their capture, she'd been haunted by her coldness toward Cailin. No, his offer of marriage wasn't the romantic one she'd envisioned, but he cared for her deeply, and though he hadn't admitted love, 'twas more than many women received.

If nothing else, their capture had taught her that life was too short. Should he revive and once they were free—if that miracle happened—she would marry him.

She tugged the moth-eaten blanket tighter and ignored the suspicious stains on the floor within the cell, refusing to try to decipher their contemptible origin.

In several of the cells, men moaned in agony, their ramblings interrupted only when guards stormed in and hauled a prisoner away. She closed her eyes against the memories of the men's pleas for mercy, entreaties ignored by the stone-faced sentries.

The distant tap of steps grew. Moments later, the wooden door scraped open.

Elspet braced herself, prayed the Earl of Odhran had returned and demanded that she and Cailin be freed.

An elder with stringy gray hair, bushy eyebrows, and age lines dredged deep across his face limped forward, a bucket in his hands. He paused at each cell, filled a battered clay bowl with foul-looking stew, shoved it beneath the iron bars, then shuffled on.

He paused before her. Lumps of unidentifiable brownish-gray meat plopped into the bowl.

Bile rose in her throat. "Has the Earl of Odhran returned?"

He sniffed with disdain. "If he had, he wouldna be speaking with the likes of anyone plotting treason against the Earl of Dalkirk."

She shoved to her feet. "Cailin MacHugh is the rightful Earl of Dalkirk."

"A lie the steward said you'd claim," the elder sneered. "Nor when Lord Odhran returns will he find amusement in your deception."

Cailin moaned.

Thank God! She rushed to the bars. "Cailin!"

The elder grunted, limped over, filled the bowl outside Cailin's cell, kicked it into the dank cell, then moved on.

Body trembling, Cailin wove slightly as he shoved to a sitting position. Eyes dark with pain, he looked around, paused when his gaze met hers. "Are you well?"

"Aye," she breathed.

He rubbed the back of his head where he'd been hit, pushed to his feet. "How long have we been here?"

"Since yesterday."

The elder who'd delivered the vile substance meant to pass as edible ambled past, casting a scathing look toward Cailin before departing the dungeon.

The door slammed shut, and she rubbed her arms. "The steward believes we are traitors plotting against Dalkirk."

He grunted. "Nay doubt a result of what my uncle penned to the Earl of Odhran, and he isna here." Legs aching, he made his way to the bars, frowned. "Why would the steward open the missive?"

So caught up in her worry for Cailin, a point she hadn't considered. "Do you think Odhran's man is in league with your uncle?"

* * * *

"I do, which means the steward isna a man we can trust, and Odhran must be warned. Then again, it could be gossip the runner passed." On a muttered curse, Cailin braced himself against the iron and rubbed his throbbing head.

He needed to talk to the earl, but what if he couldna convince him of his uncle's lies? God's teeth, what if, upon the earl's return, he was never informed of their arrival?

No, with the many people gathered when they were seized, Odhran would be informed. The only question remaining was when.

Cailin scanned the dungeon, where men sat huddled in their cells shivering, moaning, with several laying lifeless. Regardless of Elspet's friendship with the earl, never should he have brought her to Syridan Castle. Though he damn well knew why he'd allowed her to accompany him.

He'd wanted her near him. Bedamned, he'd wanted her.

A shameful admission for a warrior, more so for a Knight Templar to allow his decisions to be swayed by lust. It mattered not that she was beautiful, intelligent, or a strong woman who drew him like no other.

He'd sworn to protect those in harm's way. Instead, not only had he placed her in danger, but however drawn to her, never should he have allowed them to make love.

Chest tight with self-condemnation, he stared at the woman who had tossed his life upside down, ignited feelings he'd never experienced, a lass who in his arms made him feel whole. Though she wore his mother's cross, in truth, he didna need a sign to know that however wrong, he couldna imagine a life without her.

Cailin's breath caught in his throat.

He loved her.

Why hadn't he realized it sooner? Or, maybe deep inside he'd known, the part of him determined to keep his distance from her. As if it mattered now. God's sword, he must have sounded like a fool. Instead of the ultimatum he'd delivered, he should have taken her into his arms.

Elspet's eyes dark with worry narrowed. "What is wrong?"

His fingers tightened on the bars. Heart filled with love, he stared at her, wanting to tell her, but not like this. After everything she'd sacrificed, everything she had given him, she deserved to know. It was a small penance he could satisfy.

"Never did I believe I would find a woman who would touch my life, who would make me want more than I have ever wanted someone in my entire life. Nor did I ever plan on telling you something of such vital importance here."

Fear jumped in her eyes. "You think we are going to die?"

Frustrated, he shook his head. "Nay, I am doing this poorly. Elspet, I—"

Voices echoed from the corridor, then the door scraped open. A large man sporting a thick black beard and wearing finely tailored attire entered, a fierce scowl upon his face. He scanned the dungeon, and his eyes paused on Cailin. "Sir Cailin MacHugh?"

Cailin drew himself to his full height, furious that locked within, he couldna protect Elspet. "Aye."

The stately man's gaze shifted to Elspet. Shock, then anger widened his gaze. "Sir Cailin, Elspet, my deepest regrets."

Her shoulders sagged, but her voice was clear and firm. "Lord Odhran, thank God you are here."

Odhran nodded to the guard. "Release them!"

The guard hurried forward. Keys rattled as he opened the door to his cell, then hers.

Ignoring the pain, his face taut, Cailin moved beside her, his limbs stiff.

"I wasna aware of your or Elspet's arrival until moments ago." Anger flashed in the earl's eyes. "I assure you, an oversight my steward deeply regrets. Come with me." He exited the dungeon.

Cailin followed at a pace his body allowed. After the rotting stench of the dungeon, he savored the fresh air of the corridor edged with the tang of winter. "What of the runner from my uncle?"

"He is under guard. 'Twould seem my steward has been supporting your uncle in secret, but he erred in believing I wouldna discover his deceit." He glanced at Cailin. "When I first learned that you were still alive, I couldna believe 'twas true. Tell me what happened."

As they walked, with Elspet at his side, Cailin explained his uncle's plan to claim the title of Dalkirk. Of how Gaufrid had killed his brother and sister-in-law, paid a sailor to kill Cailin, who'd sold him to pirates, and then how he was freed.

Odhran grunted with disgust. "It makes my skin crawl that a man would destroy his family for greed. I will help you to regain Tiran Castle. 'Tis long past time for your uncle's treachery to end."

"The earl has sent runners to other lords," Elspet said, worry etched in her voice.

"A fact I discovered during my *discussion* with Dalkirk's runner." He met Cailin's gaze. "I will pen writs to all who the earl asked for aid, informing them of your uncle's duplicity and request that they deny him support. As I am acquainted with all the lords who were mentioned, I am confident all will agree."

"I thank you." With Rónán's arrival leading a contingent of King Robert's knights, combined with Taog's men and Odhran's support, little doubt remained that soon Cailin would have control of his legacy.

Grief lined the earl's face as he turned to Elspet. "My deepest sympathies on the loss of your stepfather and mother. They were both wonderful people and will be missed."

She nodded. "'Tis hard to believe they are gone."

"I am always here if I can be of help." His expression somber, he shook his head. "I struggle to accept the charges brought against Sir Angus."

Anger flashed in her eyes. "'Twas Lord Dalkirk's lies!"

Cailin listened as she explained, the outrage on Odhran's face feelings he shared. "I assure you," he said when Elspet finished, "my uncle has much to pay for, penance I will serve."

"Aye," the earl agreed with a low growl. "I will send word to my master-at-arms to ready the troops. Though 'twill take them through the night to prepare, we will ride at first light."

"I thank you," Cailin said.

The earl met Elspet's gaze. "You will remain here, where you will be safe."

She angled her jaw. "I will accompany you."

His instincts urged Cailin to deny her participation, but 'twas right to honor her wishes. "After all she has endured, as well as fighting alongside me during my uncle's attack, 'tis her right to face the man who murdered her parents. Nor, surrounded by my troops and yours, is there a chance she will be harmed."

"Aye, she will be safe, but I would rather she remain here until Tiran Castle is seized. But—" Pride twinkled in the man's eyes—"well I remember your stepfather speaking of your stubborn streak. If I am correct, unless I return her to the dungeon, she willna remain."

She didn't deny it.

"Indeed." Cailin agreed, "'tis a fool who tries to stop her. Truth be told, without her, we would not have achieved this much."

A blush burned her cheeks.

The earl gave her a tender smile as they started up the turret. "Sir Angus was so proud of you."

Her lips trembled. "I–I loved him so much."

The earl glanced at Cailin, shook his head. "You look so much like your father. If I hadna been informed 'twas you in the cell, when I saw you, I would have known."

At the third floor, Lord Odhran paused at the first chamber, turned to Elspet. "This is where you stayed when you and your stepfather last visited. I thought perhaps being here would ease your loss."

"'Tis thoughtful of you."

"'Tis the least I can do. 'Twill be several hours before we sup. A warm bath has been readied for you, then you can rest until we eat."

"I thank you." She gave a long look to Cailin, then slipped inside.

Once she'd closed the door, the earl continued down the corridor, strategically placed torches illuminating paintings of a lord from his ancestry. "A warm bath awaits you as well." He paused. "I didna want to upset her, but when I heard of my steward's perfidy, I had the traitor flogged. Nor will your uncle's runner be allowed to depart until my master-at-arms receives word that Tiran Castle is in your control."

"I thank you for all you have done."

"Your father helped me on many occasions, 'tis an honor to aid his son." He halted before a chamber several paces from Elspet's. "Rest now. We will speak further about the best way to seize Tiran Castle after we sup."

* * * *

Hours later, with supper behind her, an exhausted Elspet sank onto her bed, tugged up the covers.

A soft tap sounded at her door

Lids heavy with sleep and lured by the softness of the feather mattress, with a groan she glanced toward the entry.

Another knock sounded, this time louder.

As the castle lay silent, with no gongs from church bells warning of an attack, they were safe, so who could it be?

"Elspet, let me in," Cailin whispered.

At the urgency in his voice, she shoved from the bed, hurried across the chamber, and tugged opened the door.

Her heart thumped. Bathed with torchlight, his rugged good looks and muscled body stole her breath. Loving him, 'twould always be so. "Is something wrong?"

"We need to talk."

Chapter 17

At the look on Cailin's face, Elspet stepped back into the chamber. Once he'd entered, he closed the door. "What did you need to talk about?"

"This." Cailin drew her body flush against his and claimed her mouth. Instead of the previous heated demand, he took his time, skimming his tongue across her lips in slow torture, teasing until her body ached for him.

Moaning, wanting only to stay in his arms, she forced herself to tear her mouth from his and stepped back. "We canna make love here."

"I think," he said as he swept her into his arms and strode toward the bed, "'tis the perfect place."

His erotic kiss smothered any reply. Lost in his touch, her mind hazed. At what moment he'd discarded her garb as well as his, she wasn't sure, but with his hard length pressed intimately against her, she welcomed him into her heat.

With each stroke, her heart ached at the beauty of his touch, of how he took his time, as if this entire moment was for her.

Was that why he was here? Was this his way of convincing her to marry him? The rush of her dreams of love collided with reality.

Cailin's pace increased, and he drove deep.

Waves of sensation flooded her, stealing every thought as he filled her over and again. As she cried out her release, he found his own.

Breath coming fast, he collapsed on top of her.

Elspet savored the feel of his nakedness, the subsequent ripples of pleasure, until 'twas as if every part of her was humming with pleasure. She should feel elated, pleased. Though she might never have his love, they would be together.

"I know why you are here—to convince me to wed you because I might carry your child, an heir to Dalkirk." At the smile in his eyes, irritation filled her that when she should be overjoyed to have such a man in her life, a part of her felt empty. "I see little humorous about this situation."

"Elspet, I—"

She pushed against his muscled chest; he didn't move. "Let me go."

"Never." Eyes dark with intention, he rolled to his side and lifted her chin until their eyes met. "Elspet, what I have to tell you is that I need you and want you in my life. Not because you may carry my child, though that would have been a discussion we would have had…if I had not fallen in love with you."

"Merciful saints, I willna be…" She stared at him as his words sifted through her mind, igniting hope in her soul. Though she'd wished, prayed for Cailin's love, to hear the words, the immense feeling within them, she struggled to breathe. "Y–you love me?"

"Aye." He caressed her cheek. "Never did I expect to find a woman who I couldna live without before I met you. I was a fool to nae realize what I felt for you before, and I am never going to let you go." He released her and knelt on the bed. As she sat up, he clasped her hand. "Marry me, Elspet. I love you and want to spend the rest of my life with you."

Joy exploded inside as she threw herself into his arms. "Aye!"

* * * *

Several days later, at the camp outside Tiran Castle, Elspet glanced at Cailin as he stood before his destrier. Desire swept through her as she recalled how they'd made love at Syridan Castle. Most of all, of the memories of how he'd confessed his love, and asked for her hand in marriage.

Happiness surged through her at thoughts of being his wife, of the children they would have. Aye, he would have to return to fight for King Robert. With most of Scotland beneath the rightful sovereign's rule, she prayed that Cailin would be away a brief time.

Cailin drew her to him, gave her a deep kiss, then swung up on his destrier. "I will return shortly." He cantered to where the Earl of Odhran and Rónán awaited him at the edge of the forest.

From the shelter of the thick pine boughs, Elspet watched as Cailin, carrying a white flag of truce, rode with the other men toward the stronghold.

Taog stepped next to her, rested his hand on the hilt of his sword. "Dinna worry. The fortress is surrounded. Even if the earl tried to attack us, his forces are greatly outnumbered. I have little doubt the earl will be forced to surrender."

"I pray so, but we dinna know how long his uncle will hold out."

He grunted. "Once he learns that nay reinforcements will be coming, with his supplies running low, he will last naught more than a fortnight before he cedes."

"You are right." She gave a slow breath. "I wish 'twas all over."

"As I, but the time will come."

The distant figures disappeared down the incline, then appeared as they rode the incline toward the castle. "Cailin's decision to wait out his uncle to spare loss of life on both sides and avoid rebuilding the stronghold is wise."

"'Tis."

"Taog," a man a distance behind them called.

The Romani leader turned. "'Tis my smithy. Wait here. I will be but a moment."

"'Tis unnecessary," Elspet said. "I promised to help the healer replenish her stock of herbs."

He nodded. "Take care, lass."

Moved by his friendship, with sunlight warm upon her face, Elspet said a prayer for Cailin's safety, then headed toward the healer's tent.

* * * *

Cailin glared up at his uncle standing on the wall walk of Tiran Castle, then reined his horse toward where his combined forces lay across the field. Rónán and the Earl of Odhran fell in beside him, his uncle's laughter in his wake.

Once out of arrow range, Cailin slowed his mount. "The selfish bastard. He doesna care for those who will suffer if he refuses to surrender."

"A trait common in men like him," Odhran called out. "To them, all that matters is that in the end they hold the power."

"With you at my side, how could my uncle dismiss my claim that none of the other nobles will send him reinforcements? Blast it, there is something I am missing."

A frown worked across Rónán's brow as he glanced up. "Such as?"

"I am unsure, 'tis a feeling I canna shake off." After years as a warrior, it was an intuition he refused to dismiss. Too many times in the past, such instincts had saved his life.

Taog stood at the edge of the trees as Cailin and the others guided their horses close, drew to a halt, then dismounted.

The Romani leader folded his arms across his chest. "What did Dalkirk say?"

"He refuses to surrender," Cailin said.

"Which doesna make sense." Jaw tight, Taog glanced toward the stronghold. "He is surrounded, has lost a significant number of knights, and the secret tunnels are guarded to ensure that no one escapes."

"Aye," Cailin agreed, "and they have naught more than a fortnight of supplies at best."

The Earl of Odhran approached. "As our combined forces overwhelm theirs. We can attack."

"Nay," Cailin said. "Though we would have the upper hand, the lives of people innocent of my uncle's treachery are at risk. In the end, once Gaufrid cedes, naught will be lost but days." He looked around, frowned. "Where is Elspet?"

The Romani leader gestured toward the healer's tent. "She is helping her restock herbs and—"

The flap pushed aside, and Elspet glanced out. Her shoulders sagged with relief, then a smile curved her lips. She turned back toward the healer a moment, then hurried toward Cailin.

Taog chuckled. "She has been watching for you."

Snowflakes tossed within the breeze swirled around her as she halted a pace away. Emerald eyes studied his, and the warmth within faded. "Your uncle refused your offer."

"Aye, what we are discussing. Considering his lack of options, a decision that doesna make sense." Cailin rubbed the back of his neck, the prickling of unease growing. "Until he surrenders, I want extra scouts posted around the castle."

The Earl of Odhran nodded. "'Twill be done."

* * * *

The snap of flames and hushed voices filled the cool night air as Cailin settled beside Elspet. Worry filled her at the deep lines of exhaustion on his face. After everyone had taken care of their duties and retired, he'd checked that all points of the encampment were secure.

She filled a large bowl with stew and held it out to him. "You must be needing this."

Tired eyes grew tender. "I think I must be needing this more." He leaned in, gently cupping her face. Cailin captured her mouth in a heated kiss that had desire storming her.

With a soft moan, he drew her against him. "If I dinna stop, I will be taking you here."

Pulse racing, she smiled. "If you dinna stop, I could lose hold of the bowl and you will be wearing the stew."

He chuckled. "There is that." After one more kiss, he leaned back, accepted the fare and took a bit. "'Tis wonderful."

She arched a brow as he gulped down the food. "As hungry as you are, I could have given you a bit of leather and you wouldna have noticed."

With a wink, Cailin downed the last of the stew, the easy gesture stealing her heart. With him, it would always be so. A simple touch, a look would make her want him and be thankful they'd share a life together.

Warmth filled her of thoughts of the day they would say their vows, and of the nights to come. His love was more that she could have ever wished.

Three heavily armed guards strode past, the wavering torchlight rippling across the weapons carried at their sides.

A chill crept through her and she rubbed her arms. "I pray your uncle yields soon."

"As I," he said, his voice grim, "but as I rode away from the castle today, he laughed. Not the action of a man who believes himself doomed."

Her fingers shook at this disclosure, and the ladle she'd lifted clattered into the bubbling stew. "You believe he will attack?"

"However inconceivable, 'tis the only thing that makes sense." He finished a second bowl, then set it aside. "Which is why, before I came here, I walked the circle of troops to see all was secure and doubled the guard around the main camp."

"But he is greatly outnumbered. With the castle and secret tunnel exits guarded, even if he tried to ride from Tiran Castle, he and his men would quickly be seen."

"Reasons why he should have already surrendered. That he didna tells me that he doesna plan to."

"So, what do we do now?" she asked, strain threading through her voice.

"We remain on alert." He wiped his hands and tossed the cloth aside. "We know Gaufrid hasna received any additional support. Whatever his plan, 'twill happen soon."

The thought of them waiting for his uncle to strike left her on edge. Nor would worrying about the upcoming days change anything. She waved Cailin away. "You are tired. Go rest."

"Only if," he said, drawing her against him, "you accompany—"

"Dalkirk's men are attacking from the south!" a man shouted from across the field, where Odhran and Taog's guards were stationed.

Curses and the scrape of steel filled the air as men scrambled from their tents and grabbed their swords.

In the flicker of the fire, fury slashed Cailin's face. "Bloody hell, we had every castle exit guarded. The bastard must have another tunnel no one knew of!" He glanced at the Romani leader rushing toward him. "Taog, take twenty men and back up your guard. With the pitiful amount of men my uncle has, that should be enough to hold them. I will check the remainder of the camp's defenses."

The Romani leader nodded, headed out with his men.

Cailin gave Elspet a hard kiss, stepped back, and withdrew his sword. "Stay here and keep your weapon ready. This should be over soon."

Pulse racing, she nodded as Rónán and Odhran ran over.

"Lord Odhran," Cailin said as he withdrew his broadsword, "select four guards and—"

A scream near the forest had Elspet unsheathing her sword. Illuminated in the wash of torchlight, several men bearing Dalkirk's colors stormed the camp from the east. On the opposite side of the main camp, a small contingent charged from the north.

"Get them!" Cailin roared.

Blades clashed and screams filled the air.

Breath coming fast, Elspet clutched her sword, moved closer to Cailin. Horrified, she watched as Dalkirk's men were cut down with brutal efficiency, their screams of pain wrenching her heart. Damn the earl that he could cast away the lives of those who served him without care.

"Behind you, Cailin!" Rónán shouted.

Cailin whirled as two knights rushed him. In an incredible display of skill, he blocked the first swing and drove his dagger into that assailant, before driving his sword into the other man.

Stunned disbelief fell over the warriors' faces as they crumpled to the bloodstained snow.

Movement from behind Cailin caught her attention. She glanced over. Dalkirk's warriors were creeping toward Cailin. "Cailin, three men are behind you!"

He whirled as the first man charged. Cailin slashed his blade across the assailant's throat; the attacker collapsed.

Screaming Lord Dalkirk's name, the last two men charged.

Cailin swung hard, deflecting the first aggressor's strike, then rammed his blade against the other man. The second knight stumbled back as the first man again charged.

From the corner of her eye, Elspet caught sight of a new assailant behind the others, his knife raised, aimed straight toward Cailin, threw; the dagger sliced through the night toward Cailin's heart.

Merciful saints! As Cailin's sword shoved deep into the second attacker, he didn't see the threat, nor was there time to warn him.

Terrified for his life, refusing to allow the man she loved to die, she shoved Cailin out of the way. Hot, burning pain sliced through her side and her world faded away.

Chapter 18

Cailin knelt beside Elspet as she lay near one of the fires at the Romani camp. Eyes closed, sweat beaded her brow and her face was deathly pale. Opposite him, the healer secured a new bandage over the dagger thrust she'd taken in her abdomen the night before.

His gut wrenched at memories of their struggle to stop the bleeding. In the end, they'd cauterized the wound. Thankfully, Elspet had fainted, only to develop a fever hours later.

God's teeth, he couldna lose her. He lifted his eyes to the heavens, where a soft tinge of purple smeared the sky. *Please God, let her live. She is my life.*

The healer secured the last knot and sat back, her face haggard. "She has lost much blood, and the fever has me worried. God help her if the wound begins to fester."

Cailin strangled on the words lodged in his throat, too aware that she barely clung to life but needing a wisp of hope. "Do you think she will live?"

Eyes dark with anguish were lifted to his. The woman sighed. "I am unsure."

Like a wounded animal, a deep cry built within against the soul-tearing fear. Breath trembling, Cailin brushed his thumb against her pale cheek. "I love you, Elspet, come back to me."

Instead, she lay still, a large bruise peeking from the bandage at her side.

A hand settled on Cailin's shoulder. He glanced up.

Rónán's somber gaze held his. "You have been with Elspet all night. Go and rest; I will sit with her. If there is any change, I will wake you."

As if a dam collapsed, the frustration and rage boiling within him was unleashed. Cailin shoved to his feet. "Wake me? As if I give a damn if I am tired when Elspeth may…" He stalked off, whirled and stormed back.

"God's teeth, if I had attacked Tiran Castle yesterday, as Lord Odhran suggested, she wouldna have taken a dagger meant for me!"

"Blast it," Rónán snarled. "You thought to spare those within the stronghold innocent of your uncle's treachery, a noble decision."

"A fact that, in the end, with the number of his guard we killed, matters little." Cailin looked toward the ravine, where Taog's men had moved the deceased knights from last night's assault, the ground too frozen to give them a proper burial. "They all died in an effort to get to me."

"A command given by Lord Dalkirk."

He grunted. "Now I understand why my uncle laughed as I departed. He had built a secret tunnel to set up an attack that nay one, including Father Lamond, knew of."

"And he failed," Taog said as he stalked over.

Anger built in Cailin's chest as he gazed upon Elspet. She hadn't roused for hours and looked lifeless on her pallet. "If she dies," he rasped, "my uncle will have won. Naught matters without her."

Expression hard, the Earl of Odhran stepped up beside the Romani leader. "We can attack Tiran Castle now. Though we followed their tracks and found the secret tunnel caved in to forbid us entry, nor is it critical. After the loss of Dalkirk's troops last night, his ranks are decimated and the stronghold can be taken with ease."

Taog and Rónán nodded.

Cailin dragged his gaze away from Elspet. "And if we do, because of Gaufrid's greed, more people will die."

"Then we must wait until their supplies run out," Rónán said.

Blood pounding hot, Cailin struggled against the rage pouring through him, fury so vile that 'twas as if it blackened his soul. He damned his uncle, whose greed had driven him to kill Cailin's mother and father. But destroying the lives of his brother and sister-in-law wasn't enough. He'd arranged for his only nephew who held the title of Earl of Dalkirk, to die.

Gaufrid had ruled with a brutal hand, spreading fear among those within his control, torturing and murdering any he considered a threat, including Elspet's mother and stepfather. Under his hand, no one was safe.

A tremor whipped through Cailin as he lowered his gaze to Elspet, her face fragile, like if he reached out and touched her, she'd break.

He closed his eyes against the burst of pain, then slowly opened them. She'd suffered so much, lost so much—her home and family. When most women would have given in, she'd stood her ground and sought revenge. God's blade, what an incredible lass. Such bravado. To dare confront a Knight Templar. Confront? No, steal from him to save a stepbrother she loved.

A man who, in the end, had betrayed her.

By God, she, as others, had suffered enough!

Jaw tight, he met Rónán's gaze, shifted to Taog, then to Odhran. "From this day," he stated, "nay more will die beneath my uncle's deceitful hand save one—him." With a last tender look toward Elspet, Cailin stormed to his warhorse.

Rónán caught up with him. "What in God's name are you going to do?"

He jerked the reins of his horse free. "I intend to issue an honor challenge to my uncle."

The Templar stepped in front of him. "'Tis a challenge used for tournaments, nay battle."

"I know what 'tis for." Cailin started to walk around him.

Rónán caught his arm. "God in heaven, your uncle isna a man of honor!"

"A fact I well know, but my decision is made." He glared at the fingers upon his forearm. "Release me."

"Cailin—"

"Of anyone," he growled, aware of his friend's own tumultuous youth, "you understand why I must go."

Pain flashed in his friend's face, and Rónán released him.

Cailin checked his mount's saddle. "If for some reason I dinna return and Elspet lives, take care of her. If I fail, ensure my uncle receives his due."

"I will," Rónán rasped. "That I swear. God go with you."

The many things that could go wrong when he arrived at Tiran Castle flooded Cailin's mind. Not giving a damn, he swung up on his horse.

The thrum of hooves shattered the silence as he cantered across the snow-smeared expanse. A short distance from the gatehouse, he halted his destrier. Clouds smothered the sun as he glared up at where his uncle stood, Elspet's stepbrother, Blar at his side. "Your pathetic plan to kill me failed," Cailin called up, finding a small bit of satisfaction as his uncle's face darkened with outrage that he still lived.

"Come inside and we will talk." The earl nodded toward a guard. "Sir Donnach, call to open the gate."

The knight turned toward the bailey. "Raise the gate!"

Chains rattled, then the scrape of wood and steel.

Cailin didn't move.

"Enter!" his uncle demanded.

Did Gaufrid believe him a fool? If he rode into the stronghold, he would be killed. "The fight isna between those within the castle," Cailin shouted so everyone along the wall walk and within the bailey could hear. "Just us. I challenge you to an honor challenge of single combat to the death, with the weapon of your choice!"

"Challenge me?" his uncle scoffed. "To a foolish tournament game for a title *I* already *possess*? Enter, before I order my guard to kill you."

Blar smirked.

The bastard, he'd... Cailin's gaze settled on the knight near his uncle, the one he'd called Donnach. Though years had passed, he recognized the strong cut of his jaw, the lean frame now crowded with muscle, and the black hair of his childhood friend.

Cailin met the warrior's hard stare, prayed their youthful bond still held firm.

He slanted his gaze to his uncle. "I offered my challenge." He kicked his steed to walk parallel to the castle wall where the guards standing above watched. "But," he shouted, "are you a man of honor?"

Gaufrid's face grew redder. "I gave you an order!"

"A command," Cailin called out, meeting the gazes of those above who watched, "from a man who killed my father and mother, his brother and his sister-in-law, a man who paid to have me murdered at sea as a lad." He turned his horse, rode back along the castle. "Enough people have died for something that is between us. Through this last confrontation, I seek by honor to reclaim my birthright. A challenge, as I am the rightful heir, that is mine to demand!"

Murmurs filtered through the castle, and his uncle slashed his hand in the air. "You had your chance." He nodded to Sir Donnach. "Kill him!"

At his uncle's order, Cailin's heart slammed against his chest.

The knight didn't move.

"You bloody traitor!" Blar withdrew his dagger, lunged for Sir Donnach.

In a violent slash, the warrior drove his broadsword into Blar's chest, jerked the blade free.

Shock melded with pain on Blar's face as he stumbled back, collapsed.

Bloody sword in hand, Sir Donnach's gaze narrowed on Lord Dalkirk; then he pivoted to address his fellow guards. "Sir Cailin has made a just challenge, one I support."

Murmurs of assent rumbled from the wall walk, and Cailin blew out a relieved breath.

His uncle motioned to the knights near Sir Donnach. "Seize him!"

No one moved.

Gaufrid stared around in disbelief.

Satisfaction filled Cailin the moment his uncle realized that if he refused to fight, he'd lost any hope to reclaim his people's loyalty.

Jaw tight, the earl withdrew his blade, glared at those around him, before meeting Cailin's gaze. "I accept your challenge, one you will regret!"

That Cailin doubted. He glanced back toward the main camp, noted that Rónán and the others had ridden beyond the line of trees in a show of force.

Gaufrid stormed toward the turret. Moments later, the thud of hooves sounded, then the clatter of wood as his uncle rode over the drawbridge.

Several riders followed, including Sir Donnach.

Paces away, the noble dismounted, then unsheathed his weapon, his gaunt face weathered by age, his stocky frame sporting layers of fat absent in his youth. One of the guards led his horse away.

Cailin dismounted, unsheathed his blade as he kept his eye on his uncle, his skill with a broadsword well known, nor would he trust Gaufrid to fight fair. As with the ruthless decisions of his past, the scoundrel would use any means, however deceitful, to win.

Ready to end his uncle's tyranny, to avenge his parents' deaths, his grip firm on his sword, Cailin slowly began to step sideways in a circle.

His uncle mimicked his action, keeping his weapon ready. The noble feigned to the right, then thrust.

Cailin's blade blocked his strike. With a snarl, he shoved him back, swung.

The cacophony of steel crashing filled the air as each attacked over and again. A long while later, sweat streaming down his uncle's face, Gaufrid ducked, slashed his blade in a small arc.

Cloth fluttered in the wind as a thick line of red lay across Cailin's arm. Blast it! He stepped away, avoided his uncle's next strike.

Growling, the earl rounded on Cailin. "I should have killed you myself!" Gaufrid attacked with punishing blows.

Honed steel scraped with a violent hiss as Cailin met each assault, delivered his own, damned the pain screaming in his leg from his earlier injury. An image of Elspet's pale face swam to his mind. He gritted his teeth and swung hard.

His uncle stumbled back.

As Cailin moved forward, the earl regained his balance, rounded his sword in a vicious swing toward Cailin's legs.

He jumped. Forged iron slid a hand's width beneath his boots. Before he could gain his feet, his uncle slammed against him, his foot jamming into his injured leg. Pain screamed through him as he fell to the ground, his uncle's body landing hard on top of him, trapping his sword arm.

Nay! Cailin kneed his uncle in the gut, rolled and pinned Gaufrid. In a move honed by his years of fighting with the Templars, he withdrew his blade and pressed a dagger to Gaufrid's throat.

Eyes frantic with fear widened. "Spare me!"

Fury pouring through him, Cailin ached to shove harder until every last drop of blood was emptied from his worthless carcass. "However much I want to kill you, shame is a fitting penance." He hauled him to his feet, shoved.

Gasping for breath, his uncle stumbled back.

"From this moment on," Cailin roared, "as Earl of Dalkirk, I banish you from my lands, and all will know your shame!"

Desperation darkened his uncle's gaze. "I have naught."

"You have your life." Cailin sheathed his sword. "Which is more than I should allow after you killed my parents."

Hand trembling, his uncle reached for his broadsword on the ground.

Cailin stepped on his weapon. "Keep your dagger, nay more. Go!" Gritting his teeth against the pain in his leg, he picked up the broadsword, then strode past Gaufrid, ignoring his eyes dark with hate. 'Twas done. Now to check on Elspet, then he would—

"Cailin, behind you!" Sir Donnach called.

Cailin whirled as he withdrew his blade.

Dagger clutched between his fingers, a merciless smile creasing his face, Gaufrid angled his hand as he started to throw.

Before the blade could leave his uncle's hand, Sir Donnach's dagger whipped past Cailin, sank deep in the earl's chest. Blood trickled down his garb as he gripped his chest and collapsed.

Silence fell upon those on the wall walk.

"The earl is dead," a man shouted from above.

"The true Earl of Dalkirk lives!" Sir Donnach walked over to Cailin, bowed in deference, then stood. "Long live the earl!"

Cheers rose from the castle, and the church bell began to ring.

Cailin stared at his uncle, a man whose entire life was devoted to power, to evil. "'Tis over." He nodded to one of the guards. "Take him away."

"Aye, my lord." The guard hurried toward Gaufrid's body.

Cailin met Donnach's gaze. "I thank you."

"'Tis unnecessary," the knight said. "You won the challenge."

"You saved my life, an act I willna forget."

A wry smile touched Sir Donnach's mouth. "As I remember, you rescued me when I almost drowned in our youth. We are even." He knelt. "I swear my fealty to you, my lord."

The other knights dismounted and followed suit.

* * * *

Streaks of dawn broke through the sky before Elspet was settled in his chamber at Tiran Castle. At her moan, Cailin strode over and sat beside the bed, his combat with his uncle but a memory. "I am here."

A frown wedged upon her sweat-laden brow, then smoothed as she continued to sleep.

"Elspet," he rasped, the hours of watching her, praying for her fever to break strangling his every thought.

The thick, deep gray blanket seemed to swallow her as she remained still, the dark hues of the weave at odds against her pallor.

Panic rising, he glanced at the healer, wanting to scream his frustration, understanding too well that caught in the throes of fever, her life could be lost in a trice.

Aged eyes dark with concern held his. "You havena left her side all night. The bed in the next chamber awaits you. Try to rest, my lord. If she awakens, I will alert you."

My lord. A title he'd yet to become used to. And with Elspet's life in the balance, the legacy he'd fought for meant little. At this moment, he'd give up everything for her life.

He shook his head. "I canna sleep."

A soft rap sounded on the door.

He glanced up. "Enter."

Rónán stepped inside, followed by Lord Odhran and Taog.

"How is she?" the Templar asked.

"Still asleep."

His friends halted near the bed. "Has she woken at all?"

"Nay," he rasped.

"I willna ask if you have tried to sleep," Rónán said. "You look like Hades."

Cailin rubbed the back of his neck, gave a rough exhale. "I closed my eyes a time or two, but all I see is her taking the dagger meant for me. If only I had attacked the castle earlier, she would be—"

"'Tis done," Taog snapped. "You made the decision you believed best at the time, a choice I supported."

"As I." Lord Odhran stepped forward. "Your people await you. They have heard naught but lies fed to them by your uncle and need to know you are a man they can trust, one who will treat them fairly, a leader they can turn to."

His people.

He glanced at Elspet. Face pale, her breath came in the slow, steady rhythm of sleep.

Aye, 'twas his castle, the people within his responsibility. After all that was sacrificed, never would he fail them. As well, familiarizing himself with his stronghold, getting to know residents, making a list of things that needed to be done would keep his mind busy.

Cailin turned to the healer. "After I meet with my people, I will be going through the castle ledgers with the steward. If Elspet wakens, send for me."

She nodded. "Aye, my lord."

* * * *

Late afternoon sunlight spilled through the crenellations, leaving shadows like jagged teeth as Cailin forced his legs to move as he crossed the wall walk. The day's events had aggravated his injury and every step was painful.

Rónán opened the door to the turret leading to the dungeon. "You are all but stumbling on your feet. Go, sleep. I will check the dungeon and report to you later."

Caught in the golden rays of sunset, the entry blurred before him. Gritting his teeth, Cailin entered, started up the steps, using the wall for support. "After I am done, I will check on Elspet, then try to rest."

"With the way you are weaving on your feet, I may have to carry you back."

Cailin grunted, shoved up another carved stone step.

"Bloody stubborn."

"Nay, irritated that I havena been here earlier." Torchlight wavered upon the dank, curved walls as he went. "After I spoke with the people of Tiran Castle, I visited Sir Petrus. God's blade, after the beating he took, 'tis a miracle he still lives." He shook his head. "Gaufrid died too quickly, but at least he is dead. To think, I was going to do naught but banish him. I was a fool."

"You are an honorable man. However horrific your uncle's actions, you didna want family blood on your hands. When most would have slain him without question, you offered mercy."

"Which the bastard discarded." Cailin jerked open the dungeon door. The stench hit him first. Their progress tangled with the moans of men as the scrape of sodden wood reverberated within the dank, cold chambers. "God in heaven, to allow anyone to live in such filth. Rónán, fetch the steward. Tell him to bring me a list of every man within and the charges against them immediately."

"Aye." Face grim, his friend hurried out the entry, pulling the door behind him.

Bile rose in his throat as he slowly walked the length of the dungeon, noting the fear in the men's eyes, those who dared to look at him. He shuddered to think what they had endured beneath his uncle's cruelty.

Near the end of the walkway, chained in a cell, an elderly man stood stooped, leaning against the wall.

He remembered briefly seeing the man when they'd slipped in to rescue Sir Petrus. Regardless of his fate, though dressed in rags, his frame thin and his face streaked with bruises, he held himself with pride.

Familiarity crept up Cailin's spine. He stilled. God's blade, he knew him. He struggled to remember the names of men he'd known as a child. The few that came to mind he dismissed as they'd be the wrong age.

Legs trembling, Cailin braced his feet and held the man's gaze, furious that even an elder wasn't spared his uncle's torture.

The old man coughed, a deep, rattling sound. Eyes bright with intelligence narrowed.

"Gaufrid is dead," Cailin said, finding it important that the man should know. "I have come to free you."

"A bloody lie." With a snarl, the prisoner glared at the door. "Gaufrid is out there, 'tis yet another of the bastard's tricks."

The rough, familiar voice had Cailin's pulse racing. "Who are you?"

Nostrils flared with fury. "As if you dinna bloody know. What is Gaufrid's plan this time?" he snarled. "Nay doubt he has invented another punishment to appease his warped mind."

"Your name," Cailin demanded, chilled by the sense of urgency.

His gray hair and beard hanging in oily strands, he drew himself to his full height. "The rightful Earl of Dalkirk!"

Chapter 19

Cailin's knees almost buckled as he stared at the man behind the forged bars, chained to the wall like an animal. A man he'd loved, a man due to his uncle's treachery he'd believed dead. "Father!" he cried.

The elder's face wrinkled with suspicion, then he moved as far forward toward the door as his chains would allow. His mouth parted, and tears began to roll down his face. "S–son, can it really be you?"

"Aye." He struggled to breathe, expecting any minute to awaken and find 'twas all a dream. Ever since his youth, he'd believed him dead. But here, now, he'd been blessed with the most precious gift. "Gaufrid told me you were dead."

His father wiped the tears from his eyes. "My brother told me you had died at sea. 'Twould seem," he spat, "the bastard lied to us both."

Metal scraped as Cailin fumbled the key into the lock, turned it. Hands shaking, he jerked open the door and wrapped his arms around his father, and for the first time since he'd been told of his father's death years before, he cried.

When his body stilled, Cailin freed him from his chains and stepped back, taking in his gaunt frame, the ragged, filthy garb, the worn holes in his cracked boots. "How long have you been here?"

"Since the day your mother and I and Gaufrid went hunting when you were a lad."

"Is she alive?" he asked, praying for another miracle.

The joy in father's eyes faded. "She is dead. While I was out of sight during the hunt, Gaufrid killed her. A fact I didna learn until I woke up in the dungeon. 'Twas then that my brother revealed how he had crept up and hit me while I held her lifeless body." His mouth curled into a snarl.

"Over the years, my brother found perverse pleasure in keeping me alive, trying to break me."

After the reports of his uncle's twisted ways, something Cailin could believe.

"For several years, he kept me in a secret location," he continued. "At times he would beat me, leave me without food or water for days. I will never forget when he strode in, declaring that he had paid to see you murdered. I..." A tremor shook his thin body. "I refused the bastard the satisfaction of knowing how I crumpled inside. A few years ago, after having installed younger guards in the dungeon who wouldna know me, and with them believing I was dead, Gaufrid brought me to this cell through the secret tunnel."

"I never knew," Cailin whispered, aching at the misery he'd endured, the ultimate betrayal.

He stilled, glared at the door. "Gaufrid?"

"Dead," Cailin growled. "Had I but known you were locked here, of how you had suffered over the years, I would have ensured the bastard died a slow and painful death."

His father's shoulders sagged as if a weight had been lifted. "When did he die?"

"Yesterday. After his men attacked my camp, trying to kill me, but almost killed Elspet instead..." Even as he yearned for hours with his father, Cailin looked away. He had to get back to her.

"Who?"

"The woman I love." He shook his head and shifted to relieve the weight on his injured leg. "Father, there is much I need to tell you, to explain, but not here. After a bath and a hot meal, you need to rest. We have plenty of time to talk. Years."

With care, he led his father to the lord's chamber, opened the door, pleased to discover all signs of his uncle had been cleared away as he'd requested earlier this day.

Instead of Gaufrid's rich silks and gaudy statues, a portrait of his father and mother graced the wall above the hearth. A cream handcrafted cover woven in a complex Celtic pattern lay atop the bed, and several wool blankets lay folded at the foot. To its right sat a table laden with a bowl of water, a flask of wine, bread, cheese, and sliced meats. In the far corner stood a tub filled with steaming water.

He'd intended to use this room with Elspet, but thanked God he could hand the chamber to the man to whom it belonged. "I will leave you until we sup."

After another embrace, he departed. Urgency had him hurrying down the corridor. He couldna discover his father was alive then lose Elspet. 'Twould be fate's cruelest joke to gift him with a long-lost parent while stealing the woman who'd won his heart.

Please God, let her live!

The potent scent of herbs filled the air as he stepped inside her chamber. Shimmers of golden light spilling from the hearth illuminated her pale face, exposing how her chest barely rose and fell with each breath. Heart in his throat, he glanced toward Rónán, who sat nearby. "Any change?"

Deep lines dug across his friend's brow. "None since you left."

He nodded. She hadna died. He'd find solace in that. "I just returned from the dungeon and..." His throat tightened with emotion.

Face taut with concern, his friend shoved to his feet. "What has happened?"

"'Tis my father; he is alive." Voice rough, Cailin explained the events of a short while before.

Rónán shook his head. "God's truth, 'tis an incredible blessing."

"'Tis." He swallowed hard. "Once he and Elspet awaken, I look forward to introducing them." Cailin glanced toward the bed. "Go and rest. I will stay beside her."

Rónán sighed. "I would argue that you need to find your own bed, but from your stubborn look, 'twill achieve naught."

"It willna."

"I shall be in my chamber if you need me." He departed.

The snap and crackle of the fire filled the silence as Cailin walked over to her side, the beads of sweat on her face shimmering in the firelight, as if mocking his fear. Cupping her hand, he knelt before her, made the sign of the cross, and began to pray.

* * * *

Heat seemed to engulf her, to fill her every breath, the inferno a dark companion to the pain lancing her side. Rousing from a groggy haze, Elspet shifted, trying to find a comfortable position, bumped against hewn muscle.

Confused, she forced her lids open. Struggling against the incessant throbbing throughout her body, she turned her head to find Cailin lying beside her, then frowned at the unfamiliar chamber. Where were they?

Memories rolled through her of the attack, of the terror at the assailant hurling his dagger toward Cailin, of how she'd jumped before him, then naught.

By the soreness in her side, 'twas where the knife had sunk in.

She scanned the chamber, noted the flag bearing the crest of Dalkirk hanging near the hearth. Several large chests lay stacked against one wall, no doubt Cailin's mail filling the largest, others holding garb and his belongings. Several bottles of wine stood upon a nearby table, a bowl of water lay near the bed, and to its side sat a basket filled with herbs.

Was this Cailin's room from his childhood? As if it mattered. Wherever they were, he was alive.

Love filled her as she skimmed her gaze over his muscled body, clad in naught but a shirt and trews. From his slow, deep breaths, he was asleep. Needing to touch him, she smoothed her hand over the rough stubble upon his face, a man she would love forever.

Blue eyes opened. Relief flickered in his gaze, then a tender smile curved his mouth. "Your fever has broken."

"I had a fever?"

"Ever since the attack two days past."

Her hand trembled as she lowered it to the comforter. "I have been asleep for two days?"

"Aye."

"Where are we?"

"Tiran Castle."

Her mind whirling, Elspet listened as he described the events since the attack, gasping at the last. "Your father is alive?"

Fury coiled in her gut as he explained how his uncle had killed Cailin's mother, allowing everyone to believe the earl had died in the hunting accident as well. But he'd imprisoned his brother and found twisted enjoyment in tormenting him since.

"I am glad the scoundrel is dead!"

"As I. Gaufrid can *never* hurt anyone again." Cailin skimmed his thumb along the curve of her jaw, the tension on his face easing. "I canna wait until you meet my father. He will love you."

"Will he?" Caught up in the mayhem of the past few weeks, until this moment she'd forgotten one simple fact. She shifted, ignoring the radiating pain, then took a steadying breath. "I am a simple lass without a family, much less a dowry."

"That willna matter to him."

"How can you be sure?" she whispered, her unease growing. "What if he disapproves? What if he—"

Cailin smothered her words with a tender kiss. A twinkle in his eyes, he cupped her face. "My mother was the daughter of a Viking blacksmith. They met when he was traveling."

Her mouth fell open. "'Tis incredible."

"As are you." Cailin rolled to his side. "However much I wish to stay and talk, to be with you in every way, for now you need to rest."

He started to move back, and she caught his arm. "Stay with me."

"I—"

"Please. I dinna want to be alone, at least for a while."

Love filled his eyes as he settled beside her and drew her into his arms. "I couldna think of being anywhere else. I love you, Elspet, and plan on spending the rest of my life with you."

* * * *

A fortnight later, in the solar, Cailin secured his sword and turned toward his father, thankful that in the passing days, his gaunt form had filled out and he now glowed with good health. Nor did he move with difficulty. Food and rest had allowed his body to heal.

The scent of fresh rushes filled the air and flames danced cheerfully in the hearth as Lord Dalkirk poured a cup of wine, then another. With a smile he passed the latter to Cailin. "A toast to your upcoming wedding!"

Cailin lifted his goblet, took a sip of the tangy brew. "There is one more thing I must share." Aware his next words might drive a wedge between them, he hesitated. Blast it, he should have broached the matter before.

At his somber tone, the earl lowered his cup.

Cailin's fingers tightened on the stem of the goblet. "My fealty is nay longer to Lord Comyn, but to King Robert."

His father's brow raised. "I met the Bruce years ago during a meeting with Bishop Wishart in regards to Scotland's fight for independence."

"You never told me. Nor did the king."

"You were a young lad. The day would come when I could explain, or so I believed." He swirled the ruby liquid in the crafted goblet before taking a sip. "As for the Bruce, I wasna surprised to learn he'd become Scotland's king. 'Twas his rightful place, the crown stolen from his grandfather through King Edward's interference years before."

"Then you arena angry that I have given the Bruce my fealty?"

A smile creased his father's face. "Nay. I assure you, 'tis one I pledge as well. I never respected Lord Comyn."

Cailin's relief faded against the hard knowledge that soon he would depart. "There is one more thing. I will be sending a writ to the king, explaining that you are alive and Tiran Castle is seized. Soon after, I expect a missive with his orders instructing me where I must go to support his fight to claim Scotland."

His father gave a solemn nod. "A battle I will join once I am in full health."

"Nay, your place is here. I ask that while I am away, you keep watch over Elspet."

Somber eyes held his. "'Twould be an honor. She is a fine lass, one who knows her own mind."

Warmth filled Cailin at how she and his father had liked each other from the start. During their mutual recovery, their frequent chess matches had turned into more of a challenge of wills. "She does."

A soft knock sounded on the door.

"Enter," Lord Dalkirk called.

Decked in his finest attire, his sword gleaming, Rónán stepped inside. "Father Lamond has arrived."

Eyes beaming with pride, his father set aside his goblet. "Let us be on our way, son. 'Tis time for you to wed."

Cailin met his father's gaze as he set aside his cup, then joined him as he headed for the door. Indeed, he couldna wait to make Elspet his wife. A lingering sadness filled him as he wished his mother could be there. Then he recalled that Elspet wore his mother's cross and realized in spirit she was. A tale that Cailin relayed to his father as they walked.

* * * *

"And do you, Sir Cailin MacHugh, take Elspet to be your lawfully wedded wife?" Father Lamond asked, his rich tones echoing throughout the chapel.

Love filled Cailin as he held Elspet's hands, amazed that, within a few weeks, his life had changed completely. Gone was the loneliness, of days filled with thoughts of naught but battle. However unconventional their meeting, in the end she'd stolen more than his sword but his heart. "I do."

"And do you, Elspet," the priest asked, "take Sir Cailin for your husband?"

Emerald-green eyes sparkled with happiness. "I do."

Father Lamond made the sign of the cross. "In the name of the Father, the Son, and the Holy Spirit, with your consent declared before God, you are now bound as husband and wife!"

The crowd cheered as Cailin drew her into his arms for a deep kiss. "I love you, Elspet."

"And I love you, Cailin, and will forever."

His heart full, he laced his fingers with hers as they turned to the crowd.

"May I present Sir Cailin and Elspet MacHugh!" Cailin's father boomed out.

Cheers again filled the holy chamber.

A short while later, with the celebration having moved to the great room, Rónán handed goblets of wine to Elspet, Cailin, Lord Dalkirk, Lord Odhran, and Taog as the aromas of roast boar, mutton, hart, and sweets sifted through the air. "A toast for a long and happy life!"

His friends lifted their cups and downed the spirit. Calls for Cailin to again kiss the bride rang out.

Laughter fading, the door of the keep opened. Snow whirled inside as a man bearing King Robert's colors entered.

Body tense, Cailin lowered his goblet. Only one reason came to mind for the runner's appearance. His sovereign was requesting his immediate presence.

His father frowned. "'Tis the king's man."

Any scrap of color on Elspet's face faded.

Cailin's chest squeezed tight. 'Twas to be their wedding night, the hours ahead filled with soft whispers, making love, and creating memories to cherish for a lifetime, not for thoughts of war.

As quickly, he smothered the feelings. He was a warrior, and 'twas the king's support that had allowed him to seize Tiran Castle, discover his father lived, and, more, meet and fall in love with Elspet. "Nay doubt he bears news that I am needed and must leave to rejoin the fight."

A guard led the messenger to the dais.

"He wouldna ask you to depart on the day of your wedding," Taog said.

Lord Odhran nodded his agreement.

"He will want me to return posthaste," Cailin said, resigned to his duty.

Rónán nodded. "I will go with you."

"Sir Cailin?" the runner asked.

"Aye." Cailin stepped forward and accepted the writ. As the others waited in silence, he broke open the king's seal, skimmed the parchment, stilled. "God in heaven!"

Elspet stepped closer. "What is wrong?"

In disbelief, he reread the missive, rolled it up, then met the runner's gaze. "I will draft a reply to the king on the morrow. For now, I invite you to partake in the wedding celebration."

"Aye, my lord." The messenger was handed a cup of wine as he stepped from the dais.

Face grim, his father moved to Cailin's side. "When do you go?"

"I dinna, at least for now. King Robert commands me to stay and ensure Dalkirk, as well as the surrounding lands, remain secure from those loyal to Lord Comyn."

"'Tis wonderful," Elspet said amid the group of happy murmurs, "but what will he do once he learns your father is alive?"

"A question I willna know until he replies to my writ. I will ask to stay here for another month to ensure my father is in full health." He glanced at Rónán. "As well, the Earl of Sionn has arrived at the Bruce's castle, and the king commands you to return posthaste."

Brows narrowed, Rónán's thumb slid across the stem of his goblet. "What is a powerful Irish lord doing in Scotland?"

Cailin shrugged. "King Robert didna say more. Do you know Lord Sionn?"

"Of him," the Templar replied. "He is revered as an intelligent and fierce warrior. One, 'twould seem, who supports our king, a boon indeed. Nor is tonight for discussing war, but to celebrate your wedding." He lifted his cup. "I wish you and Elspet every blessing!"

"Hear, hear!" Lord Dalkirk agreed.

Warmth filled Cailin as he claimed Elspet's mouth in a deep, slow kiss filled with promise, with the heat of the night to come. He drew away, stared into her eyes, wanting her with his every breath. "I think," he said as he swept her into his arms, never wanting to let her go, "'tis time we retire to our chamber."

Shouts and cheers of approval rang out as Cailin strode toward the turret.

* * * *

Through the window, a full moon shimmered in the clear sky as Elspet lay sated in his arms. Cailin nudged a strand of damp hair from her cheek, drew her into a deep kiss, savored her quick shudder, how she accepted him fully, gave, demanded until he lost himself in her.

Only after she found her release did he follow, then draw her against him. Her heartbeat pounded, matched hers, and a sense of completeness filled him. Aye, he'd truly come home.

Epilogue

Two months later

Laughter echoed from the solar, and warmth filled Elspet as she reached the entry. Cailin sat beside his father, a satisfied expression on his face. In the time since her marriage, she'd come to know Lord Dalkirk—Fergus, as he'd insisted she call him. Though she'd learned of his wife's simple roots, it still felt strange. Of all the gifts he'd bestowed upon her and Cailin for their wedding, none could be finer than his love and acceptance.

Cailin glanced over, and his eyes flickered with awareness.

Heat swept through her, and she wanted him. 'Twould always be thus. Both men stood as she stepped inside.

Fergus lifted a bottle. "Would you like a glass of wine, Elspet?"

Her heart squeezed as she walked over, took both of her husband's hands, thankful that in the past sennight they'd received a missive from the king instructing her husband to remain at Tiran Castle to help his father fend off any resistance from Lord Comyn. "I think," she said with a grin, reveling in this moment, one that would transform their lives, "'twould be a proper choice to celebrate the announcement that I am with child."

"A babe?" Cailin rasped.

A look of awe so intense filled his gaze that tears blurred her eyes. "Aye."

With a shout, he whirled her in his arms.

"Let your wife down," his father huffed. "You must treat her with care. The lass carries your heir."

Cailin winked at her. "Indeed, 'tis my duty to see to her *every* need," he whispered in her ear. "A duty that I will ensure begins now."

Heat inflamed her cheeks as he swept her from the room and strode toward their chamber. "Put me down. Your father will know where you are taking me."

Blue eyes twinkled with sensual delight as he pushed open their chamber door, then closed it behind them. He set her on her feet and began untying her gown. "I care not what my father thinks. 'Tis you that I love. Come to bed with me, Elspet. I need you now and forever."

Moved by the intensity of how she needed him, of how her life had changed, as his mouth caught hers and his hands began to work their magic, she gave into his touch. Though he needed her now and forever, she couldna imagine her life without him, one that would now include their child.

With love filling her heart, she slipped off her gown and pressed her naked body against his. He wanted her, loved her, 'twas simple as that. Aye, who was she to argue?

Preview

Eager for more adventures with
The Knights Templar?
Keep reading for a sneak peek at
FORBIDDEN REALM
the next in
The Forbidden Series
coming soon
from
Diana Cosby
and
Lyrical Press

Chapter 1

Scotland, March 1309

The late afternoon sun provided little warmth as a frigid blast of wind hurled past Sir Rónán O'Connor. He glanced toward Stephan MacQuistan, Earl of Dunsmore, a friend and a fellow Knight Templar, then nodded to the guard holding open the intricately carved arched door of St. Andrews Cathedral as they strode past.

The rich scents of frankincense and myrrh filled the air as he halted inside, then dusted off the thin layer of falling snow from his cape. However thankful to be out of the cold, unease rumbled through him at King Robert's request for his presence, more so that it involved the Earl of Sionn, a powerful Irish noble.

A soft groan sounded as the guard pulled the entry door shut, then the man glanced to the earl. "My Lord." Then he turned to Rónán. "Sir Rónán, King Robert is meeting with the Bishop of Dunblane. He bids you to wait in the solar until I bring word that he will receive you."

Rónán nodded.

The guard stepped back. "If you would follow me."

"'Tis unnecessary," Stephan said. "My wife is there. I will show him the way."

"I thank you, my lord." The steady thud of steps faded as the guard departed the massive entry and headed toward a nearby corridor.

Waning rays of golden sunlight streaming through an ornate arched window entwined with torchlight illuminating the grand interior. In awe, Rónán studied the massive columns lining each side of the cathedral. He glanced toward the nave, framed within the rows of highly polished pews leading to the chancel adorned with carvings of Christ and other well-crafted tributes honoring the Lord surrounding the grand altar.

"'Tis beautiful," he breathed, "and incredible craftsmanship. Nay doubt Templars were involved in the construction."

"Aye, 'twas my thought the first time I came here." Stephan headed in the opposite direction the guard had taken. "This way."

They passed a fresco mural of Christ. "With the significant number of clergy and nobles arriving for King Robert's first parliament," Rónán said, "I should have expected to find you here."

"I arrived two days ago with the Bishop of Dunblane. We are to listen to the Bruce's strategy for quelling the English and Lord Comyn's resistance, and to offer insight."

"With Lord Comyn believing he is the rightful claimant to the Scottish throne, 'tis a fight he will never abandon. Unlike King Edward II, who hasna the taste for power like his father."

"Indeed," Stephan agreed. "'Tis the blasted lords who have the young sovereign's ear who press him to continue the battle to conquer Scotland."

Rónán shot him a wry smile. "Nay doubt they are furious that King Philip of France has recognized the Bruce as the King of Scots."

A satisfied look settled on Stephan's face. "'Tis certain that news put a burr in their arse." He nodded respectfully to a monk garbed in a brown robe as he passed, then glanced at Rónán. "I didna expect to see you here. Did you travel with one of the representatives in support of King Robert?"

"Nay. 'Tis an unexpected trip. I was at Tiran Castle, attending Sir Cailin's wedding—"

"Wedding?"

"Aye." In brief Rónán explained having been sent to aid Cailin in reclaiming his birthright, Tiran Castle, and discovering Cailin's father hadn't been murdered in Cailin's youth as he'd been told by his treacherous uncle, but was alive and locked within the dungeon. Then Rónán told Stephan the unusual circumstance of how their friend had met and fallen in love with Elspet McReynolds.

Stephan shook his head in disbelief. "'Tis remarkable."

"Indeed. I was there, and I am still stunned by the extraordinary chain of events." Thoughts of their friend—also a Knight Templar—made Rónán smile, due to the happiness Cailin had found in his lovely and spirited bride. "'Twas after the wedding when the king's runner delivered a missive that the Bruce requested my presence in matters concerning the Earl of Sionn."

The faint murmur of voices echoed from down a corridor, and the scent of venison, onions, and herbs sifted through the air.

Rónán's stomach rumbled, a reminder he hadn't eaten since dawn. But that would have to wait until after he'd met with his sovereign.

His friend guided him down another hallway, this one smaller but as grand. From the ornately framed paintings, the discreet carvings straddling the walls, 'twas clearly the king's private area.

"Have you ever met the Earl of Sionn?" his friend asked.

"Nay, only heard that he is a man well respected by his warriors." During a time in his brutal youth he'd rather forget, a place filled with naught but pain and fear. Nor did he ever intend to return to Ireland, a promise he'd kept after his adventures had brought him to join the galloglass, where a year later, he'd met and given his vow to the Brotherhood in France. He'd sailed away with a Templar crew and never looked back.

Cold fury lanced his gut as he thought of the Knights Templar, who'd been betrayed by King Philip, of the false charges leveled upon an elite Christian force who'd displayed naught but the highest ideals and principles for nearly two centuries.

Yet, for all of the French king's conniving to replenish his coffers with Templar wealth, in the end he'd claimed naught but a pittance of their gold.

Warned in advance of King Philip's nefarious intent, Rónán, along with a sizable portion of the Brotherhood, had loaded most of the Templar treasures aboard their ships and sailed from La Rochelle before the arrests began. Five galleys and their crews had headed to Scotland, led by the fierce warrior at his side. The remainder of the fleet had traveled to Portugal.

Though a year and a half had passed since the arrests had begun, heartache still filled Rónán at the loss of men who were like brothers. Nor could he forget the brutality endured by those still imprisoned in France.

"During my last meeting with King Robert," Stephan said, drawing Rónán from his somber musings, "he mentioned that he is seeking support from Ireland."

"'Twould explain why Lord Sionn is here, but not the reason the Bruce would request my presence."

"Perhaps the king seeks a trusted Irish adviser."

Rónán shot his friend a skeptical look. "As I havena been in Ireland since my childhood, that I doubt."

"But with your Irish roots, along with our king's Templar ties, the motive makes sense."

Learning King Robert was of the Brotherhood over a year earlier had left Rónán stunned. Stephan's reasoning could indeed explain why the monarch had asked him here, a rationale Rónán prayed was wrong. The very thought of returning to the land of his youth chilled him.

"If Lord Sionn has joined the Bruce's cause," Rónán said, shoving aside the dreaded possibility, "Lord Comyn and the English will be irate."

His friend grunted. "There is that."

Paces ahead, torchlight illuminated a statue of Jesus and another of the Virgin Mary.

"I regret to have missed Sir Cailin's wedding," Stephan said.

Rónán smiled at memories of his friend's marital vows. "You would like Elspet. In addition to being beautiful, she is an intelligent and strong woman. A fine match for Cailin."

Humor twinkled in his friend's eyes. "Mayhap a union in which our king had a hand?"

"A thought I considered. Though Cailin protests that fact, he canna deny that King Robert sent him to meet with her father." In brief, Rónán explained.

Sadness edged Stephan's face as he passed below an arched, stained-glass window softly illuminated by the last rays of sunset. "I regret the lass had to endure such treachery by her liege lord and stepbrother. That justice has been served, and she and Cailin have found love, is what is important."

"Indeed."

Eyes softening with humor, his friend arched a brow. "Mayhap 'tis why the king has called you here, not to have you meet the Earl of Sionn but to announce the lass you are to wed."

At his friend's teasing, Rónán shook off the claw of dread sliding through him and forced himself to shrug. "With the Bruce preparing for his first parliament and nobles and clergy arriving in force, I hardly think he has time to ponder the future of an unwed knight."

"Mayhap." Stephan waggled his brows. "But the earl has a beautiful daughter, one who accompanied him to St. Andrews."

Far from worried, a smile touched Rónán's mouth. "A woman who I will never meet, nor will she play a part in my life."

"Given the dangerous situation created by those seeking to dethrone King Robert, that her father allowed her to travel with him is surprising." Stephan shot him a wry look. "Unless her presence here, like yours, was requested by the Bruce."

"I am without a title, a rank her station demands when she weds. Nor does this conversation hold any relevance. 'Twas only the Earl of Sionn who was mentioned in the Bruce's writ." He held up his hand as Stephan started to speak, missing their verbal spars over the years, appreciating that regardless whether his friend had reclaimed his father's title, their strong bond of friendship hadn't changed. "As for a reason she accompanied her father, I remember another stubborn lass who confronted our king in her efforts to accompany our force as we sailed to seize her home."

Stephan turned a corner, the waning sheen of colored light sifting through the crafted glass window lending a demure cast over the corridor. "'Twas a difference circumstance."

"Indeed, but unlike you, I willna marry the lass, much less meet her," Rónán said, amused at his friend's attempt to make him worry about Lord Sionn's daughter. "Speaking of beautiful women, when I first saw you in the stable, you mentioned that Lady Katherine is here. Nor have I congratulated you on the birth of your son."

Pure joy swept Stephan's face. "I thank you. Three years ago, I never could have imagined myself married with a child; now I canna imagine myself without them. And King Robert has agreed to be Colbán's godfather."

"Wonderful," Rónán said, surprised by the tug of envy. Why? He'd never pondered thoughts of marrying, much less of having a family. That his friend had found both was a blessing, but not a life for him.

With Scotland far from united, the years ahead would be dedicated to fighting beneath King Robert's standard. Though Rónán had somehow managed to retain a sense of humor and an appreciation for friendship, 'twas a foil against the bitterness in his heart, one forged by his brutal youth, many battles faced, and of witnessing too many of his friends dying beneath a blade.

A familiar trickle of laughter sounded from an open door ahead, where an elaborate crucifix was centered above the entry.

"'Twould seem," Stephan said, "that my wife has found something to amuse her."

Recalling Katherine's humor during the time they'd spent aboard ship with Stephan and the other Templars over a year ago, an idea sprung to mind. "Does your wife know I was summoned by the king?"

"Nay, neither of us was informed you were to arrive. The only reason I saw you was because I was outside when you rode in."

"Is your son with her?"

He shook his head. "Colbán is asleep in our chamber, his nursemaid nearby."

"Then," he said with a smile, "wait here and let me surprise her."

His friend chuckled. "If you think you can. I doubt you will get the best of her."

"We will see. 'Tis time for me to pay her back for the last prank she played on me." With stealth, Rónán crept to the entry, but his view was blocked by a large carved statue. He peered between the figure and the wall.

A slender woman stood with her back toward him. She had long blond hair, and wore a stunning blue wool gown that hung to her ankles. Celtic designs braided in gold decorated the hem, a *sgian dubh* was secured at her waist, and an intricate silver torque encircled her neck.

Though over a year had passed, he'd recognize Katherine anywhere. Pride filled him as he thought of their time on board the Templar cog. And when attacking her castle to reclaim it, she'd proven over and again that she was a woman who, when determined, could accomplish all she set out to achieve. To find a lass of such integrity, oh were he to be so fortunate...

Stunned, he smothered the thought. Nay, he sought naught but the life of a warrior. That his friends had found women to love was a fate he didn't seek.

The soft murmur of another woman's voice had him glancing over, but with his limited view, he couldn't see further into the room. Nor did it matter. Rónán glanced back at Stephan.

Down the corridor, a smile curved his friend's mouth as he leaned against the hewn stone wall and folded his arms across his chest.

Turning, Rónán focused on Katherine's back. With a plan in mind, he crept around the statue and started to lay his hands over her eyes. "Guess wh—"

In a blur of movement, blond hair slapped his face as a woman he'd never seen before whirled to confront him. He caught a brief glimpse of smooth features and glittering eyes a second before her leg swept out and hooked his knees.

Off balance, Rónán caught her shoulders to steady himself.

She jerked back.

Air rushed down his throat as they started to fall. Blast it! He shifted his body, taking the brunt of the impact as they landed.

Sprawled atop him, gray eyes narrowed with fury, she unsheathed her dagger.

God's truth! Rónán caught her wrist. "Lass—"

"Release me!" she warned.

Her rich, lyrical brogue had him hesitating. With the Bruce's first parliament soon to be held within these walls, he'd expected to find travelers from Ireland. So why did her body pressed to his, combined with the wild flash in her eyes, make him hesitate? "With pleasure." He caught her blade with his free hand, jerked it away, then let her go.

Her breath coming fast, she scrambled up.

Considering the speed and accuracy with which the woman had withdrawn her *sgian dubh* and aimed it at his throat, she must be trained in combat. Nor was he surprised by this discovery. 'Twas naught uncommon for women in Ireland to hold rank, be educated, and be trained for war.

"My mistake for surprising you," Rónán said, pushing himself to his feet. He extended her weapon to her handle first.

Eyes wary, she snatched her dagger.

"Sir Rónán?"

He glanced right to find Lady Katherine stepping toward him, her eyes warm with surprised welcome, the reaction he'd anticipated a moment before.

"Whoever this stranger is," the lass snapped, "he has the manners of a lout."

"Lady Lathir," Lady Katherine said with a chuckle, her voice growing fond. She walked over and rested her hand upon his arm. "May I introduce you to Sir Rónán, a friend and a man I would trust with my life."

The lady took an almost insulting length of time securing her blade, then gave him a cool nod. "Sir Rónán."

"Sir Rónán," Katherine continued, "I am pleased to introduce to you Lady Lathir. Though you two have only just met, I believe that you will get along well."

With the daggers shooting from the other woman's eyes, that Rónán doubted. Intrigued now that their scuffle was over, he studied her. Wary gray eyes, ones he noted held a hint of lavender, held his without apology. She was fair, even-featured, with lush lips. A beauty by all standards. And she had felt very soft and womanly in those brief moments she'd lay upon him on the floor.

Most women would have jumped or screamed at his unexpected presence, but like a trained knight, she'd gone on the attack. A mystery. Nor did this incident hold importance in the grand scheme of things. Once he'd spoken with the king and was given his mission, he would depart and, thankfully, he and the lass would never again see the other.

But he did owe her an explanation. "My lady, I regret startling you. Lady Katherine and I have a history of playing pranks upon each other. As you have a similar appearance and height, and I heard her voice, I believed you were she." He offered her a warm smile that had charmed many a lass. "I had meant to surprise her."

"I see," she said, her words clipped.

From her prickly manner, he suspected otherwise. He shifted his gaze to Katherine. "'Tis wonderful to see you, my lady."

"And I you." Katherine smiled. "I wasna informed you would be here."

"Which is what I explained to Rónán when I saw him," Stephan said as he entered the solar. He crossed to his wife, then nodded to Lady Lathir.

"My lady, 'tis good to see you again. I regret the confusion. These two can be like scrapping siblings trying to outdo the other."

"Lord Dunsmore," she said, her tone warming to a sincere welcome. "The knight's error is inconsequential, and as he explained, 'twas a mistake." She took a step toward the door, a tight smile on her lips. "Nay doubt you wish to reminisce with your friend."

Worry filtered into Katherine's gaze. "Please stay. Once Sir Rónán learns that—"

"An explanation that is unnecessary. Enjoy your reunion. We will talk later." She nodded. "If you will excuse me."

With exquisite grace, she exited the solar, her blue robe swirling around her slender curves with a royal flare. Without a glance toward him, Rónán noted, though he found himself watching her departure. As the last tantalizing wisp of the lass disappeared from view, he grimaced. "She is skittish."

"Nay, anxious," Stephan said. "En route, her party was attacked a league outside St. Andrews. During the fray, two men rushed Lady Lathir."

"God's truth," Rónán hissed, "they tried to kill her?"

"We believe the warriors meant to abduct her for ransom," Stephan said, "or to use her to force her father to withdraw his support for King Robert."

"Except," Katherine said with pride, "she killed them both."

Given her skill with her blade, that he believed. "Serves the scoundrels right and explains her reaction when I snuck up on her."

"It does," Stephan said.

Katherine poured a cup of wine, held it out to him. "She is only now beginning to relax."

"I wish I had known."

"You couldna," Stephan said, "but during your stay at St. Andrews, you can speak with her again."

"I will make a point to make amends before I depart." A point he hadna counted on including in his schedule, but 'twas proper. "Were Comyn's men behind the attack?"

"King Robert believes 'twas some of John of Lorn's men still hidden about and seeking retribution after their stinging defeat at Brander Pass," Stephan said. "That they somehow discovered Lord Sionn was traveling from Ireland to meet with the Bruce and were determined to stop him."

"Lord Sionn?" Rónán repeated, a sinking feeling in his gut as he recalled her brogue. "What has Lady Lathir to do with the earl?"

Katherine laced her fingers together. "She is his daughter."

Bloody hell. If the powerful Irish noble learned of the incident, Rónán hoped he found it amusing. As for King Robert, he would surely find hilarity in the misstep.

Katherine walked to a table by a grand stone hearth. A banner displaying a red lion rampant sporting blue claws and tongue, woven on a yellow background, hung centered above. Beeswax candles seated in skillfully crafted holders flickered a soft golden glow on either side. She poured three goblets of wine, then returned.

Rónán thought of when they'd first met, and he'd admired her fiery demeanor, more so when in the end she'd fallen in love and married his close friend. So much had changed since, except that their love had prevailed, and now they had a son.

He accepted a cup, waited until she'd handed her husband his, then raised his vessel. "A toast to your son. I wish Colbán God's blessings."

Pride filled their eyes as Stephan and Katherine raised their goblets and drank.

She lowered her cup, her countenance glowing with a mother's love. "Colbán is a handsome lad, with his father's good looks and"—laughter shimmered in her eyes—"also his stubbornness."

Stephan grunted. "The willfulness, my lady wife, comes from you."

At their teasing, the last of Rónán's tension eased. He'd missed his friends and would enjoy the time with them until he departed.

A soft knock sounded at the entry.

"Enter," Stephan said.

The king's runner stepped inside. "My lord, my lady." His gaze shifted to Rónán. "King Robert requests your presence."

* * * *

Rónán entered the throne room. Through an arched window, inky swaths of the oncoming night marred the fading shimmers of orange-gold painting the sky. The warm spill of golden light, along with the torches placed inside sconces positioned upon the wall, illuminated the chamber. In a massive stone hearth sparks popped from the fire and swirled within a plume of smoke before disappearing up the chimney.

Stepping onto the plum carpet, he strode toward King Robert, seated upon his throne. Behind him stood intricately carved columns, and stone lions stood positioned discreetly on either side of the platform.

A powerful setting for a formidable monarch, a man who'd gained his loyalty and respect, and, as a fellow Knight Templar, one he would die to protect.

Over a year had passed since Rónán was part of Stephan's crew which had sailed to the monarch's stronghold, Urquhart Castle, and learned the Bruce was part of the Brotherhood. A tie that had proven critical.

King Edward I had gone to great lengths to ensure Scotland was excommunicated. But the religious exclusion secured by the English monarch, and the Scottish clergy's refusal to acknowledge it, had allowed King Robert to offer all Knights Templar entry into his realm with impunity. A move, much to the English sovereign's chagrin, that had strengthened King Robert's efforts in reclaiming Scotland's freedom.

Before the dais, Rónán halted. That the Bruce had made time to see him during the harried preparations for his first parliament revealed the grave nature of the mission.

He bowed, then met his king's gaze "I am here as you commanded, Your Grace."

Shrewd eyes held his. "How fared the contingent you led to aid Sir Cailin?"

"We arrived in time and aided him in overthrowing his uncle and seizing Tiran Castle." Pride filled him. "And to discover his father, the rightful Earl of Dalkirk, was locked in the dungeon." The formidable ruler's eyes widened. "God in heaven, 'tis a miracle!"

"'Tis." He handed the king the writ from Cailin. "'Twill explain the events."

"I thank you."

"I have more news you may find of interest," Rónán added, "Sir Cailin has wed Elspet, the stepdaughter of one of your loyal confidantes, Sir Angus McReynolds."

The king's eyes widened with satisfied delight. "A fine match, and one I would have encouraged had I the time."

Aware of the king's penchant for matchmaking, and confident the ruler had indeed played a hand in his friend's marriage, Rónán only nodded. "Though," he continued, damning the news he was next to impart, "I regret to inform you that Sir Angus and Elspet's mother were murdered during the series of events."

Anger whipped across the monarch's face. "Is the bastard who killed them dead?"

"Aye, Your Majesty." He gave a brief explanation of what had occurred.

King Robert blew out a rough breath as he rubbed the back of his neck and took a moment of silence for their sacrifice. "I will be happy when Lord Comyn accepts me as Scotland's king and English ambitions to seize our country end. The latter," he said, his voice dry, "with the young king far from concerned with issues of war but a matter of time."

The Bruce stood, strode to a table, lifted an elegant glass carafe. Dark amber liquid sloshed inside. Mouth grim, he filled a pair of goblets inlaid with a Celtic weave, a ruby centered between the breaks in the complex design.

The king handed him a cup. "The Earl of Sionn has arrived at St. Andrews. Unknown to most, he is a trusted Templar supporter and has a large cache of Templar weapons hidden in his realm. Arms I need to force the English from Scotland and quell Lord Comyn's attempts to seize the throne."

Which explained the powerful Irish lord's presence. Rónán took a sip, recognized the potent slide of *uisge beatha*, the spirit distilled by the monks of the Border Abbeys.

"With your expertise in strategy, battlefield experience, and Templar background, you will accompany the earl to his home in Ireland and oversee the transport of the Templar cache to my castle in Aberdeen."

"Aye, Your Grace." Blast it, the last thing he'd ever intended was to return to Ireland. There was naught in his homeland he wished to ever see again. Even the nightmares that had haunted him as a child were long since gone. Nor did he miss the pride in the king's voice at the mention of the recently captured northern stronghold, boasting an easily accessible sea port to the north. "When do we leave?"

"At first light." The monarch took a sip from his goblet, then shot him a hard look. "The earl's party was attacked about a league from St. Andrews by a band of John of Lorn's men."

"The Earl of Dunsmore explained the details of the assault, Sire. With John of Lorn's forces severely cut, and his begging the young English king for supplies, 'twas a brazen move."

"'Twas. I have ordered a contingent to accompany your party to ensure you reach their ship. My guard will remain in port until you have sailed. Once at sea, keep watch for English ships intent on severing my attempt to gain Irish support. If they see Lord Sionn's ship departing Scotland, they will attack."

Rónán nodded. "Aye, Your Grace."

His face relaxed, and on a slow exhale he sat back. Mischief sparkled in the king's eyes as he swirled the amber liquid in his cup. "Did Lord Dunsmore also mention that Lord Sionn has a beautiful daughter?"

At the king's measuring look, Rónán stilled. Was he now the subject of the king's next matchmaking ploy? No, he was being oversensitive. His thoughts shifted to Stephan's amusement at Rónán's thwarted attempt to surprise Katherine.

"Aye, we have met," Rónán said with reluctance.

The Bruce set his goblet down. "How so?"

In brief, he shared the chaos of his and Lathir's encounter.

With a smile, the king laughed. "An intriguing way to meet a lass. She is a strong and intelligent woman." He took a deep drink. "One who needs a man of caliber at her side."

Rónán cleared his throat. "With the dreadful impression I made, Sire, I assure you, I have far from earned her favor." Her *sgian dubh* pointed at him was, he recalled grimly, proof.

"Mayhap a feisty lass is exactly what you need."

In midsip, Rónán almost choked on the powerful spirit. "I am here to serve you, Your Grace, not seek a wife." God's truth, he needed to change the subject before his sovereign became enamored with the idea of pairing him with Lady Lathir.

With the monarch's power of persuasion, ability to bestow upon him a title, and Lord Sionn's Templar ties, 'twould take little to convince the Irish noble to agree to such a union. The disappointment of having to leave in the morning and not spend time with Stephan and Katherine faded against thoughts of escaping before the king decided he and the earl's daughter should wed.

* * * *

A thin mist clung to the air as Lathir dismounted. The strong scent of fish, decaying seaweed, and salt filled the air as the first rays of sunlight struggled through the dense layer.

She glanced around, thankful to arrive safely at their ship, anxious to be out to sea. After their party's attack a short while before, only when the shore faded from sight would she relax.

"I will take your mount, my lady," her personal guard said.

"I thank you, Gearalt." The soft thud of hooves on dirt and the guards' voices rumbled around them as she joined the tall, stocky man who'd raised her.

Blond hair, secured behind his neck in a leather strip framed his intimidating features, and his face settled into a harsh frown as he strode toward the ship. Eyes sharp with intelligence shifted toward her. "You were quiet during the trip."

"I am anxious to be home." The truth.

"The attack still troubles you."

She grimaced and said with equal candor, "I doubt that I will ever forget taking a life, regardless if 'tis an enemy and deserved."

He grunted, leaving her to her silence. Nor would she reveal that what disturbed her as well were her dreams the previous night of Sir Rónán. Something about him had left her off kilter. Several times she'd woken with images of him filling her mind.

To be fair, their first meeting had been something, well, unusual. In those few heated moments, how could she not notice his well-muscled form, confident air, or grayish-green eyes that'd pierced her with such intensity 'twas as if he could see to her soul. His every move proclaimed him a warrior, a man who did naught without purpose, and one who, with his smooth words and manner, no doubt drew many a woman's eye.

Since her betrothed, Domhnall Ruadh mac Cormaic, had died in battle against the English more than two years before, never had another man earned more than her passing interest. That this Irish knight had the audacity to invade her dreams was unacceptable.

Though they hadn't spoken since they'd departed St. Andrews, she was aware that he rode with their soldiers.

Unwittingly, she glanced around and found him. The knight was talking with the leader of the contingent King Robert had provided as protection for their journey to their cog.

Her father followed her gaze. "The Bruce speaks highly of him."

Lathir sighed, understanding his intent. A year after Domhnall's death, he'd advised her 'twas time to seek another man to wed. Her heart still hurting, she'd refused, doubting she'd ever recover from the heartbreak. Nor had he given up pressing her on the issue, a frequent discussion that left her weary. The knight's lack of title mattered little to her father. He judged men by their caliber, not the title they bore. For a king's favorite, nobility could be granted with but a wave of the hand.

Lathir met her father's gaze, blinked. "Of whom?"

His lips thinned. "Sir Rónán O'Connor."

"Which," she said as she started up the gangway, "I would expect of the knight as King Robert chose the warrior to oversee the transfer of arms."

"Lathir—"

"Father, my marital status, or lack of, isna something I wish to discuss, especially," she said, keeping her voice low, "as we prepare to sail."

A deep frown settled upon his mouth. "'Tis time for you to marry."

"I dinna need a man to accept responsibility for the realm of Tír Sèitheach when the time comes."

"You are as stubborn as your mother," he blustered.

She arched an amused brow. "Mother said I acquired my obstinacy from you."

"Aye, she did," he said, his face softening. "I miss her and want you happy."

An ache built in her chest, and she lay her hand upon his arm. "I know, Da."

He covered her hand with his, winked. "What do you say we set sail and return home?"

She smiled. "I would like that very much."

* * * *

"The fog is thicker than mud," Rónán said as he stood at the bow of The Aodh, scanning the thick, dense gray that had moved in several hours after they departed. The soft slap of waves against the thin layer of ice upon the hull played in eerie harmony to the ghostly cries of distant gulls.

"Aye," Lord Sionn agreed at his side, sounding equally displeased. "Nor with the wind having decreased to a light breeze in the last few hours have we traveled far."

"'Tis clearing overhead," Lathir said from her father's other side. "Mayhap the fog will break soon."

Rónán rolled his shoulders and wished that unease didn't trail up his spine as it was wont to do in times of danger.

He allowed his gaze to skim over her plaited gold hair adorned with a weave of silver, accenting the silver torque around her neck clasping an emerald at the base of her throat, before meeting her gaze. "Fog formed over the sea is not something that tends to fade beneath the sun's rays. I expect we may be in the thick of it for a while."

She gazed at him and opened her mouth as if to answer, then looked away, leaving him to wonder what he'd done anew to offend her.

A distant creak, the faint rattle of a chain, and the muted tangle of voices echoed in the murky setting.

On alert, Rónán scanned the dense swath toward the sound. "Someone is out there." He glanced toward the earl and said under his breath, "Did you leave ships farther from port for protection?"

"Nay," the earl replied, his jaw tight. "We saw several English ships en route, but they were at a distance, and we were still in Irish waters."

"King Robert warned me that the English are determined to sever any attempt for the Irish to support his cause."

"Aye, but they will fail," the noble replied.

A soft splash sounded, this time closer. The outline of a ship sailed into view, men running to the rail, their swords drawn.

Lathir gasped. "Their standard is English."

"God's truth," Rónán hissed, "prepare for an attack!"

About the Author

A retired Navy Chief, AGC (AW), Diana Cosby is an international bestselling author of Scottish medieval romantic suspense. Diana has spoken at the Library of Congress, appeared at Lady Jane's Salon NYC, in *Woman's Day*, on Texoma *Living! Magazine*, *USA Today*'s romance blog, "Happily Ever After," and MSN.com.

After retiring from the Navy, Diana dove into her passion—writing romance novels. With thirty-four moves behind her, she was anxious to create characters who reflected the amazing cultures and people she's met throughout the world. Diana looks forward to the years ahead of writing and meeting the amazing people who will share this journey.

Diana Cosby, International Bestselling Author
www.dianacosby.com

Forbidden Vow

In battle-torn Scotland, a castle's mistress awaits her groom, a warrior she has never met . . .

Lady Gwendolyn Murphy's fiancé has finally arrived at Latharn Castle, but she expects no joy in their introduction. Gwendolyn is well aware of Bróccín MacRaith's cold reputation. Yet from first glance, she is drawn to the intimidating stranger. Impossible! How could she be dazzled by such a callous man?

Little does she know, Bróccín is dead. The man Gwendolyn believes to be her intended is actually Sir Aiden MacConnell, a member of the Knights Templar and her enemy, masquerading as the earl to gain access to the castle. His soul is dedicated to God and war; he has no time for luxuries of the flesh. But Gwendolyn's intoxicating beauty, intellect, and fortitude lures him to want the forbidden.

With the wedding date quickly approaching and the future of Scotland at stake, Aiden gathers critical intelligence and steels himself for his departure, vowing to avoid an illicit liaison. But a twist of fate forces him to choose—move forward with a life built on a lie, or risk everything for the heart of one woman?

Forbidden Legacy

A betrothal neither wants . . . a passion neither can resist.

When the English murder Lady Katherine Calbraith's family, she refuses their demands to wed an English noble to retain her home. Avalon Castle is her birthright, one she's determined to keep. After Katherine's daring escape, she's stunned when Scotland's king agrees to allow her to return to Avalon, but under the protection of Sir Stephan MacQuistan . . . as the knight's wife. To reclaim her heritage, Katherine agrees. She accepts her married fate, certain that regardless of the caliber of the man, Stephan may earn her trust, but he'll never win her love.

One of the Knights Templar, Stephan desires no bride, only vengeance for a family lost and a legacy stolen. A profound twist of fate tears apart the Brotherhood he loves, but offers him an opportunity to reclaim his legacy—Avalon Castle. Except to procure his childhood home along with a place to store Templar treasures, he must wed the unsuspecting daughter of the man who killed his family. To settle old scores, Stephan agrees, aware Katherine is merely a means to an end.

The passion that arises between them is as dangerous as it is unexpected. When mortal enemies find themselves locked in love's embrace, Stephan and Katherine must reconsider their mission and everything they once thought to be true . . .

Forbidden Knight

Deep within Scotland, a healer and a warrior join forces to protect Scotland's future . . .

There is an intruder in the woods near King Robert Bruce's camp, but when Sir Thomas MacKelloch comes face-to-face with the interloper, he is shocked to discover his assailant is a woman. The fair lady is skilled with a bow and arrow and defiant in her responses. The wary Knight Templar dare not allow her beauty to lower his guard. Irritated by his attraction, he hauls her before his sovereign to expose her nefarious intent.

Outraged Sir Thomas dismissed her claim, Mistress Alesone MacNiven awaits the shock on the arrogant knight's face when he learns that she has told the truth. But it is she who is shocked, and then horrified, as it is revealed that her father, the king's mortal enemy, has betrothed her to a powerful noble, a deal that could jeopardize the king's efforts to unite Scotland. Robert Bruce orders Sir Thomas to escort Alesone to safety. As they embark on a harrowing journey through the Highlands, Alesone tries to ignore her attraction to the intimidating warrior, but as she burns beneath Thomas's kiss she realizes this fearless knight could steal her heart.

An Oath Taken

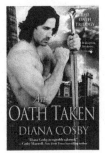

As the new castellan, Sir Nicholas Beringar has the daunting task of rebuilding Ravenmoor Castle on the Scottish border and gaining the trust of the locals—one of whom wastes no time in trying to rob him. Instead of punishing the boy, Nicholas decides to make him his squire. Little does he know the thieving young lad is really . . . a lady.

Lady Elizabet Armstrong had donned a disguise in an attempt to free her brother from Ravenmoor's dungeons. Although intimidated by the confident Englishman with his well-honed muscles and beguiling eyes, she cannot refuse his offer.

Nicholas senses that his new squire is not what he seems. His gentle attempts to break through the boy's defenses leave Elizabet powerless to stem the desire that engulfs her. And when the truth is exposed, she'll have to trust in Nicholas's honor to help her people—and to surrender to his touch . . .

An Oath Broken

Lady Sarra Bellacote would sooner marry a boar than a countryman of the bloodthirsty brutes who killed her parents. And yet, despite—or perhaps because of—her valuable holdings, she is being dragged to Scotland to be wed against her will. To complicate the desperate situation, the knight hired to do the dragging is dark, wild, irresistible. And he, too, is intolerably Scottish.

Giric Armstrong, Earl of Terrick, takes no pleasure in escorting a feisty English lass to her betrothed. But he needs the coin to rebuild his castle, and his tenants need to eat. Yet the trip will not be the simple matter he imagined. For Lady Sarra isn't the only one determined to see her engagement fail. Men with darker motives want to stop the wedding—even if they must kill the bride in the process.

Now, in close quarters with this beautiful English heiress, Terrick must fight his mounting desire, and somehow keep Sarra alive long enough to lose her forever to another man . . .

An Oath Sworn

The bastard daughter of the French king, Marie Alesia Serouge has just one chance at freedom when she escapes her captor in the Scottish highlands. A mere pawn in a scheme to destroy relations between France and Scotland, Marie must reach her father and reveal the Englishman's treacherous plot. But she can't abandon the wounded warrior she stumbles upon—and she can't deny that his fierce masculinity, Scottish or not, stirs something wild inside her.

Colyne MacKerran is on a mission for his king, and he's well aware that spies are lying in wait for him everywhere. Wounded en route, he escapes his attackers and is aided by an alluring Frenchwoman...whose explanation for her presence in the Highlands rings false. Even if she saved his life, he cannot trust her with his secrets. But he won't leave her to the mercy of brigands, either—and as they race for the coast, he can't help but wonder if her kiss is as passionate as she is.

With nothing in common but their honor, Colyne and Marie face a dangerous journey to safety through the untamed Scottish landscape—and their own reckless hearts . . .

Printed in the United States
by Baker & Taylor Publisher Services